1979

CHILDREN OF THE HOLOCAUST
THE COLLECTED WORKS OF ARNOST LUSTIG

DIAMONDS OF THE NIGHT

BOOKS BY ARNOST LUSTIG

DIAMONDS OF THE NIGHT

by Arnost Lustig

Translated By
Jeanne Němcová

INSCAPE / PUBLISHERS / Washington, D.C. / San Francisco

Copyright © 1978 by Arnost Lustig

*Printed in the United States of America. All rights reserved.
No part of this book may be used or reproduced in any manner
whatsoever without written permission except in the case of brief
quotations embodied in critical articles and reviews. For information address INSCAPE Corporation, 1629 K Street, N.W.,
Washington, D.C. 20006*

International Standard Book Number: ISBN 0-87953-407-9

Library of Congress Cataloging in Publication Data

Lustig, Arnost.
Diamonds of the night.

(His Children of the Holocause; v.3)
Translation of Demanty noci.
CONTENTS: The lemon.—The second round.—The white
rabbit. (etc.)
1. Holocaust, Jewish (1939-1945—Fiction. I. Title. II. Series.
PZ4.L97Ch vol. 3 [PG5038.L85] 891.8'6'35s
ISBN 0-87953-407-9   [891.8'6'35]   77-10807

For Pepi and Eva

Contents

*

What's good in a man, expresses itself in action.

The Lemon

Ervin was scowling. His feline eyes, set in a narrow skull, shifted nervously and his lips were pressed angrily into a thin blue arch. He hardly answered Chicky's greeting. Under his arm he was clutching a pair of pants rolled into a bundle.

"What'll you give me for these?" he demanded, unrolling the trousers, which were made of a thin nut-brown cloth. The seat and knees were shiny.

Chicky grinned. "Ye gods, where did you pick those up?" He inspected the cuffs and seams. "Jesus Christ himself wouldn't be caught dead in such a low-class shroud."

Ervin ignored the sneer. "I'm only interested in one thing, Chicky, and that's what I can get for them." He spoke fast.

"Listen, not even a resurrected Jesus Christ on the crummiest street in Lodz would wear a pair of pants like that," Chicky went on with the air of an expert.

He noticed the nerve twitching in Ervin's jaw. "Well, the knees still look pretty good, though," he reconsidered. "Where did you get them?"

It was cloudy and the sun was like a big translucent ball. The barn swallows were flying low. Ervin looked up at the sky and at the swallows swooping toward unseen nests. He'd been expecting Chicky to ask that and he'd prepared himself on the way.

He displayed his rather unimpressive wares again. He knew he had to go through with it now, even if the pants were full of holes. The skin on Chicky's face was thin, almost transparent; he had a small chin and rheumy eyes.

A member of the local security force came around the corner.

11

"Hey, you little brats," he snapped, casting a quick glance at their skinny bodies, "go on, get out of here!"

They turned around. Fortunately, a battered yellow street-car that was set aside for the Jews came along just then and diverted the security guard's attention.

"Don't tell me it's a big secret!" Chicky said. "Anybody can easily see those pants belonged to some grown-up. What're you so scared of?"

"What should I be scared of?" Ervin retorted, clutching the trousers close. "I've got to cash in on them, that's all."

"They're rags."

"They're English material, they're no rags."

"Well, I might see what I can do for you," Chicky relented. "But on a fifty-fifty basis."

Ervin handed over the bundle, and Chicky took a piece of twine from his pocket and tied up the trousers to suit himself, making a fancy knot. He looked up and down the street.

The security guard was at the other end of the street with his back to the boys. They were on the corner of an alley which hadn't had a name for a long time. It was intermittently paved with cobblestones. People hurried on; Ervin and Chicky moved closer to the wall. The streetcar now took a different route. The next stop was out of sight.

Chicky, the smaller of the two, the one with the shaved head, was clutching the brown checkered pants under his arm as Ervin had done.

"But don't you go having second thoughts, Ervin. Don't let me go ahead and work my ass off and then...."

"My dad died," Ervin said.

"Hm...well," Chicky remarked. "It's taken a lot of people these last few weeks," he observed.

"Now there's only one important thing, and that's how you're going to cash in on those pants."

It occurred to Chicky that Ervin might want a bigger share of the take because the pants had been his father's.

"Who's your customer, Chicky?"

"Old Moses," Chicky lied.

"Do I know him?"

"Little short guy."

"First time I've heard of him."

"He just comes up as high as my waist. He's absolutely the biggest bastard in town. But he kind of likes me. Maybe it's because I remind him of somebody."

"He's interested in pants?"

"He's interested in absolutely everything, Ervin."

"Funny I never heard of him."

"Well, I guess I'd better be going," Chicky said.

"What do you suppose your friend would give me for these pants?" Ervin asked.

"Give *us*, you mean," Chicky corrected.

"Anyway, go on and see what you can do," said Ervin, dodging a direct answer.

"He might cough up some bread in exchange for these pants. Or a couple ounces of flour." He unrolled the trousers again. "Like I told you, the knees are still pretty good and the lining's passable. The fly isn't stained yellow like it is in old men's pants. In that respect, these trousers are in good shape and that tells you something about the person who wore them. I'll try to get as much as I can for them, Ervin." He bared his teeth in a tiger grin.

"I need a lemon, Chicky."

"What about a big hunk of nothing?"

"I'm not joking," Ervin said curtly. "All right, then half a lemon, if you can't get a whole one." The expression on Chicky's face changed.

"You know what *I* need, Ervin?" he began. "I need an uncle in Florida where the sun shines all year long and trained fish dance in the water. I need an uncle who would send me an affidavit and money for my boat ticket so I could go over there and see those fish and talk to them." He paused. "A *lemon*! Listen, Ervin, where do you get those ideas, huh, tell me, will you?"

Chicky gazed up into the sky and imagined a blue and white ocean liner and elegant fish poking their noses up out of the silver water, smiling at him, wishing him bon voyage.

Swallows, white-breasted and sharp-winged, darted across the sullen sky. Chicky whistled at them, noticing that Ervin didn't smile.

"That lemon's not for me," said Ervin.

"Where do you think you are? Where do you think Old Moses'd get a lemon? It's harder to find a lemon in this place than...."

But he couldn't think of a good comparison.

Chicky's expression changed to one of mute refusal. He thought to himself, Ervin is something better than I am. His father died, Ervin took his trousers, so now he can talk big about lemons. Chicky's mouth dropped sourly. .

"It's for Miriam," Ervin said flatly. "If she doesn't get a lemon, she's finished."

"What's wrong with her?"

"I'm not sure...."

"Just in general. I know you're no doctor."

"Some kind of vitamin deficiency, but it's real bad."

"Are her teeth falling out?"

"The doctor examined her this morning when he came to see my mother. The old man was already out in the hall. There's no point talking about it."

"It's better to be healthy, I grant you that," Chicky agreed. He rolled up the pants again. "At best, I may be able to get you a piece of bread." He tied the twine into a bow again. "If there were four of us getting a share of this rag, Ervin—your mom, your sister, and you and me, nobody would get anything out of it in the end."

"If I didn't need it, I'd keep my mouth shut," Ervin repeated.

"I can tell we won't see eye to eye, even on Judgment Day."

A Polish streetcar rattled and wheezed along behind them. The town was divided into Polish and Jewish sectors. The streetcar line always reminded Ervin that there were still people who could move around and take a streetcar ride through the ghetto, even if it was just along a corridor of barbed wire with sentries in German uniforms so nobody would get any ideas about jumping off—or on.

"It's got to be something more than that. Everybody's got a vitamin deficiency here. What if it's something contagious, Ervin, and here I am fussing around with these pants of yours?" He gulped back his words. "And I've already caught whatever it is?"

"Nobody knows *what* it is," said Ervin.

14

"Well, I'm going, Ervin...."

"When are you coming back?"

"What if we both went to see what we could do?"

"No," said Ervin quietly.

"Why not?"

Ervin knew what it was he had been carrying around inside him on his way to meet Chicky. *It was everything that had happened when he'd stripped off those trousers. His father's body had begun to stiffen and it felt strange. He kept telling himself it was all right, that it didn't matter.* Instead, he kept reciting the alphabet and jingles.

This was your father, a living person. And now he's dead. Chicky was the only one he could have talked to.

"I haven't got a dad or a mother even," Chicky said suddenly. A grin flickered. "That's my tough luck. They went up the chimney long ago."

The sky above the low rooftops was like a shallow, stagnant sea.

Chicky lingered, uncertain.

It was just his body, Ervin told himself. *Maybe memory is like the earth and sky and ocean, like all the seashores and the mountains, like a fish swimming up out of the water to some island, poking out its big glassy eyes just to see how things look. Like that fish Chicky had been talking about. Nobody knows, not even the smartest rabbi in the world. And not the bad rabbis either. But while he was taking his father's trousers off, he knew what he was doing. He wasn't thinking about his father, but about an old Italian tune he used to sing and which Miriam loved. Father sang off key, but it sounded pretty. Prettier than a lot of other things. It was about love and flowers and his father had learned it during the war when he fought in the Piave campaign.*

He already had the trousers halfway off. And he knew the reasons he loved his father would never go away.

The swallows flew quietly in low, skidding arches. Ervin looked around to see how the weather was, and finally his gaze dropped. The rounded cobblestones melted away.

"All right then, I'll bring it around to your place later," Chicky said.

"By when do you think you can do it?"

15

"In two or three hours."

"But, Chicky...."

Chicky turned and disappeared around the corner as another streetcar came clanging along.

Now Ervin could think ahead, instead of going back to what had been on his mind before. He set off down the alley in the opposite direction, toward the house where he and his family had been living for two years.

The tiny shops upstairs and in the basement had been hardly more than market stalls which had been converted into apartments for several families.

He remembered how he discovered that his father no longer wore underpants. The stringy thighs. The darkened penis, the reddish pubic hair. Rigid legs. Scars on the shin bone. His father had gotten those scars when he was wounded fighting in Italy.

Then that old tune came back to him, sung off key again, the song from somewhere around Trieste that he and Miriam had liked so much.

Hell, who needed those pants more than they did? Father had probably traded in his underpants long ago. Who knows for what?

So Father died, he is no more, Ervin thought to himself.

He reached home, one of the dwarfish shops where he and his mother and sister lived.

The corrugated iron shutter over the entry had broken a spring, so it wouldn't go all the way up or down. He could see a mouse.

He squeezed through a crack in the wall. Mother was scared of mice, so he'd repaired the wall boards through which the mice came in and out. Pressing against the wall, Ervin was suddenly aware of his body, and that reminded him of his father again.

"It's me," he called out.

It had occurred to him that there was nothing to be proud of, being unable to cash in on the trousers *himself.* (Even so, his mother must have known what he had done.) He had to take a deep breath and adjust to the musty smell in the room. It was easier to get used to the difference between the light outside and the darkness inside.

Mother greeted him with a snore. She had long since lost any resemblance to the woman who had come here with him. He peered around him. He had been almost proud of having such a pretty mother. On top of everything else, her legs had swollen. She hadn't been able to get out of bed for the past eight weeks. She'd waited on everything for Father, and now for him.

"Where've you been?" his mother asked.

"Out," he answered.

He crawled into his corner where he could turn his back on everything, including his father who lay out in the hall wrapped in a blanket. Miriam, too, was curled up next to the wall, so he couldn't see her face. He heard her coughing.

He bundled his legs into the tattered rug that used to be his father's. *He'd always had the worst covers. He didn't want to admit he was a loser, and as long as he was able to give up something for them, maybe it wasn't so obvious. The dim light made its way through the thin fabric of dust and dampness and the breath of all three of them. When he lost, he put on the smile of a beautiful woman. He was making a point of being a graceful loser. As if it made any difference to anybody except himself.*

"Did you find anything?" his mother asked.

"No...."

"What are we going to do?"

"Maybe this afternoon," he said, his face to the wall.

"Miriam!" his mother called out to his sister. "Don't cough! It wears you out."

"Mirrie," Ervin said. "Miriam!" She didn't answer.

"Can't she speak?" he asked his mother.

"It wears her out," she repeated. "You really ought to look around and see if you can't scrape up something."

"There's no point so early in the afternoon."

"You ought to try at least," his mother insisted.

That's how it used to be with Father, Ervin recalled. *She always kept sending him somewhere. But Father had gone out just as he'd done now, and, like him, he almost felt better out-side; he also may have believed that just by going out he was getting back in shape, that he'd be able to do what he used to do in the beginning. Then Mother started saying things couldn't get any worse. She never went wrong about that. That's because there is no limit to what's "worse." The limit was in his father. And now Ervin had to find it, just like his father.*

"I already told you, I can't find anything just now," he said.

"You ought to go out and try, dear," his mother went on. *This was what Father had had to put up with.* "You see how Miriam looks, don't you?" his mother persisted.

"I can see her," he answered. "But I can't find anything now."

"This can't help but finish badly."

"Oh, cut it out! I'm not going anywhere," Ervin declared flatly. "I've already tried. There's nothing to be had."

"For God's sake, listen to me!" his mother cried sharply. "Go on out and *try!* Miriam hasn't had a thing to eat today."

The stains on the plaster were close to his eyes. The room was damp, and it almost swallowed up the sound of his mother's voice and his own. The dampness didn't bother him, though. He could hear faint scratching noises in the walls.

The boards he'd put up didn't help much. He almost envied mice. Just as he'd felt a certain envy for trees when he was outside. Ervin suddenly wished he could catch one of those sad little animals. Pet it, then kill it. Father had told them about the time they were besieged during the First World War and the soldiers ate mice.

To kill and caress. Or simply kill, so you're not always bothered by something or somebody.

But if Chicky was right, a trained mouse should get along great.

"I wonder if I shouldn't air out the room a bit," he said into the silence.

"Have they been here already?" he asked after a while.

"No."

"They're taking their time about it."

Now, in her turn, his mother was silent. "Who knows how many calls they have to make today?"

"Why don't you want to go out, son?"

"I will. In a while," he answered gently. "It doesn't make any sense now, though."

"Ervin, son...."

The room was quiet, the silence broken only by Miriam's coughing.

Ervin put his head between his knees, trying to guess where the mouse was and what it was doing. He stuck his fingers in his ears. The scratching continued. *So Father's still lying out there in the hall. He doesn't have any pants and Mother doesn't even know it. He's naked, but that doesn't bother his old Piave scars. Mother could use that extra blanket now,* he thought to himself. *But he left it around his father for some reason which he didn't know himself. So I don't have the feeling that I've stolen everything from him, including our second tattered blanket,* he thought to himself. *It was lucky she couldn't get out of bed now, even if she wanted to. Her legs wouldn't support her. She'd see that Father had no pants. They'll probably take him along with the blanket. What the hell? They were certainly taking their time. They should have been here an hour ago. It was a regulation of the commanding officer and the self-government committee that corpses must be removed promptly. Everybody was scared of infection. The corpse collectors were kept busy. They probably didn't miss a chance to take anything they could get. Everybody knew they stole like bluejays.*

Miriam would probably have been afraid to sleep with a dead person in the same room, even if it was Father, Ervin decided.

"There's some rabbi here who works miracles, I heard," his mother said. "Why don't you go and see him?"

"What would I say to him?"

"Tell him that I'm your mother."

"I don't have any idea where he lives. And even if he could perform a miracle, he certainly won't put himself out to come over here. He waits for people to come to him."

"I feel so weak," his mother told him.

Suddenly it occurred to him that maybe his mother would have been better off lying out in the hall beside his father. It would be better for Miriam too. Mother's gestures and the things she told him were getting more and more indecisive.

"Why don't you want to go anywhere?" Mother said.

"Because there's no point," he replied, "I'd be wearing myself out in vain. I'll find something, but not until this afternoon."

19

"Miriam won't last long. She can hardly talk anymore."

"Miriam?" Ervin called out.

Miriam was silent and his mother added: "You know how it was with Daddy."

"He'd been sick for a long time."

And when her son said nothing, she tried again. "Ervin...."

"It doesn't make any sense," he growled. "I'm not going anywhere now. Not till later."

He sat quite still for a while, staring at the blotches and shadows moving on the wall. He could hear mice scampering across the floor toward the mattress where Mother and Miriam were lying. Mother screeched, then Miriam.

Ervin was bored.

It might be more comfortable and pleasant to wait outside. But there was something in here that made him stay. He remembered how he and Chicky used to play poker. They always pretended there was some stake. That made it more interesting. You could bluff and pretend to have a full house when you didn't even have a pair. But there was always the chance—which they'd invented—that you might win something.

He remembered how he and Miriam used to go ice-skating. She was little and her knees were wobbly. He'd drag her around the rink for a while, then take her into the restaurant where you could have a cup of tea for ten hellers. Miriam's nose would be running, and she'd stay there for an hour with her tea so he could have a good time out on the ice. Once his mother had given them money to buy two ham sandwiches. His arches always ached when he'd been skating. So did Miriam's.

If they'd come for Father—and he wished it were over with—he wouldn't have to worry that the body would start to decay or that his mother would find out he didn't have any pants on.

"Why don't you go out and see that miracle rabbi?"

"Because it doesn't make any sense."

At first, Mother only had trouble with her legs. And Miriam hadn't coughed *quite* as much.

The sentries along the streetcar line always looked comfortably well-fed, with nice round bellies, as though they had everything they needed. When these sentries passed through

20

the ghetto, they acted as though victory was already theirs, even if they might lose this little skirmish with the Jews. *Daddy once said that this was their world, whether they won or lost.*

Ervin's stomach growled. It was like the noise the mice made. He stretched and waited for his mother to start nagging him again. But she didn't, and it was almost as though something were missing. *He didn't want to think about his father's body wrapped in that blanket out in the hall. Daddy had been sick long enough. He was certainly better off this way.*

After a while, he wasn't sure whether his stomach was making the noise or the mice. His mother groaned. He thought about a nap. Just then he heard someone banging on the iron shutter. He got up.

"Well, I'll be on my way," he said.

"Come back soon," his mother replied. "Come back safe and sound."

"Sure," he answered. As he approached the shutter, he asked, "Is that you, Chicky?"

"No," a voice replied. "It's the miracle-working rabbi with a pitcher of milk."

Ervin pushed the broken shutter and slipped through. It was easy. His body was nothing but skin and bones now. He had a long narrow skull, with bulging greenish blue eyes. He could feel his mother's eyes on him as he squeezed out. Outside in the courtyard he pulled down his shirt and his bones cracked. Chicky was waiting on the sidewalk.

"So?" asked Ervin.

"Even with those stains on the seat," Chicky started.

"What're you trying to tell me?"

"He gave me more than I expected." He smiled slyly and happily.

Chicky produced a piece of bread, carefully wrapped in a dirty scarf. He handed it to Ervin. "This is for you. I already ate my share on the way, like we agreed."

"Just this measly piece?"

"Maybe you forgot those stains on the seat of those pants."

"Such a little hunk?"

"What else did you expect, hm? Or maybe you think I ought to come back with a whole moving van full of stuff for one pair of pants?"

21

Chicky wiped his nose, offended.

"You just better not forget about those stains on the seat. Besides, almost everybody's selling off clothes now."

Ervin took the bread. Neither one mentioned the lemon. Ervin hesitated before crawling back into the room, half-hoping Chicky was going to surprise him. Chicky liked to show off.

"Wait here for me," he blurted. "I'll be right back."

Ervin squinted through the dimness to where his mother lay on the mattress.

"Here, catch," he said maliciously. He threw the bread at her. It struck her face, bounced, and slid away. He could hear her groping anxiously over the blanket and across the floor. As soon as she had grabbed it, she began to wheeze loudly.

She broke the bread into three pieces in the dark.

"Here, this is for you," she said.

"I don't want it."

"Why not?" she asked. He heard something else in her voice. "Ervin?"

He stared at the cracks in the wall where the mice crawled through. He was afraid his mother was going to ask him again.

"My God, Ervin, don't you hear me?"

"I've already had mine," he said.

"How much did you take?"

"Don't worry, just my share." He felt mice paws pattering across the tops of his shoes. Again, he had the urge to catch one and throw it on the bed.

"Miriam!" his mother called.

Ervin left before he could hear his sister's reply. He knew what his mother was thinking.

Chicky was waiting, his hands in his pockets, leaning against the wall. He was picking his teeth. He was looking up at the sky trying to guess which way the clouds were going. There must be wind currents that kept changing.

For a while the two boys strolled along in silence. Then just for something to say, Chicky remarked: "You know what that little crook told me? He says you can't take everything away from everybody."

Everything melted together: father, bread, mother, sister, the moment he was imagining what Chicky might bring back for them. Mice.

"He says we can *hope* without *believing*." Chicky laughed, remembering something else.

"Do you feel like bragging all day?"

"If you could see into me the way I can see into you, you could afford to talk. When my dad went up the chimney, I told myself I was still lucky to have my mother. And when I lost Mother, I told myself that at least I was lucky to have a brother left. He was weaker than a fly. And I said to myself, it's great to have your health at least."

Ervin was silent, so Chicky continued: "Still, we're pretty lucky, Ervin. Even if that's what my little businessman says too. Don't get the idea the world's going to stop turning just because one person in it is feeling miserable at this particular moment. You'd be exaggerating."

They didn't talk about it anymore. They could walk along like this together, so close their elbows or shoulders almost touched, and sometimes as they took a step together, their hips. The mice and the chameleon were gone; Chicky was really more like a barn swallow. Chicky was just slightly crooked. The thought suddenly put him in a better mood. Like when the sun came out or when he looked at a tree or the blue sky.

"He's full of wise sayings," Chicky resumed. "According to him, we have to pay for everything. And money and *things* aren't the worst way to pay."

"Aw, forget it. You're sticking as close to me as a fag."

"What about you?" Chicky's little face stretched.

"They haven't come to get him yet, the bastards."

"I can probably tell you why," Chicky declared. "Would you believe it, my dad's beard grew for two days after he was already dead?"

"Do you ever think you might have been a swallow?"

"Say, you're really outdoing yourself today," Chicky remarked. "But if you want to know something, I *have* thought about it."

Ervin looked up into the sky again. He might have known Chicky would have ideas like that. Ervin himself sometimes

23

had the feeling that he was up there being blown around among the raindrops when there was a thunderstorm. The sky looked like an iron shutter. Sometimes he could also imagine himself jumping through the sky, using his arms and legs to steer with.

"Ervin...." Chicky interrupted.

"What?"

"That old guy gave me a tremendous piece of advice."

"So be glad."

"No, Ervin, I mean it."

"Who's arguing?"

"Aren't you interested? He asked me if your old man had anything else."

"What else could he have?"

"He was just hinting."

"These have been hungry days for us. That crooked second-hand man of yours, his brains are going soft. I hope he can tell the difference between dogs and cats."

"Considering we're not their people, Ervin, what he told me wasn't just talk."

"My dad was the cleanest person in this whole dump," said Ervin.

"He didn't mean that and neither did I, Ervin."

"What's with all this suspense?"

"Just say you're not interested and we'll drop it," Chicky said.

"Come on, spill it, will you? What *did* he mean then?"

"Maybe there was a ring or something?"

"Do you really think he'd have let Mother and Miriam die right in front of his eyes if he'd had anything like a *ring*?"

"He wasn't talking only about a ring. He meant gold."

"Dad had to turn over everything he had that was even gilded."

"He hinted at it only after I tried to explain to him about the lemon."

"You know how it was. Mother doesn't have anything either."

"He only hinted at it when I told him how important it was for you to have that lemon, Ervin."

"Well, what was it he hinted, then?" Ervin noticed the expectant look on Chicky's face.

"He hinted that it wasn't impossible, but only in exchange for something made of pure gold. And that he didn't care what it was."

"Don't be a bastard," said Ervin slowly. "Forget it. My dad didn't have anything like that. Go on, get lost!"

"He even indicated exactly *what* and *how*."

"Look, come on—kindly spill it," Ervin said with irritation. *Once again he saw his father lying there wrapped in the blanket. It flooded through him in a dark tide, like when his mother didn't believe that he hadn't taken more than his share of the bread. He'd known right from the start what Chicky was talking about.*

Ervin didn't say anything.

"Gold teeth, for instance. It's simply something in the mouth he doesn't need anymore, something nobody needs except maybe you and me."

Ervin remained silent.

"Well, I wasn't the one who said anything about a lemon," he concluded.

Ervin stopped and so did Chicky. Then Ervin turned and looked him up and down, eyes bulging.

"Aw, cut it out," Chicky said wearily. "Don't look at me as though I killed your dad."

Suddenly Ervin slapped him. Chicky's face was small and triangular, tapering off crookedly at the top. It was very obvious because his head was shaved. Then Ervin slapped him again and began to punch his face and chest. When his fist struck Chicky's Adam's apple, Ervin could feel how fragile everything about him was.

Again he saw himself stripping those brown checkered trousers off his father's body. The undertakers would be coming along any minute. [They should have been here long ago.] He thought of how he'd managed to do that before they came and how he'd probably manage to do even this if he wanted to. And he knew that he couldn't have swallowed that piece of bread even if his mother had given it to him without those second thoughts of hers. He kept pounding his fists into Chicky, and it was as if he were striking at himself and his

25

mother. *He kept telling himself that his father was dead anyway and that it didn't matter much and that it didn't have any bearing on the future either.*

Then he felt everything slowing down. Chicky began to fight back. Ervin got in two fast punches, one on the chin, the other in the belly. Chicky hit Ervin twice before people gathered and tried to break it up, threatening to call the security guards.

Ervin picked himself up off the sidewalk as fast as he could. He shook himself like a dog and went home through the courtyard.

"Ervin?" his mother called out. "Is that you?"

"Yeah," he answered.

"Did you find anything else?"

He was shivering as he sometimes did when he was cold because he'd loaned his blanket to his mother or Miriam.

"Mirrie...." he tried.

He bundled himself up into the rug. He was glad Chicky had hit him back. It was hard to explain why. It was different from wanting to catch a mouse and kill it. He touched his cheek and chin, fingering the swollen places. Again he waited for his mother to say something. But she didn't. Mother only knows as much as I tell her, he said to himself. Mother's quite innocent, Ervin decided. Despite everything she's still innocent. Would she have been able to do what she had criticized him for? He wished she'd say something, give at least an echo. He thought of Miriam. For a moment he could see her, tall and slender, her breasts and blond hair.

The twilight began to melt into the dampness of the cellar. The spider webs disappeared in the darkness. He wished they'd muffle the edge of his mother's voice. He waited for Miriam's cough. The silence was like a muddy path where nobody wants to walk. *And his father was still lying out there in the hall.*

When someone dies, Ervin thought to himself, *it means not expecting, not worrying about anything, not hoping for something that turns out to be futile. It means not forcing yourself into something you don't really want, while you go on behaving as though you did. It means not being dependent on anybody or anything. It means being rid of what's bothering you. It's like when you close your eyes and see things and people in your own way.*

That idea of a path leading from the dead to the living and back again is just a lot of foolishness I thought up by myself. To be dead means to expect nothing, not to expect somebody to say something, not to wait for someone's voice. Not to stare enviously after a streetcar going somewhere from somewhere else.

He looked around. Miriam had begun to cough again. She's coughing almost gently, he thought to himself. She probably doesn't have enough strength left to cough anymore.

My God, that lying, thieving, sly old man, that bastard who's fed for six thousand years on Jewish wisdom and maybe would for another half an hour—but maybe not even that long! That dirty louse, full of phony maxims and dreams as complicated as clockwork, lofty as a rose, rank as an onion, who perhaps wasn't quite as imaginary as I wanted to think he was, judging from Chicky's descriptions which made him sound as though he'd swallowed all the holy books. That slimy crook with his miserable messages, that you have to pay for everything and that money and things aren't the most precious currency. But he also said you can't take everything away from everybody, as though he wanted to confuse you by contradicting himself in the same breath. Where did he get those ideas?

"No, I don't have anything," he said suddenly, as if he knew his mother was still waiting for an answer.

He heard her sigh. From his sister's bed he heard a stifled cough. (She's probably ashamed of coughing by now.)

Nothing's plaguing Father anymore either. Not even the craving for a bowl of soup. He wasn't looking forward anymore to seeing Ervin dash out onto the field in a freshly laundered uniform and shiny football boots, which he took care of, in front of crowds of people waiting for entertainment and thrills and a chance to yell their lungs out. If they come for Father now, they'll do just what Chicky said they would. Anyway, the undertakers themselves do it to the old people. He remembered his father's smile which got on his mother's nerves.

He stared into the darkness. His mother was bandaging her swollen legs. Her eyes were very bright. She's probably feverish, he thought. She made a few inexplicable gestures. What if the rabbis are right and there is some *afterwards? Then his father must be able to see him. Where do you suppose he really is,* Ervin wondered, *and where am I? Does anybody know? Inwardly he tried to smile at his father. It would be nice if I could really smile at him. To be on the safe side, Ervin tried smiling at his father again.*

"I'm going out and take another look around," he said.

Mother ceased her strange movements. "Where do you want to go in the dark?"

"I want to have a look at something."

"Be careful, child."

He went out into the hall and the place he had avoided before, so he wouldn't have to look at the wall beside which his father's body was still lying. He was squeezing through the crack in the wall. For a short while an insurance agent had lived in the corner shop. *But this isn't your father anymore,* he told himself; *he was only until yesterday. Now there is nothing but a weight and the task of carrying it away,* he reminded himself immediately. *But I'll think of him only in good ways. And Mother and Miriam will think about him as if nothing's happened.*

He threw off the old blanket. He closed his eyes for a second. I won't be able to eat very much, he realized, as though he wanted to convince himself that this was the only difference it would make. Everything moved stiffly. He had to turn the head and open its mouth. He grabbed it by the chin and hair and that was how he managed. He couldn't remember exactly which tooth it was. He tried one after another. He was hurrying. He didn't want Chicky and the men with the coffins to catch him at it. Instead, he tried to imagine that lemon. It was like a yellow sphere at the end of the hall. Suddenly he couldn't remember where lemons came from, except that it was somewhere in the south, and whether they grew on trees or bushes. He'd never really known anyway.

He picked up a sharp stone. He had a sticky feeling as though he were robbing somebody. He tried to decide which was the best way to knock it out. He tried several times without success. Then he stopped trying to get at just that one tooth.

Finally something in the jaw loosened. Ervin could smell his own breath. He tossed the stone away. He was glad nobody had seen him. Into the palm of his hand he scooped what he'd been seeking. (He was squatting and the head dropped back to the floor.)

Ervin stood up slowly. He felt as though his body and thoughts were flowing into a dark river, and he didn't know where it came from and where it was going. He wiped his hands on his pants. The cellar was dark, like the last place a person can retreat to. For a moment he closed his eyes. He had to take it out into the light. He headed for the other end of the corridor.

He'd hardly stepped out into the street when he saw Chicky's face in the twilight. There, you see, Ervin said to himself. He was keeping watch after all. Chicky would have done what he'd just done if he'd had the chance.

"Hello, kid," Chicky began. "Hello, you Jew bastard." Then Chicky exploded: "You lousy hyena! You son of a bitch! I suppose you've come to apologize. At least I hope so."

Ervin was clutching the thing tightly in his fist. He stared at Chicky for a long time.

"But I got in two good punches, didn't I? Like Max Schmeling." Chicky sounded pleased with himself. His eyes shone.

But then he noticed that the skin under Ervin's eyes was bluer than any bruise could have made it. He noticed, too, the pale blotches on Ervin's face. And how he kept his hand in his pocket.

"No hard feelings," Chicky said.

"I have it."

"I was sure you'd manage...."

Ervin pulled his hand out of his pocket and Chicky's glance shifted swiftly.

"Bring me that lemon, Chicky, but the whole thing!" He unclenched his fist. It lay there cupped in his palm, a rather unattractive shell of gold the color of old copper, and very dirty.

"You won't take the tiniest slice for yourself."

"If it's pure, Ervin, you're in luck," Chicky said.

When Ervin did not respond he continued: "Sometimes it's just iron or some ersatz. Then it's worn through on top. The old man warned me about that in advance. But if it isn't, then you're damned lucky, Ervin, honest."

"When will you bring me that lemon?" Ervin asked, getting to the point.

"First hand it over and let me take a look."

Impatiently, Chicky inspected the crown, acting as though he hadn't heard Ervin. He scraped away the blood that had dried around the root and removed bits of cement. He blew on it and rubbed the dull gold between his fingers, then let it rest in his palm again.

"For this, the old runt will jump like a toad."

"I hope so."

"But first, Ervin, it's fifty-fifty."

"The hell it is," he answered firmly.

"I'll only do it for half."

"If Miriam doesn't get that lemon, she won't even last out till evening."

"Why shouldn't she last out? I'm keeping half."

"You're not keeping anything," repeated Ervin. "Now get going before it's too late."

Ervin glared at him, but there was a question in his eyes. Chicky acted calm. None of his self-satisfaction had filtered through to Ervin. His throat tightened. He began to shiver. He could feel the goose pimples on his neck and arms. It wasn't the way he wanted to think it was, *that his father had died and otherwise everything was just the same as before.* And when Chicky looked at him, Ervin could read in his eyes that instead of bringing a lemon or some kind of pills that have the same effect as lemons, Chicky would probably bring another piece of bread.

Ervin heard a quiet gurgle rising in his throat. He tried thinking about that runty second-hand dealer.

"I'd be crazy to do it for nothing," said Chicky slowly. He squinted warily and his nostrils flared. He bared his teeth. There were big gaps between them.

"Either we go halves or I tell your mom how you're treating me."

"You're not such a bastard, Chicky, are you?"

"Well, I'd have to be," replied Chicky.

"Get going," Ervin said.

"That sounds more like it."

"I'll wait at home."

"All right."

"And hurry up. Honestly, it's very important."

"Fast as a dog can do you know what," grinned Chicky.

Small and nimble, he dodged among the pedestrians. In the meantime, two men with tubs had appeared. Chicky must have passed them. The tubs were covered with tattered sheets and something bulged underneath. Everybody stepped aside as the porters passed. They knew what they were carrying.

Ervin didn't feel like going back home. He crawled into the opening of a cement culvert pipe. His long skinny head stuck out as he sat there watching the sun set behind the clouds. It dropped slowly. The barn swallows were flying lower now than they had been earlier that afternoon, flying in flocks, suddenly soaring up, then back toward earth.

He kept looking up and down the alley so he wouldn't miss Chicky when he came back.

It all began to melt together before his eyes: the silhouettes of the buildings and the cobblestones that had been pounded into the earth and then washed loose by long-gone rains. He watched the sky which was full of barn swallows and the sun disappeared. Rain was gathering in the clouds as their colors changed.

I ought to be like a rock, he told himself. Even harder than a rock.

And he wept, quietly and without tears, in some little crevice which was inside.

The Second Round

"It's going to be me," said the one in the middle, the one they called Marquis.

"Don't try to be a prophet," replied the second, a tall man of about forty. "Where's it say it'll be you?"

"I know what I'm talking about," Marquis growled. "Quit stalling and get started!"

The third, who stood beside him, was small for his nineteen years. He had not spoken yet. He shifted his feet impatiently while the other two argued. He turned from one to the other, watching their faces as they talked.

"Maybe it'll be me," the little man piped up.

"We'll soon see," the tall man said. He was gaunt, the way people are who haven't had enought to eat or enough sleep for years. He was covered with scars and scratches which blurred into each other so you couldn't tell which were new and which were old.

"Listen, don't dawdle around!" Marquis repeated.

"We all stand absolutely the same chance—nobody has any advantage or disadvantage when we draw lots this way," the tall man went on.

The little one looked up at him. Fear had set in. He could see in his mind's eye what the person who won (or lost?) would have to do. And what would happen if he didn't succeed. There were at least a hundred reasons why he might fail, but these were outweighed by the thing they were risking this for. The little one didn't like to hear the others fight. They'd been edgy for the last few days. At first, they'd gone a bit wild, then apathy took over, but finally they'd pulled themselves together as they always did. They were more fidgety than they used to be, though. It wasn't just because they were hungry and cold at night and wet during the daytime. It wasn't the feeling in the air, either.

From beginning to end, it was always that other possibility.

The little one studied the older man's face. His skin, carved with irregular, curving furrows, looked like a map of the moon filmed from a great distance. He reddened, then turned pale again. There was doubt in the eyes of the older one, along with an indefatigable determination. The little one had a bellyache after six days of nothing to eat but roots and grass. You could almost see through his skin, as Marquis had told him that morning. He envied the older man for having skin that gave some protection against dampness and cold, against sunshine and bugs, skin that was as tough as the hide of an old rhinoceros.

The little one had wanted them to count him in when they drew lots, but he hoped it wouldn't fall to him. He felt a mixture of embarrassment and fear and self-reproach. He didn't want them to notice what was going on inside him. His belly started to ache again.

The tall man turned to the others, "Whoever pulls the shortest twig," he said, "is the one who's going to have to do it. Unless he chickens out at the last minute."

The little one was silent.

"O.K., now, get going, all right?" Marquis mumbled. "You expect us to listen to you make speeches all night? We've heard it a hundred times."

"I've been ready for ages," the tall one answered.

He was at least twice as old as Marquis and he had noticed that it made Marquis feel good when he could talk back to him. He could see right through him. They'd been together too long, and yet there was no one else they were closer to and they all realized that they had nobody else besides each other. This bothered Marquis, as the older man knew. He also knew that if it fell to Marquis, he'd do a better job of it than the rest of them. That was what he wanted to happen and that's why he forgave himself in advance, even though deep inside, he was resentful. Marquis must have realized it, because they knew each other inside out, without having to say a word.

So the tall man put up with Marquis's insolence. Maybe he would have been more straightforward and uncompromising too, twenty years ago. Sometimes, being that way looks like self-confidence, but the two things were quite different. He used to be a lot like Marquis. It had evaporated over the years. Some unexpected experiences had evaporated into thin air too. Nothing is ever really lost, he told himself. Not even here.

Before the war, the tall one had worked as a janitor at the Astronomy Institute. He liked to talk about it. Sometimes he'd act as though he used to be responsible for the stars and for setting things straight among the galaxies. During the winter, when he and Marquis and the little one worked on the ramp unloading coal and cement and sheet metal, they'd baptized him Big Dipper.

He'd been warming himself one day in front of an iron brazier full of hot coals. It was intended for the German sentries. He'd moved over to make a place for the two of them and that had made them feel closer. He told them about the stars as they stared into the molten coals. He was probably the first person to tell them that the Milky Way had nothing to do with milk, just as the Spanish flu, which spread all over Europe after the Great War, had nothing to do with the Iberian Peninsula.

But more important than the stars had been the warmth he'd transmitted to them within two minutes, the experience that went together with his age. His eyes mirrored a strong will, and something else which even the past few years had not been able to destroy.

Even after the sentries came and drove them all away from the brazier, they'd stuck together. Later, it was because he grew so haggard, because of that wrinkled, furrowed skin which looked like it belonged to an animal, rather than to a man. Because of all the things that happen to a man who's always a loser.

"We know you," said Marquis. "We know you too damn well! You even envy a dog by now. But do you know whether a dog envies you?"

Marquis eyed the older one with caution. Just like the little one (who was shivering), he could see the three twigs he was

35

holding, one of them shorter than the others. Birch twigs, carefully peeled. He opened his palm so they could see them lying there—no special markings, except that one was shorter.

Now all there was to do was to decide who would draw lots first. The oldest lifted his thumb from the twigs. When he lowered it over the ends, they all looked the same. The tall man held his fist closer so Marquis and the little one could see better.

The little one could feel his whole body tense up. They were going to have to choose one of those little sticks under the dirty thumb of the oldest. It wasn't a dress rehearsal anymore. Big Dipper had shuffled the twigs with his eyes shut. He knew which was which, but even so, he couldn't foresee which twig either of the other two would pick and which would be left for him.

His hands moved nimbly, as though the twigs were cards or dice. He evened them without glancing at his hands; he didn't even open his palm. They couldn't see what he was doing and maybe they didn't want to. He shuffled the twigs again to confuse even himself. With his left thumb, he could feel that the protruding twigs were now even.

"It's going to be me, I know it already," the little one babbled softly. He tried to overcome his fears by talking.

"Shut up," grumbled Marquis, but his tone was different than when he talked to the tall one.

The oldest one said nothing. He stared up at the sky, looking for stars the others couldn't see. He wanted to convince them that this was absolutely fair—no fraud.

He wasn't thinking about the twigs. He was thinking about what a miracle it would be if they survived until spring. If they lived through it till the end. Spring was already well advanced, though, even if it didn't look like it, there by the railroad tracks in the middle of the woods. He was also thinking how lucky it was that nothing was happening just then, because everything that had happened during each of those three hundred and sixty-five days in every single one of the past three years had contained not just the seeds of other misfortunes, but the absence of what they were still looking forward to.

"Swear to God," breathed the little one.

The other two threw him a scornful glance, as though they were mutely letting him know that even if the lot fell to him, it would be better for all three if they didn't have to depend on him.

He looked like a dwarf beside the others. He'd just gotten over typhus, so he had a right to speak of the favors of fate, since he'd survived—with his frail little body. His hair had fallen out and the smooth, thin skin on his skull made him look like he'd been scalped. His lips, purplish from fever, were full of cold sores and scabs. If you only saw his lips, you might have thought he was an old man.

The little one could hardly stand on his feet. But he was quite right to think that if he allowed himself to be excluded from this lottery, he'd have to count himself out too from what was supposed to happen afterwards, regardless of all the possible obstacles. He was still very weak, even though Marquis had given him his share of beets on a few occasions and shared the water from his canteen. As long as the beets and water lasted. He wished they'd go ahead and get this over with so he could go out behind the train, unbutton his pants, and relieve himself in the bushes.

"What're you waiting for?" Marquis demanded. "Why do you want to turn this into a circus?" He faced the little one. "You wish he wouldn't stall too, don't you?"

He looks like a sick, overage baby, Marquis thought to himself. He knew that if he got anything in his stomach, it'd go right through and out his pants. Judging from the way he was shivering.

Marquis spat in the grass. But he couldn't help admiring the little one for having gotten over a bout of typhus. A lot of people had been done in by dysentery, pneumonia, or less serious diseases. The little one must have a very strong will woven among the tiny fibers inside that funny-looking skull of his. Evidently it wasn't enough just to *want* to die.

Maybe next time, he'd be knocked out by the first fever that came along. Or just by a hint of what might happen to him. The same as it had happened to other people.

Marquis looked out across the field. It was lovely, covered with last year's grass. For Marquis, it had a marvelous kind of indifference—like rocks and rivers which go on un-touched by everything that happens. He'd never been able to put it into words. Then he looked up at the sky. Clouds drifted with the wind, going somewhere. It was that *somewhere,* unattainable for human beings, which almost drove him crazy sometimes.

"Look here," said the older one. "We'll start with the youngest. Or alphabetically. Although . . ." He turned to Marquis. "You fit both categories. It's your right to have first go."

When he noticed his expression, he went on, "Let's go over the whole thing one more time, right? Whoever draws the shortest twig, or whoever gets stuck with it, is the one who's going to do the job. The twig you draw is for all day. Or all night. And all day tomorrow. In other words, for as long as we stay here and until the job gets done, right? Is that clear to everybody?"

"I've heard it a million times," Marquis interrupted. "If it's something that's written in the stars, then try reading them and tell us where the next star's going to fall. By now, I couldn't care less. You don't need to drag this thing out the way you're doing. Let's see your hand!"

The wrinkled man was clever enough, he realized, to convince him he ought to begin because he was the youngest, as if it were something to proud of. But he still didn't seem to be in a hurry. Perhaps he was doing it on purpose. He wanted to make sure everybody was quite clear about the rules, because that was the only part of the whole exercise that was fair. He noticed that the little one's chin was quivering. He was dying of anxiety, knowing that if Marquis didn't pull the shortest twig, it was going to be up to him.

"It's written in the stars," the oldest one declared. "This is fair and square, honest to God. It's the fairest way we could do it."

"Nobody's arguing with you and nobody needs to bother drawing after me," said Marquis. "Come on, let's get over with!"

He looked like he had last autumn, when the tall one had introduced him around in the fortress. There were girls there who looked after the horses and who shared themselves with everybody. Except the little one. Finally, even he got his share too.

That was when Marquis acted as if that bedraggled, much-handled, Jewish stablegirl meant something more to him than just feeling high for a few seconds, followed by ten hours of disenchantment and half a year of worry.

They hadn't succeeded in knocking it out of his head. There were some things he'd hung on to, things that were important to him—like hair for that poor guy centuries ago who ended up wishing for just enough strength to pull everything down around his own ears, along with the people who had first robbed him of the source of his strength and everything that was connected with it. But there was betrayal there, and Big Dipper had been careful during the past three years, so nobody could say he'd been involved.

They didn't talk about it, but Big Dipper understood what it meant for Marquis, even in such circumstances, to hold to his principles, never underestimating anybody, but not over-estimating them either. Not to brag and not to let yourself be put down by every fool that comes along. It took a lot of effort.

The little one watched Marquis's lips and then he glanced at Big Dipper's hands. He could feel how hard his heart was thumping.

"All right, come on, for God's sake, I'm telling you for the third time!" Marquis snapped. He took his thumb from his belt loop through which an old piece of rope was threaded to hold up his pants.

The tall one shoved his clenched fist under Marquis's nose. He glanced around quickly to see if there wasn't a guard or the *scharführer* nearby.

Marquis gave a cursory glance at the tips of the three twigs sticking out of Big Dipper's fist and made his choice, picking it out with his dirty fingers.

The oldest one's fist was like an open wound or a big, leathery hill.

One of the twigs was shorter than the others. They all saw it. Marquis felt a sudden wave of anger toward the wrinkled one. It wasn't unadulterated wrath or jealousy or impatience. It had to do with the ancient, crippled yearning he'd sensed in

39

the tall man, like a sum of failures he'd never admitted, a stubborn effort to act like somebody who can take it as well as dish it out, someone who doesn't see betrayal everywhere, and who can still trust in his own destiny. The yearning was warped with someone who doesn't know the dimensions of reality, who doesn't recognize the obstacles, but who goes on putting up a brave front.

Everything inside Marquis was seeking a scapegoat now so he wouldn't have to apply to himself the things he held against the tall one. He looked at the tall man's toothless gums as though they were accusations of his former greediness. Or as though the very fact of his standing there were a reminder of the pit we dig for ourselves.

"I'll take this one," said Marquis.

"O.K., you take that one," echoed Big Dipper. He looked at the little one as though he were asking him to be a witness.

"Sure, you take that one," the little one repeated.

The wrinkled one relaxed his fingers, but kept a careful hold on the two remaining twigs.

Then the little one drew. "This is mine," he said, pointing to the twig at the left. He held his breath.

"All right," said the wrinkled one. "The third and last is mine. Everything that's lucky and unlucky comes in threes. Now let's compare . . ."

He opened his hand and held up his twig as though it were a scalpel or a gold coin.

The little one was the first to notice that his twig was the same length as the wrinkled one's as they lay side by side in the middle of the grubby, calloused palm. When Marquis lay his twig next to the other two, they could see at once that it was the shortest.

"You were right," said the wrinkled one. "It's up to you." He tried not to sound too relieved. But he couldn't contain the tension inside his throat. He didn't want to make Marquis angry or nervous. "It had to be somebody," he went on.

The little one couldn't even speak. He couldn't get over what he'd escaped.

"Don't worry about it," murmured Marquis. "It's as clear as day. It's me, and no sense talking about it." Then he laughed, to shake off the same fears the little one was feeling. I'm not going to slash my wrists on account of this, he told himself. It had been clear to him for a long time that when you want the best, you've got to be prepared to give the best you've got in yourself.

Marquis's smile wasn't a happy smile. For a long time he'd known what it was, that particular kind of anxiety that comes over you at times and you don't know why. It comes just before dawn, around four o'clock in the morning. Later, it starts in the middle of the day. Even when there is no immediate cause for fear.

The little one squatted down.

"I'm not complaining, am I?" Marquis demanded. "It's not such a big deal."

"The important thing is breath control," said the wrinkled one.

"You two lie down over there so nobody sees you," Marquis said. "If I can't do it on the first round, I'll try with the second, at my own risk. I don't want anyone drawing lots, all right?"

"But try to do it the first round," said the one with wrinkles. "You know why I tell you that. I don't want to scare you, but . . ."

"Well, all right, then shut up! I can't stand it when somebody nags even before you get started. You know as well as I do that I'll try my damndest to do it on the first round. I'm not doing this for the fun of it."

"Sure you can do it," the other murmured. "I know what I'm talking about when I say that."

"I'm in good shape," Marquis went on.

"If it'd been me, I'd have tried too, but I've got a belly-ache," put in the little one. "I wouldn't like for us to draw lots a second time if I failed. Like I was dead already."

"I don't take such a gloomy view of it," said Marquis.

"Nobody does," replied Big Dipper.

Marquis was silent. There was always a difference between what the little one said and what the one with wrinkles said. You could stand not eating for six days when you could drink, but if this were to go on twice as long, they'd be finished. It'd be easy for the Germans. They wouldn't need to fire a single bullet. All they'd need to do would be to allow them all to lie down at the edge of the woods on the ninth or tenth day, and after that, their worries would be over. By the time summer was over, they'd all have rotted. Anybody who found them in their rags and tattered shoes, before their flesh was entirely gone, would say "good riddance!"

He looked up at the sky again as though he were trying to forecast the weather. Actually, he was. Looking at the old man's scabrous face, he felt like yelling that everybody is a crook, even if he doesn't cheat anybody but himself, and even if he swears he's honest now. He wouldn't believe anyone again.

He inspected the terrain again, although he knew it by heart now. It looked the same as before. That was good.

Postponing it would only be temporary relief. The tall one read his mind.

"Like we said—just watch your step and look out for the *scharführer*. We're pretty sure of his movements by now. I've kept my eye out. Nobody gets out of the train at this time."

The wrinkled one, Marquis, and the little fellow could all see the German in his riding boots as he passed the staff coach and the supply car, which were coupled together, but uncoupled from the locomotive and the rest of the prison transport train.

"I know what you mean," Marquis said.

The German officer finished his rounds and disappeared behind the train.

"All he'd need to do would be to stop to take a leak and then it would take longer than usual," the older man observed. "But if you keep count for yourself, you won't go wrong. Well, O.K., you know what you're supposed to do. I don't need to give you advice."

Marquis suddenly realized that Big Dipper was usually right, no matter what he said. Not just today.

There were empty fields on both sides of the train. The woods were some distance away. That was why the Germans had left the two coaches there, out in the open. Marquis's thoughts turned back to the little one. Scared little sissy. He'd probably been that way ever since he was born. It must be an awful effort for him to get through each day. Every minute must be a trial of will.

After Marquis had succeeded in dissolving within himself the rage he felt toward the older man, he could feel something like resignation flowing through him. Or calmness. Or the remnants of inner strength. He was simply concentrating now on what came next. He used to admire that kind of concentration in grown-ups.

The railroad track ran through a green meadow at the bottom of a valley between two steep hillsides that resembled two camels. There was a culvert in the middle with a concrete bridge. The ditch along the tracks wasn't deep. It was choked with mud, dead leaves, and last year's pine needles. There were woods on either side. One hill curved away as though it were leading off into some dead-end spur and ended abruptly with wooden buffers set into old cement blocks.

The tall man and the little one lay alongside the tracks. At first, they pretended to be searching for something to eat in the underbrush.

"Keep you eyes open!" whispered the tall one. "Count! Keep counting just to be on the safe side."

"Quit nagging," murmured Marquis, as though he had his mind on other things now. "Don't worry. Relax! Get some rest. You're going to need it." After a pause, he went on, "Well, here I go! Wait here. A jaguar is never scared . . ." He watched the *scharführer* as he finished his round again. As soon as he turned away from the supply car, Marquis moved out, hunched forward, taking long, swift strides. Then he broke into a run. He started counting.

He couldn't see the other two anymore, but they were watching him—small, dark brown, timid eyes lost in a face which seemed to be getting smaller and smaller. Big, cautious eyes of an aging man.

The one with wrinkles put his arm around the little one's shoulders. He was shivering. They lay next to the tracks like creatures exhausted after a day of grazing and troubled by something they'd eaten. Or hadn't. Most of the other prisoners from the transport were lying next to the tracks too or along the banks of the creek. They were the ones who had made it, who hadn't been left along the wayside yet. The two men stared fixedly across the silver tracks, watching Marquis run, counting to themselves, wondering how it was going to turn out.

They knew as well as Marquis did that he had sixty seconds to get to the supply car. If there were no complications, he had eighty seconds to fumble with the tarpaulin which covered the car and with the loaves of bread inside. He had to do it so the *scharführer* wouldn't see. Then he had to run back to the tracks where the other two were waiting for him. He'd have to act as if he'd just been out for a stroll in the field.

If the *scharführer* saw him, he'd shoot. That had happened to two other prisoners yesterday. A freight car full of bread was too great a temptation for people who hadn't had anything to eat for six days. No one else had tried it since yesterday, though, so they figured the *scharführer* wasn't worried anymore.

Marquis ran on. He could feel Big Dipper's eyes boring into his back like bright daggers, sharp knives. Or raw gashes in his skin. He could feel the little one watching him listlessly.

So far, so good. He was doing better than he'd expected. He didn't have to worry as much as the little one or even Big Dipper, who would have a hard time if he had to make a break for it late some afternoon without having anything to eat. He'd probably pass out in the middle of a swamp some night, exhausted from hunger.

Marquis was making good time, even though this was just a brief spurt of force, powered by his fear of getting caught. It gave fleetness to his feet. He'd stick it out for two rounds. But there was that thing that had happened yesterday, when the *scharführer* had subtracted two from their number. He'd shot two kids who had tried the same trick. Afterwards, he'd ordered a couple of Orthodox Poles with side curls to drag the bodies off into the woods, where they were left lying. Like dogs. Being able to lie down somewhere like a dead dog wasn't the kind of rest Marquis was interested in yet. Like every living being, he had a spark of hope inside him that he would survive simply because he was still alive.

The *scharführer* enjoyed shooting. He took particular pleasure in shooting people at close range.

Marquis certainly didn't identify himself with the two boys who'd been shot. But he could still see them, as though he had a third eye in addition to the two that were keeping a careful watch on the field and on the freight car. He could see the *scharführer* ordering them to get undressed. They were naked when he shot them. It probably gave him a bigger kick to shoot naked men. As if they were being born instead of dying. Well, it was over for those two now. Two rounds, Marquis repeated to himself. He makes two rounds and then he turns. That gives me twenty seconds. Like a one-man marathon.

He counted up to fifty as he ran and he counted fast. That made it twenty seconds instead of forty. One to forty. After that, he wouldn't need to bother counting anymore.

He jumped over the oil-smeared axle. Now he didn't have time to imagine himself naked, before they'd shoot him.

If this had been the end of the first lap in a race, people would have been crowding around, slapping him on the back and congratulating him.

He was careful not to slip on the oily axle. He held on tight to the straps of the canvas tarpaulin which was stiff as a board after the rain. Then he grabbed the tarpaulin itself and tried to fold it back, but it resisted. His feet felt solid on the six-sided grease cup in the middle of the freight car's wheel. There were rainbows in the puddle of leaked oil underneath.

He slid his right arm easily under the tarpaulin. But then he had trouble. He stuck it in up to his elbow. He couln't reach far enough to get the bread. He couldn't even touch it. He'd been glad everything had gone so well so far—even though the tarpaulin was stiff—but now he suddenly felt let down.

The bread was farther back in the car than he'd expected. At first he thought maybe the bread was all gone, and he wished he could shinny up and see for himself to make sure there was cause for panic. Then he put himself in the place of the *scharführer* or any German officer. They were going to need a lot of bread, even though they were the only ones on the whole train who had eaten any during the past six days.

Marquis had a skinny arm. He wasn't really as strong as he liked to think he was. He tried to reach as far as he could and then he saw there was no point, that he was simply wasting time.

It was a good thing he was as skinny as he was, but it was too bad his arms were too short. He stood on tiptoes on the slippery grease cup. He stretched as far as he could and poked into the darkness. One good thing about not having had anything to eat for such a long time was that he wasn't very fat. This little old hand of mine isn't just a hand, he told himself encouragingly. It's a crane. It's a miraculous tool made of flesh and blood and bone, a fantastically sensitive and delicate affair, a handy thing to have around when you're in a hurry.

He was in a feverish hurry now, but that didn't make any difference in the depth he had to reach. And couldn't. It's an elephant's trunk, he told himself. A monkey's paw. A pair of tweezers stitched onto my body. Seagull's claws. When a man has to, he always goes beyond his limits. But he wasn't sure that this was the case.

He tried to guess how much time had gone by. A hand and fingers aren't a strong enough magnet to pull bread out of the bottom of a freight car, that was obvious.

He groped into the emptiness. My arms are too short. I've got short legs, too. Too short for a job like this, anyway. I never realized I was born with such short arms and legs.

He stretched as far as he could, like one of those snake men he'd seen in a sideshow once. Aw, this thing's not going to fail just because I've got short arms, is it?

At last his nails grated against the bread and he touched it with his fingertips. It was like touching a nut he couldn't see. Or a turtle's shell. It was hard and dry. He had to stretch another inch. Finally he had a loaf of bread between his fingertips.

Once again he thought of all the things that were connected with bread. It wasn't just life, which is what the bread stood for and what life must have. There was death—extinction—which is what *not* having bread means.

The loaf slid out of his fingers. Don't panic!

It was a kind of extinction which no longer had anything to do with having bread or not having it, but with how he'd gotten here and with the paths that led into the future—paths he'd have to cross off his list now.

He leaned over so far that his feet barely touched the grease cup over the axle. He went through the whole procedure again, almost mechanically. Whenever I move my hand that way, I waste too much strength. You can choke your arm just as easily as you can choke another person when you squeeze his neck. He felt around for better footing.

As soon as I find a place to put my foot, I'll use my other arm. He counted to twenty. He groped for the bread again. He put his weight on the other foot. Two stabs of pain shot into his left leg in quick succession, as though the muscle were being torn in two. He tried to ignore the message his leg was sending him.

I'm counting, slowly. O.K., who am I trying to kid? . . . twenty-eight, twenty-nine, thirty . . . I can make it in fifty seconds even if the wind's against me.

A cramp grabbed at his left leg. He changed feet again and wasted a few seconds, trying to massage the pain away from his calf.

He got the bread in his grip again. Carefully, he drew it toward him. It dropped. He told himself that his fingers probably weren't strong enough, that he wasn't determined enough. But he knew it wasn't true. He was afraid to think about time now. He tried imagining time as an old rag, something you toss over your shoulder.

I can do this job even in forty seconds, he reassured himself. He wouldn't need to run. It wasn't a complete lie, although it wasn't completely true. The important thing wasn't the distance he'd have to run, but whether the *scharführer* would spot him.

He knew this wasn't just one of those little truths you scrape together into an alibi, and when you add them up, all you've got is just another lie.

He broke into a cold sweat, which had sometimes happened to him when he'd seen people shot down right beside him.

It was the kind of cold sweat that comes when you're trying to reassure yourself that it's all right to go on shooting and hanging and sending people into the showers. As long as it's not you.

The little one sweated that way because he'd had typhus and he knew that's what it was, that he couldn't kid himself or anybody else about it.

Marquis got the crazy idea of waiting until the *scharführer* came around again and hailing him with a friendly grin from the axle: "Hi, there, old buddy, how're you doing today?" Something really crazy.

But instead, he could see the *scharführer* shooting those two prisoners yesterday. Pistol shots sound different in the woods than they do in an empty field or in the courtyard of a barracks. They probably sound different too when you're standing beside a train. The results are the same, though.

Big Dipper was telling him what he thought of him, speaking wordlessly, without even opening his lips, so nobody could see or hear a thing. It wasn't just the cup of bitterness which everybody must finally drain, whether he wants to or not, and no matter how he rationalizes about the different ways of getting out of it. It wasn't just the disappointment of realizing that most people expect you to do something they can't do themselves. And prefer not to.

Then Marquis tasted the condescending scorn which would come after.

The little one would probably put in his two cents' worth also, to minimize his own fears. They'll thank me when I tell them my arms were just too short. I'll be lucky if I get to tell them anything. Unfortunately, arms aren't like a length of rope you can splice together and extend. Their anger would all boil down to one thing: that he hadn't done what he was supposed to do.

God, isn't it disgusting how little it matters what you want and why you want it? For whom and against whom? That your intentions don't mean a thing, no matter who they help or hurt?

When I start thinking like that, I'm beaten to begin with, he said to himself. If I don't stop it, I'll be dead even before they shoot me.

The *scharführer* was still making his rounds, unaware of what was going on behind his back.

Marquis told himself that he must not lose heart. He could hardly feel the pain in his left leg anymore. The thing he held between his fingers now, easing it upwards, this was just a trifle, nothing very important. Not worth getting upset about, he told himself. The loaf felt very hard. It must have been pulled out of the oven quite a while ago.

He'd seen a few people with bullet holes in their heads and it didn't take much effort to remember what they looked like. The holes looked rather innocent and harmless. As harmless as when you grab a wire, telling yourself it's not electrified, or that it won't matter.

There are some things we run after and it turns out that we run in vain. Then there are things we don't pursue, and those are the things that escape us. Marquis tried a third time. He had stopped counting or even trying to guess how much time he had left. He was staking everything on getting that loaf of bread. But he could still see the other two—the little one and the one with wrinkles. Their eyes were strained and bulging.

As long as they don't shoot you, you're still alive, he told himself. It sounded quite lucid and simple.

There isn't any loaf of bread. It's a Brazil nut, the kind we used to steal when we were kids from the grocery store in the building where I was born. Brazil nuts used to be on sale all fall until Christmas. The grocer joined the Germans in 1939. He bought his three boys Hitler-Jugend *uniforms with belts and daggers. To toughen up, they wore corduroy shorts all winter and brown shirts with neckerchiefs and braided leather rings. Dressed like that, they were absolutely sure that they were more important than they actually were.*

When you join such an organization, itself supported by another organization, you're no longer just an ordinary mortal. You belong to two intertwined organizations and that makes you twice as much—you're something to begin with and then you're part of something even bigger besides.

Dad hated that sort of thing. He used to make fun of it, before he went up the chimney. The ones who sent him there didn't do it themselves, so they'd have to bear the responsiblity—they did it for the organization that covered or embraced them.

It was a good thing he'd had practice stealing Brazil nuts. But he'd stolen them for private reasons. He'd only been risking his own skin. It had always been that way. It had been easy as pie, snatching those nuts with five fingers. The thing he was working on now felt like the cheaper Brazil nuts, the ones that used to be kept in a bag outside the store—a burlap bag that was always rolled open like a sailor's thick, turtleneck sweater.

Hastily, he tried with the other hand. It happened again—twice, a third time. He moved slowly, so he wouldn't have to accuse himself of having been in too much of a hurry if it failed. He was furious with the bread, and yet he pleaded with it, explaining things he would have easily understood if he'd been in the place of that loaf of German bread, which was getting heavier and heavier.

Extracting the bread from the freight car would be just as miraculous as *not* getting it would be terrible. Last time, when he was sure he had it in his grasp, it slipped through his fingers just as he reached out for it with his other hand.

Now all that mattered was that nobody saw him crouched next to the train. He got his hands on the bread again. Defeat is always ugly. He dug his nails into the loaf, like a weak animal clawing at a bigger, stronger one. That bread was dead, but they were still alive. But the inanimate loaf of bread probably stood a better chance than they did. Its crust cut into the flesh at the base of his nails and his cuticles. He knew it, but he paid no attention to the pain. He knew he wasn't going to drop the bread this time and he held onto it as though this were the most important thing he'd ever done. He wondered how much time he'd wasted.

Then there was no time for such thoughts, because he felt the loaf slipping from his grip again. As if his fingernails and the cramped joints and the blood which must have soaked in and softened the hard crust weren't enough to hold it.

One, two, three . . . He leaned forward as far as he could. He bent his arm up over the side of the car. He heard it crack.

Once again, he stabbed his fingernails into the loaf. Something snapped.

He pulled out the loaf just when one wave of pain had erased the first. He didn't realize quite what had happened. He thought he'd dropped it again.

He shifted the bread to the other hand and jumped down. Everything seemed to be cheering him on again, as if this were just a race with time and he'd lost a couple of seconds, that was all, and he'd be able to make up for them.

It was one of his peculiarities that in moments of acute danger he didn't think of risk, but simply about what had to be done to get out of it.

He'd found out that thinking about the risk before it comes is worse than the danger itself. It drains something out of you.

The *scharführer* was still on the other side of the train. Marquis could hear voices. He could make out whole sentences. There was a field ahead. The wind had died down. He might be able to make it back to the others in twenty seconds. As he ran with his precious prey, he decided that he could now afford to feel at least a little bit proud of himself. Like when he'd realized that a man's best accomplishments are paid for with what belongs to him alone: his bones and blood, his sweat and shredded muscles, frayed like a blade of grass.

He didn't even need to think about it; it was the substance of the years he'd spent in camps and the years before that, as though there were really nothing more between them than a thin sort of membrane. It was all part of the same life, no matter what some people said.

Just then, he heard the *scharführer* behind him.

"Hey, what's going on! What're you doing?" he yelled. "Stop! *Halt!*"

Marquis winced under the impact of the rough voice and dashed on, trying to move even faster. He knew he was making a mistake, but it was one of those mistakes you can't correct because it was part of everything that had happened to him before. He bent double and kept going. He had almost stumbled when the German yelled at him; it was as though he'd been grabbed by the collar.

Any minute, he expected the *scharführer* to pull his pistol and shoot him in the back. That would be best. He ducked instinctively. He didn't want to get shot through the head.

"*Halt!*" howled the *scharführer*.

Marquis scraped together all the strength he had left so he could throw the bread to where the other two lay waiting along the tracks.

In his mind's eye, he could see them and even hear them breathing heavily. He heard inaudible voices, cheering him on as they'd done the whole way: while he was running, while he was trying to get the bread out of the freight car, and now on the way back. He gritted his teeth and pressed his lips tight. His strength was waning fast, but he knew that if he went a few more yards, he wouldn't even be able to throw them the bread. And he'd probably get shot in the back first.

Their voices—the little fellow's and the wrinkled one's— came to him across the field, from the railroad tracks and out of the crescent-shaped clearing \hemmed in by the forest, out of the sullen afternoon sky, from the cold earth of early spring over which he ran—from everywhere he heard them.

He closed his eyes for a second and heard them more clearly than all other sounds. It was like the hum of wind and trees, as if voices were coming out of the blades of grass.

"We drew lots and it was up to you and you didn't do it," accused Big Dipper.

"You're really a goddamned sissy," drawled the little one.

"It looks like that was just dumb luck when you got that last loaf of bread from the scharführer. *It was supposed to feed ninety-two people on this transport. You know how to show off for the dead."*

"The higher you fly, the harder you fall," observed the little one.

"You're like a cat that scares birds but can't catch mice," declared Big Dipper. He said it sadly, as though it came as no surprise.

"It's really ridiculous for you to get mad at us on top of everything else," the little one went on.

"We were lying here and counting," said the tall one. *"Before he shot at you, you should have told him you wanted to have your school tuition refunded, because they obviously didn't teach you how to count. When you were right in the middle of it, you suddenly starting fooling around and I tried to signal you—I whistled La Cucaracha like we said, but you didn't hear it! My eyes were flashing like Sirius crossed with Proxima Centaur. And you were lucky the* scharführer *took eight seconds to blow his nose. And after that, he didn't walk as fast as we were counting, because he was trying to stick his handkerchief back in his pants pocket."*

He noticed that the little one wasn't sweating anymore. He didn't feel like asking them whether the only way to measure what you win is by what the other fellow loses. As if it had never stopped being true. Certainly not here and not now. He wasn't looking for justice anywhere but within himself. He was angry at himself.

"I tried. Honest," he told them. *"And finally I did it. You act like we're in a courtroom. You're so smart at arithmetic, but I broke my arm in the process, you know? I'd like to see either of you do it any better with a broken arm!"*

"You've always been a champion at alibis," said the tall one. *"Next time, Little Red Riding Hood, maybe? Aw, come on, kid."*

"I'm not a kid to you."

"For me, you're a little blue-eyed Jewish baby doll. Who was it that pitched corpses out of the train for you when you got sick to your stomach and were as white as if you had talcum powder all over your face?"

"I can't stand dead bodies, that's all," said Marquis.

"Man, there's an awful lot you can't stand. First you can't stand rats, then you can't stand dead bodies. You can't stand anti-Semites and finally you can't even stand Jews. As long as I've known you, you haven't like Jews from Poland, but you wouldn't give two cents for a German Jew either. According

to you, French Jews are degenerate and American Jews like their pocketbooks better than their poor little cousins on the battlefields of Europe. Rich people are too spoiled and poor ones are too crude. Weren't you born in the wrong century by some mistake, that you're so hypersensitive?"

"You know why I can't stand dead bodies when they're lying in big piles, looking worse than when they were alive," replied Marquis. *"It's just because they remind me of my own people who went up the chimney and I don't want to remember them in such an ugly way just because that was what happened to them.*

The tall one wrinkled his brow. "It's not up to me to pass judgment on your not being able to stand dead bodies, but you can't stand people, living or dead. You're awfully intolerant. With a character like yours, you better not rush into anything. Maybe you'll be an insect in your next life. Just be careful nobody tramps on you. And don't bite or sting anybody, like you're doing now, O.K.?" There wasn't even a shade of caring in his voice. It was an open sneer.

"It was written in the stars as soon as you pulled that shorter twig," observed the little one. *"Too bad you couldn't have seen yourself. You acted like a regular sleepwalker."*

"It's not over yet," said Marquis. *"I've still got a couple seconds before he grabs me with that free hand of his—one's enough for drawing a gun."*

"You're too slow for this sort of thing," declared the tall one. *"You couldn't have run that distance even in a thousand seconds."*

"You're really bushed, aren't you?" put in the little one. *"You're as white as if somebody'd been threatening to pump your stomach and drain your veins."*

"That little twig brought you bad luck," said the Big Dipper.

"I told you you don't need to feel sorry for me," said Marquis. *"People don't call me Marquis for nothing."*

"Nobody's going to call you that anymore, unless they're weak in the head." Big Dipper grimaced knowingly. His skin

looked like the hide of some animal that's been extinct for centuries and has reappeared by mistake or been dug out of a swamp or some ancient burial ground after roasting in the sun for a million years.

The little one's eyes got farther and farther away.

It was as though his eyes and the blotches on his face were distant stars, fading off into space so fast you couldn't even see them go.

"Catch!" Marquis mouthed the word. The sound came out as a whistle. He couldn't squeeze enough air out of his lungs.

"*Halt*!" yelled the *scharführer* behind him. "Hit the dirt! Stop those skinny pipestems of yours, you little rat, before I shoot you full of holes. Stop!"

Marquis didn't bother to answer. Even if he'd had a chance to choose between making the same mistake twice or acting differently, he wouldn't have done otherwise. He gulped for breath. His ears still rang with their angry accusations.

"*Halt*, or I'll break your neck!" shouted the *scharführer*.

That had been another one of his silly games—letting them call him Marquis in a concentration camp or on a transport from Buchenwald to Dachau. But as long as you've got the strength for it and if you're good at make-believe, it's one more proof that you're alive. You can play games even if you're hungry and thirsty and scared. But once they've killed you, you can't play anymore.

With his good arm, Marquis threw the bread as far as he could and watched it bounce and roll off the grass.

He decided to stop running. Maybe that would confuse the *scharführer*. He turned and dropped to the ground and the German almost stumbled over him.

"Give me that bread, you thief!" he screamed, and then Marquis realized that the sergeant hadn't seen what he'd done.

"I don't have any bread," he replied as he got to his feet.

"What do you mean?"

"You can see for yourself."

"Aha, so you haven't got any bread, huh?" said the German.

"No."

The veins in the sergeant's temples throbbed and his face reddened. "You think you can tell me a barefaced lie, do you?"

"I'm not telling any lies."

"Take your clothes off!"

Marquis began to get undressed. He stripped off his jacket and held his breath in pain, hoping the German wouldn't notice his disabled arm. He'd shoot him just for that, without knowing how it happened.

"I see I've got to help you remember," said the *scharführer*. "I'll have to teach you how to tell the truth."

Marquis watched the sergeant draw his pistol. He did it absently, as though he had something else on his mind. Marquis stood naked in the middle of the field.

Carefully, so the *scharführer* wouldn't notice, Marquis had his eye on the little one and the tall man, who were squatting nervously to one side. Between the railroad tracks and within sight of Marquis and the other two stood three men with side curls. They still wore the long shiny coats and furry hats they'd brought with them from Poland. They'd found the bread and had instantly torn it to pieces. The loaf was filthy, smeared with axle grease, mud, and the blood from Marquis's fingers. They crouched a few paces away from the other two and began to stuff their mouths with bread.

"I'll count to three," said the *scharführer*, "so you can change your mind. Maybe you think I'm your daddy or your mommy, that you can tell me a lie straight to my face. Well, you're wrong. There aren't any more daddies and mommies here."

As soon as the three men with the side curls had torn off a mouthful of bread, they left the rest for the oldest among them, figuring that the *scharführer* was going to be busy for a while. At least as long as it took him to count to three.

Marquis wasn't blaming anybody. He was cold, though, and that made him wish he'd get it over with. The German brushed away a gnat from his clean-shaven cheek with the muzzle of his pistol. Then Marquis heard him release the safety catch.

He felt oddly at peace, but he didn't know how to explain it. Those men with the side curls were hungry and now, after six days of nothing to eat, they'd gotten their hands on a loaf of bread. He couldn't be angry with them, even though he had a right to be. It probably wasn't normal *not* to be angry.

He looked beyond the German who was standing there, his pistol aimed right at him, and he saw the little one watching the men with the side curls, his eyes swimming with tears of rage. Marquis couldn't tell him, "Forget it, that bread doesn't belong just to us..." The little one swallowed back the urge to scream at the three Poles to at least leave them a couple crumbs. He knew he mustn't open his mouth. So he was crying.

"One..." the *scharführer* began. He eyed Marquis's scrawny body and his narrow, shaved head.

Marquis focused on the index finger, bent at the first joint and resting on the trigger. The other two were watching also. They saw the finger move, then stop.

This didn't make the men with the side curls feel any better. Or worse.

Well, I guess it's really screwed up this time, Marquis told himself.

Then he realized what the numbers on the railroad cars probably stood for. A "1" at the beginning meant load capacity or depot of origin. How can a person turn into a rail-road car?

"... two ...," the German went on.

The men with the side curls were choking on that bread. Served them right! If I didn't have to stand here waiting for the *scharführer* to count to three and shoot me and get it over with, I'd go over there and slap them on their backs. They must know that once that shot rings—two shots, maybe— their banquet will be over. And they must know how it's going to end.

Do you suppose they still think it was no more than a loaf of bread? Can't they imagine what it meant for the three of us?

The men with the side curls weren't planning on running away anymore. They had nowhere to go. Marquis stared into the muzzle of the pistol which was so close that he could see its every detail. He thought back briefly over the life he was about to lose. It really hadn't been worth much—aside from what little value it had for him. It was a very long time ago when people who'd been losing had with the last remnants of their strength still tried to put a brave face on their defeat. They knew why. To look good in defeat is the ultimate a person can want. It had something to do with the dream of a beautiful life, even though it had all evaporated. And something always happens to make you lose. It was like walking around with a veil over your eyes and when the veil is ripped away, you suddenly see what's there.

Too bad, he thought to himself. But, fortunately, only for him. This would be over quickly and he'd have no time for regrets. It didn't cross his mind now that a man can die a coward or full of courage. Although he'd thought about it often enough before.

The explosion would crack when the German got to three.

Once, as a child, he'd found an eighteenth century watch among his father's things. It had a hammered silver case with a tiny engraved design. Father had been proud of it, as he'd been proud of an old American victrola and the propeller of a German monoplane that fell on the Italian front during the Great War and which Mother used to scold him about because it just gathered dust.

The watch had been shaped like a pear, which surprised him because he had always thought watches were round. But that was just because he'd never seen any other kind. Father used to say that time is death. That wooden propeller blade, with its greenish bronze or copper edge, had something of death about it too. The victrola didn't work anymore; its spring was broken even before Dad got it.

Time reminds everybody of death, but who goes around day and night talking about it? Was this the source of that strange anxiety which sometimes comes over us, without our knowing why? Like some strange sister of joy, it was a tremor of fear, of ending, of all that begins and passes away. Was this the source of that odd loneliness we feel even when we aren't alone, and which is akin to stardust?

Marquis felt a special kind of sorrow, a quiet kind he'd never felt before, like telling himself that, regardless of everything, it was all right now. It was easier to adjust to the idea and accept it. Better than a lot of regrets.

If the *scharführer* shot him in the leg or spine, it would be worse. The pistol was two paces away, aimed at the middle of his forehead. It was funny how close it was and how clearly he could see it. His eyesight had gotten worse in camp.

". . . three," said the *scharführer.*

His index finger pressed against the trigger at the level of Marquis's eyes and pulled it back to where it would release the spring. The bolt would strike against the lock with a metallic crack, and the shot would flash out of the barrel.

Marquis thought he could smell the fragrance of the forest, of pure air scented with resin and leaf mold where pine needles and trees and moss rot away and go on living. He stared at the man's finger, as if it were hard for him to realize what was happening. He wondered whether he ought to tell the *scharführer* that these men in the long shiny coats had the bread. He'd never done anything like that in his life, but only because he's been afraid of cowardice and of what other people would say, even if he weren't around to hear it. That was stronger than any other impulse. Even now. The temptation lasted only a fraction of a second.

Marquis closed his eyes.

It all began to flood through him and it was different than he'd always heard it was and different than he'd imagined it would be. It came in a quiet swirling, like wind rushing across a field, a sensation of emptiness, or the sleep he'd been looking forward to that steals away consciousness, and now it was coming toward him like the wings of a honeybee or a dragonfly, whirring and hovering in one place. Or like the

tugging current of a river. Or the stars Big Dipper used to talk
about and which he could see in the daytime as well as at
night. It was the kind of restfulness the little one had yearned
for when he'd been all worn out after endlessly unloading
freight cars and could finally lie down under the trains.
Sometimes even under the locomotive. Just to get some rest.

Marquis wasn't looking anymore, but even with his eyes
closed, he could see that finger pressing the trigger. As if
anything else could happen now. Then he blacked out. But it
wasn't a pistol shot he heard, but the little one's voice.

"The bread's over here!"

It was more of a wheeze, sounding very close, and choked
with the bitterness and fear which timid people can never
shake off.

Marquis opened his eyes and saw the little one leap in front
of him, shielding the muzzle of the German's pistol, a dilapi-
dated human wall between the bullet and his head. The kid
was almost strangled by fear. Drops of cold sweat as big as
rosebuds stood out on his dirty, scabby skull.

"You damned shit!" said the *scharführer* and turned back
toward the train where the Poles were huddled by the wheels.
"What're you doing over there?" Then, as though he'd
recovered, he demanded, "Well, what do you think I'm here
for, just to keep an eye on you?"

It didn't make any sense, but all of a sudden, nothing did.
The little one smelled of sweat. He was soaking wet.

"Move on!" The *scharführer* prodded him with the muzzle
of his gun. "You hear me?" He looked over at the freight car
and at the three Poles, frozen to the spot, their mouths
stuffed with bread they couldn't chew. They couldn't
swallow it and they could hardly breathe.

"*Scheise!*" repeated the *scharführer.*

Everything that came into his mind collected within the
shell of that single word.

"I've only got so much patience left," the German went
on. "And nobody's going to play around with me!" He fired
a few shots in the direction of the Poles. It was impossible to
know whether he hit anybody or not.

For a moment, the *scharführer* felt that grayish urge he always got in his finger when he was holding a gun and had his sights set on a Jew. Or any prisoner, for that matter. It was like a flame that consumes, even though what it burned may have been the courage and comradeship which he knew were purely German virtues, unknown in lower, inferior races. He never had any doubt of that. It was like a brush fire, like when lightning sets fire to a field of dry grass. He had a fleeting vision of a smoldering broken rope. One, two, thousands of convicts. Yesterday he'd shot those two easily. No trouble at all, and thanks to that, he got rid of all complications. (As though everybody he didn't shoot would sooner or later poison his life.)

He spat in the grass. He felt scorn and revulsion for the little one and the others, but he wondered whether there was more to it than that.

He shoved his way between the little one and Marquis, stepped over Marquis's rags and tattered shoes, kicking them away. They watched him as he went with that strange rocking gait. He headed across the green field, watching for gopher holes or puddles, through the grass that had been flattened by the wind. He moved toward the staff car and its freight wagon, full of supplies.

He had begun his regular rounds again, once every hundred and twenty seconds.

Everything for the three of them was suddenly like many tiny flames bursting into a dazzling fire that crackled and rose higher and higher before it dropped, flickered, and swallowed itself.

Big Dipper pulled himself together. He threw himself on one of the three Poles. He started yanking from his fingers what was left of the bread. Then he pried from his mouth what he hadn't managed to swallow yet and angrily slapped him across the face.

"We drew lots, didn't we? And you got it," the little one told the middle-sized one, the boy they called Marquis. "And I felt stupid leaving you in that mess to catch hell, with nothing to show for it."

The White Rabbit

Thomas, otherwise known as Ugly, took off his glasses, then put them on again. He'd been standing there for an hour. He was waiting for Flea. She might have stuck out that little shaved head of hers by now, he thought to himself. So he wouldn't have to tramp around like this to keep warm.

They'd brought Flea here with encephalitis, the cross-eyed disease. She couldn't touch her finger to the tip of her nose.

When it was cloudy and windy, like today, the Cavalry Barracks didn't seem so big. He looked around the cobbled courtyard. Thomas was getting goose pimples.

The contagious brain disease ward was in front of him. The mental hospital was behind him. There were bars on the windows on both sides.

He was disappointed when the first patient he saw through the bars was a woman mending a stocking.

You probably couldn't escape through those bars, he decided. And even if you could, where would you go?

Red brick ramparts rose in back of the mental hospital, surrounding the star-shaped fortress town. There was a moat under the ramparts. Ammunition warehouses had been turned into stables, with crumbling loop holes in the walls. The cannons had long since disappeared. Rainwater accumulated in the gutters and storage space.

Anyway, it's all full of rats here, Thomas thought to himself.

The time Thomas had been with Flea, it had been up on the ramparts. He'd brought her a jumprope made out of string from food parcels. Girls from mixed marriages whose parents stayed in Prague were allowed to get two parcels a year. He wondered whether he could make Flea feel good by picking her a dandelion. Last year, when the dandelions went to seed, all you had to do was kick them or blow on them and the downy parachutes landed far away, burrowing their little white feet who knows where?

He began his walk. For a change, he snapped his fingernails against the fence in front of the mental hospital. The little folks with the pointed heads were still inside, but it was time for their outing. Unless the doctor thought it was too windy.

When Thomas looked through the windows into the stalls, he could smell the old horse blankets.

He flapped his arms and jumped up and down to get his blood circulating. Then he trotted around in a circle like a horse. When he stopped, he looked up at the window of the hospital ward.

"You're really taking your time today," he said out loud. "What are they doing with you there, Flea?"

With his back to the mental hospital, the barracks looked hostile, somehow. Everything seemed hostile. He took a deep breath.

"No matter where you look, it's full of anti-Semites," he said. Then he looked up at the window.

"I just hope you don't have to wait out in the hall," he said. "This morning it looked like it was going to be a cold day. The sun was like an underdone plum pie."

He tried touching the tip of his nose ten times in a row from a distance of thirty centimeters. Then he tried closing his eyes and walking a straight line as if it were a tightrope and he had to keep his balance.

He sat down on the ledge again. He leaned back and looked up at where Flea was supposed to appear at any minute.

I can't hang around here forever, he thought to himself. He rubbed his ankles to warm up. To hell with them, to hell with them, to hell with them—three times for good luck. I'm really going to have to leave in a little while, he said to himself. During the day, he had a job stacking wood behind the house of a German major, he and an old man who took

64

care of the major's rabbits. He looked up at the window again and then he got the idea of taking one of the rabbits and showing it to Flea.

"Just showing it to her, not pinching it," he said aloud.

He could just see those two young rabbits: the black one with chestnut brown eyes and his little white brother. What if I brought the white one for Flea? I bet she's never had anything like that in her hands in her life. He looked up. He took off his glasses with the rusty steel frames. He rubbed them clean. When he closed his eyes, he could see himself even more clearly, giving Flea the little rabbit.

The glasses felt cold when he put them on again. He rubbed his nose with the back of his hand. It was so cold his eyes watered. The wind was blowing toward the mental hospital. He could just see the German major's garden with its two big Canadian spruces. The old man went to work like Bismarck. He'd been a zoology professor.

Thomas wrinkled his nose and forehead. The cold slipped in through his sleeves, into his shirt and up his pants' legs. If only Flea would stick out that little shorn head of hers that looks like a dingy tennis ball, he thought to himself.

He thought about the white one. About poking his finger into its mouth, between its soft lips.

"An animal doesn't trust anybody," he muttered. "Animals just keep defending themselves," he added. And he grinned to himself.

Last time, he'd asked the old man why he put the black one and the white one in a separate cage. The old fellow explained it as if he were lecturing at a university. When Jews get old, nothing's ever a simple yes or no. For every "maybe," one hundred and twenty "but if's." The female had simply eaten one of her young. And now the major would eat her. His stomach rumbled.

He heard a noise behind him. The mental patients were coming out into the garden, much later than usual. They came two by two, women and men. They were holding each other's hands. They filed past the fence. Some of them were chewing something.

"I don't trust anybody either," said Thomas. "And if I

65

didn't defend myself, then I don't know who would."

The loonies looked peaceful. They were frail. But they always reminded him of animals and he didn't know why. But they didn't look dangerous. What were they chewing? A kick in the rear to everybody, he thought to himself. Where's Flea? For ten minutes, he stared at the toes of his shoes. Then he stared at the hard-packed earth and up at the window.

"Flea!" he said all of a sudden.

He raised his head, took off his glasses, wiped off the mist, and put them on again and blinked, his grin widening.

"Flea!" he whispered again. "Hi, there, Flea!"

A wave of warmth washed through his body. So she came after all. A good thing I waited. It's good I didn't miss her.

He called up to the girl in the window. "Like that professor I stack wood with says, Flea, a living head finally gets the hat it's been waiting for."

He looked up at the window. "How are you? What're you doing with yourself?" He wiped his nose. "How're you feeling? I hope you're all right, Flea."

He laughed. "I knew you'd show up, Flea. How are you doing? What's new?"

On the first floor, low enough for him to see but too high to hear her answer, a skinny little girl in a white flannel nightgown stood behind the grilled window. Thomas figured the window must be eight or ten meters high.

"You're barefoot, Flea," he said. "Aren't you cold?" Then he added, "You look absolutely normal, Flea."

The girl pressed her nose to the window. The tip flattened against the glass.

"You've got a cute little nose, Flea. I've got a nose like Mount Everest."

He chuckled briefly. He furrowed his brow and jutted out his chin, craning his neck. It was blue with cold. He tried to understand what her lips were saying.

"Encephalitis gets every other kid now."

Again she opened her lips and said something which he couldn't understand down below.

The girl in the window pressed her nose against the glass. Its tip flattened white. "As soon as the loonies come prancing out of the stable, you've got to show up," he said. "They operate like clockwork."

He was silent for about two minutes. He smiled at her for a while, hopping from one foot to the other. Then he rubbed his hands together. And smiled again. He had the impression that she smiled back at him.

He looked around cautiously to make sure nobody was listening. The girl opened her lips again. The glass grew misty from her breath. She drew something on the windowpane with her fingertip. She watched for a while as Thomas stared up at it. She was trying to tell him something. Her lips moved. Thomas did not respond because three people were going by. He waited until they passed behind the mental hospital. Fortunately, nobody paid much attention to anybody else in the Cavalry Courtyard.

Thomas held out his empty hands to show he didn't understand what the girl wanted. She responded with a few incomprehensible gestures.

"Just try touching your nose from a distance of thirty centimeters!" he said. "Like an exercise. You'll see, you can do it, Flea!"

The girl looked down at the mental patients as they paraded past. Then she gazed up at the treetops and the sky.

"You can't imagine how windy it is out here!" said Thomas.

Then he hugged himself to warm up. "I'm going to have to go. I'm going to have to get back to my stupid woodpile." He quickly wiped his nose. The girl didn't stir.

"What I'd like best would be for us to hibernate together, you and me," he said. He remembered crawling into his mother's bed on Sunday mornings, when she didn't have to go to work. Kick 'em all in the pants, he thought to himself.

The girl's lips moved.

"When spring comes, we'll go up on the ramparts," he said. "We'll walk over the heads of the loonies, but they won't even know it. I've investigated and found out how thick the walls are here. Can you hear me?"

But he knew she couldn't hear him. He looked up at the window.

"So long, Flea! We'll be seeing each other again."

He backed away along the fence of the mental hospital, as though he were dodging something. He watched Flea who was still standing at the window, her nose and mouth and forehead pressed against the glass. She could cut herself, he thought to himself, and waved at her to get back from the window. When he couldn't see her anymore, he turned and dashed as fast as he could across the courtyard, through the gate and down the street. He imagined that Flea was watching him, so he ran even faster.

After a while, he felt that he was getting tired. But he kept on running because he was in a hurry and also because he knew it was one way to warm up.

He bumped into several pedestrians, but he didn't bother to excuse himself. Bumping into Jews isn't a punishable offense, he said to himself. Bumping into Jews in Theresienstadt is almost a pleasure. I'm a fine anti-Semite myself by now, he thought.

He took a short-cut across the field, hoping some dumb or shortsighted German soldier wouldn't take a shot at him.

He'd already made up his mind how to do it with the white one. The professor wouldn't even notice its absence overnight, and if he came to work a little earlier than today, he'd have plenty of time to put the rabbit back where it belonged.

Even if the old man did find out, he'd pray first that nothing would happen to anybody. As if some prayer could ever have saved anybody or anything, Thomas thought to himself. He could just see the old man taking off his shoes before going up the steps into the major's house so as not to dirty his Aryan carpet.

At night, the rabbits were locked in their cage. The padlock could be pried loose and put back. Or he could take the old man's key out of his pocket. Usually, there was only the major's terrier around the cage. He was further away from being a watchdog than the old man's prayers were from his God.

The terrier licked everybody. He was particularly fond of the flies of gentlemen's trousers. The major liked to play with the terrier in the evenings. Nobody ever heard him shout at the dog. Even when he ordered the old ladies from the Hamburg

Garrison to scrub the sidewalk in front of the gates with their toothbrushes, he did it in quite a normal voice.

The rabbit was what would raise Flea's morale, he thought to himself. He was running more slowly now, still visualizing the rabbit and how he'd show it to Flea. And how she would stroke its white fur. Maybe she'd even kiss its little nose.

He slowed down to a walk, but he could just see himself and Flea, walking side by side with the white one. Flea was leading the white rabbit on a leash just as the major's wife sometimes led the fox terrier.

A few of the boys from L 218 would probably choke with envy. But they'd have to swallow it. The girls from the Home in L 408 would too. Then I'd like to see anybody dare call me Ugly!

"Don't hurt the animals," the old man reminded him.

"As if I ever did," Thomas replied. Then he said these logs were the heaviest he had ever lifted.

When the old man did not respond, he went on: "Well, so tell me what can be heavier."

"Time," the old man answered. "Time is the heaviest thing there is."

"Nobody gets the last word with you," said Thomas.

The old man eyed him suspiciously as Thomas wheezed and puffed. He was feeding the rabbits. There were just eight cages and Thomas watched him. Now he was at the pen where the two young ones were, the black and the white one.

Thomas peeked into the cage where the white one was. He knew almost every splinter by now. Its fur—the white one's—was cleaner than the old man's hands. He'd have to be careful not to break its neck. It's a very fragile animal, honest, he told himself. He tried not to think about involving the old man. They said that Jews breed like rabbits.

"I wish I knew how to tell the difference between truth and fiction the way a rooster can tell the difference between night and day," the old man said. When the old man was silent, he looked beautiful. But sometimes, he looked good even when he was talking. God knows why, Thomas thought. He looked great even when the major was beating him.

Thomas stacked the lighter birch logs on top with the oak

on the bottom. He'd already carried the kindling to the side of the house. The major liked to burn a mixture of cherry, linden, and oak. It even smelled different from outside. The oak logs still smelled of pitch.

"We only live for ourselves, but to do even that, we need others," the old man said.

"It could be worse," Thomas responded. "We're almost finished."

Rabbits are lucky, he thought to himself then. But people aren't actually so bad off either.

He was watching the rabbits. He thought about snow. Then he thought of wood and fire. He thought about the grass which would soon be hidden by the snow. About the warmth of rabbit fur.

The white one is certainly the better of the two, he thought to himself. It'd be nice if Flea could enjoy just a taste of him—just a bit. He could just imagine himself walking along the ramparts with Flea and the white one: it was spring already. In the meantime, he put words together in his head, as if he were talking to Flea. "Winter's rough. It's worst for children and animals and old folks. A long winter's a killer."

He stuck his hands into his pockets. "Winter's anti-Semitic," he told the old man. And then he added, "Transports to the east are anti-Semitic, too. I hope they will forget us."

But he was thinking about walking alongside Flea with the rabbit on a leash like a dog or cat or a weasel. They could make a little coat for him out of some old rag. When it rained Flea would pick up the white one and carry it in her arms. The way girls like to pet and nuzzle things.

He looked up and noticed how the sky was darkening. The sky was low, heavy with evening. I'll be putting the old man on the spot, he thought to himself. It's only this once. He won't even find out. Why shouldn't I be anti-Semitic too, for once, he thought to himself.

It was almost dark when Thomas opened the cage. The young rabbits' paws scrabbled in terror against the back wall of the cage.

"What're you scared of?" Thomas whispered.

He pulled out one of the animals.

70

"You aren't white," he told it.

He took the other one. He held onto it with one hand and closed the cage with the other. Then he stuck the white one inside his shirt.

"Quit wiggling," he chided. "And don't scratch!" The old man claimed they weren't far removed from rats, except in cages. He could feel its soft fur, its tiny claws, its dampness, and its smell.

At L 218, he sneaked across the courtyard and up to the room, taking the stairs two at a time. The lights had already been turned out. He slept in the corner on a three-tiered bunk, at the very top. He crawled carefully up the ladder so he wouldn't wake anybody.

He had the white one beside him. He imagined himself talking to Flea. It was as if every thought had its own wavelength which Flea could intercept and to which she responded. Or as if he were promising Flea a fire where she could warm herself and he was guarding it for her now.

Then, as if he were shivering with the cold that was really her, he whispered, "Don't worry about the nights. Look up at the trees. Maybe they know all there is to know. I don't know. Trees live a long time. Maybe they don't feel what they don't want to feel; maybe they only feel what they want to feel." He was whispering.

He couldn't sleep. He was afraid he'd smother the little beast. He touched his lips to its fur, as if he were whispering something to it, or as if he were telling Flea something.

"You're a sweet little beasty, you really are," he said to the rabbit, and he turned over on his other side, along with the rabbit, trying to find a more comfortable position on the mattress.

I'll be dead tired in the morning and so will you, but for you, it won't matter, he said to himself. The little animal trembled whenever he moved. "Quit twitching like that," he said. "And don't scratch like a cat!" He'd already accepted the fact that the white one was wetting his bed.

"Illness is the worst anti-Semite," he told the rabbit. "And then the one up there probably isn't the least of the anti-Semites, either," he added.

71

For the rest of the night, he thought about how Flea would look when she saw the white one. So he'd be able to get at least a little sleep, he carefully stuck the rabbit into a shoe box and poked a few holes in the lid with a fork. For a while, he listened to the rabbit rummaging around inside.

Get rid of 'em all, he thought to himself. Bury 'em all six feet deep. Among the rats and bedbugs, a white rabbit is the prettiest creature. Almost as pretty as one of those leather jackets worn by pilots or some of the boys who had come here and already left for the east. He was nervous, but at the same time, he smiled inwardly. He could hardly wait. Then he fell asleep.

In the morning, the rabbit was going wild inside the shoe box. Thomas went out with the box, wrapped in a pile of dirty laundry, saying he'd been told to report to the delousing station.

"I haven't been deloused for a week," he told the monitor.

When he got to the Cavalry Courtyard and looked up at the bars on the windows of the asylum, Thomas was reminded of the old man. He searched the windows. The cardboard box had come unstuck. He could feel the white one against his belly. If the major could see him here with the rabbit, he probably wouldn't feel much like singing. They'd treat the old man the same way.

Germans are careful about their belongings, he thought to himself. And they're just as fussy about the things that have now fallen into their possession, he thought finally. People are much nicer when they aren't too tidy. A lot of Jews are untidy. It's a lot better that way, he thought to himself.

The rabbit had gotten him thoroughly wet. It made him cold. He waited for Flea and inwardly counted the minutes. She really should have stuck out that little shaved head of hers by now, he thought to himself. His feet and knees and wrists were turning blue. The cold crept inside his neck and under his fingernails. His teeth chattered and he could feel his chin trembling.

He put the pile of laundry on the ground and kicked the shoe box aside. Where does a rabbit get so much heat, while

72

I'm so cold? Then he thought about the old man for a minute.

Flea always takes her time, that's for sure, he said to himself. His glasses fogged up. He took them off. He wiped them on the rabbit's fur. Then he petted the white one. He was still shivering from the cold and now he was starting to feel the urge to go to the bathroom. He peeked inside his shirt, trying to look into the white one's eyes.

"You can stand it for a little while longer, can't you?" he asked the rabbit.

He turned around, because he heard footsteps behind him. He saw the inmates from the mental hospital as they began to file out, two abreast, the men together and then the women, hand in hand.

Suddenly a small girl's head appeared in the window above. She pressed her nose and lips to the pane.

"You aren't Flea," said Thomas, disappointed. He almost choked the rabbit.

The hands on the other side of the bars and the glass made a gesture saying, no, she wasn't.

"I can see that myself. Where is she?" he asked.

The head moved, nodded goodbye, and disappeared. The window was dirty and someone had written his or her initials in the dust in the corner.

"Wait," called Thomas. "Can you hear me or can't you? Where's Flea, I'm asking you!"

"Who are you looking for?" A woman's voice behind him.

"Me?" he echoed. "For Flea."

"Who's that?"

"A girl from L 408. She has encephalitis. She can't touch the tip of her nose."

"Hasn't she got a name?"

"She has, but I don't know it," Thomas said.

"What do you want her for?"

"I brought her something."

"In which window?" the woman asked.

"You know your way around here? There, right above us."

The woman gazed at him. "A little girl with brown hair?"

73

"Yeah, but they cut it off right away," said Thomas.

"Have you been waiting a long time?"

"Not very long," he replied.

"Take it back home," the woman said suddenly. "That girl isn't here anymore. Are you her brother?"

"A friend," he told her. She ought to be able to see for herself that I'm not her grandfather, he thought.

"She's someplace else," the woman said.

"Where else?" he asked.

"Elsewhere," the woman repeated and patted his head. She noticed how he jerked away, as if he didn't want her to do that.

He looked after her for a little while as she walked away, but then she turned around once more.

How am I supposed to know where? Thomas wondered. "Am I a fortune teller?" He was talking to himself out loud. "It's really enough to make you mad, that's a fact!"

And Thomas, otherwise known as Ugly, thought about how Flea wouldn't be able to see the rabbit today, at least, and about how he'd tell the old man that he'd wanted to cheer her up by showing her the rabbit because she was a girl and had something wrong with her brain. And he took the rabbit back.

The Old Ones and Death

"I'm going to pray," said Aaron Shapiro. And when his wife did not answer, he added, "I'll say a prayer for you, too."

From the room which served as a synagogue and whose tenants had died before winter set in came the chant, "*. . . in the beginning, God created the heavens and the earth . . .*"

"If you forgive, you'll perish," said the other old woman. "Everyone who forgives will perish."

His wife still did not respond. She stared ahead with eyes where dreams no longer swam, where thoughts no longer had any life. It was that hazy stare of old people behind which was the mysterious nothingness which was drawing nearer, the absolute end, the annihilation of everything and everybody, the awful end in helplessness, grief, grief, and the sleep of everything there is.

There was also the reminder of what was waiting for him too. It no longer contained stubborn thoughts or joy or an aching heart. He couldn't help thinking about what he couldn't help being reminded of, or what he was being warned about, and what he was being prepared for. He thought about those who were dying, about dead birds, cats, and dogs, about the fallen horses he'd seen during the First World War. But no matter how far back he looked, he'd seen nothing like this. All the sense of it had been lost.

"In the beginning, God created the heavens and the earth . . ."

Her quiet resignation cast a troubling shadow over him, like her extreme frailness which couldn't be blamed only on

77

the frosts of January and February. The mind is like the body when it's tired, he decided. Like everything else. To be here or somewhere else, to live or not to live, to look out through a broken window or not to look.

"A person doesn't get much peace and quiet in this lovely and not so lovely world," said the second old woman.

He peered at his wife as though he were looking at something which reminded him of the long voyage for which we can all prepare ourselves. But we're never really ready to go. Like stepping into a dark, unheated room from which no one has ever come back.

From the room across the hall he could hear the words, *"...and the earth was without form and void, and darkness was upon the face of the deep."*

The only thing that still amazed Aaron Shapiro was the secret thought of how easy it is to betray someone or to lie to him, even to the person closest to you. All I know is I don't want to, he kept telling himself. And at the same time he knew that was just what he was doing and that he'd go on doing it for as long as they were here.

This brought back echoes of quite different thoughts. He was tired. During the past three years, the bones that held up his spine and the muscles which would not allow him to stand up straight had transformed his body almost beyond recognition. What a surprise he would be for people who had known him before!

Subconsciously, he knew very well why he didn't want to stay in the room with his wife, having to tell himself that everyone was dead long before he really died. He had learned to accept the news that someone he had known was dead. As if it had to be, as if someone always stays behind to keep looking back.

He had noticed how his wife's fever rose as darkness grew out of the light. Then he watched the moon pour across the face of the night. As long as we're young, he thought, we accept the loss of our friends as a necessary evil. Someone goes, others stay. And deep underneath it all flows the tide of complacency—that it's not *me* yet. We arm ourselves with indifference. At most, we manage to prolong the life of our best memories so we do not grieve so much, so we can hush the remnants of our conscience which resist seeing things so simply. And in the end, we're never really well enough prepared.

He looked away from the old woman. The other old woman pretended that Marketa Shapirova's fever was nothing unusual. He could imagine what it would be like when he would be left alone. Will I think back on how she lay there? No, he said to himself. We'll go back in our minds to how it was when everything was still all right. Only the most miserable are able to take comfort from the way things are. The weak believe in miracles. And the strongest accept the way things are now as if they'd never been different.

He still hung on, tooth and nail, to what he had to go back to. But it didn't comfort him. When other people's lives fall to pieces, he said to himself, and mine's been spared so far, I'd like to think I'm no exception. That the worst will avoid me.

I'm probably just an exception after all, but the other way around. When a person no longer loves his own life, he still prefers himself to anybody else. He stepped toward the gap in the damp walls where there used to be a double door. Both sides of it had been burned for firewood early in the winter. Like the floorboards, which had also kept them warm for a while. But what had been good yesterday had already evaporated. Melted away. As if it never had been. Memory preserves only the bad parts, so they can be avoided next time. Wood, fire, warmth. All that *was*. It isn't anymore.

By the time I come back from prayers, I'll be able to say that about Marketa. He tried to associate her in his mind with fire, with warmth or light. He stepped around a hole in the floor. They'd burned the doorsills in December. Nothing but ashes was left of the transom, too.

"I must go so I don't miss the prayers this evening," he said.

"I'll wait for you," she said almost inaudibly.

Her voice sounded different than it had last evening, than a year ago, than that morning. As if it were coming from another world, or as if that were where it was going. It sounded dry and crushed and betrayed. As though she saw something or as if she were afraid of something she couldn't put into words. As though it had to do with something for which there were no words, something that was still a part of life, but a step beyond it. Something she probably couldn't talk about to anybody else. It sounded as if she were still here, but it wasn't she anymore. Like the voice of an aged, frightened child.

The other old woman and Aaron Shapiro were suddenly seized by fear. Something clutched at the old woman's throat and she began to weep silently. But she was strong enough to pull herself together and, when Shapiro glanced at her, to act as if nothing in particular had happened. It took her a few moments to stop crying. Her face was smudged with tears.

"Years used to seem so long to me, then days did, and now when an hour passes, I feel as if a hundred years had gone by," said Leonie Markusova. She managed to laugh about it. Aaron Shapiro went out into the hall.

Leonie Markusova looked over at the old woman who was lying down.

"I grant you, it's not very cheerful," she said. "Snow, wind, the way it gets dark so early. Like being in the mountains somewhere."

Marketa Shapirova stared up at the ceiling. It looked like a map of some strange country. A strand of gray hair had come undone. She hadn't combed her hair for five days.

"You've skipped quite a few meals by now," observed the other old woman. "Why do you suppose they haven't come today in particular?" she went on.

She paused. "I don't like it when things are so quiet."

It seemed to her that the old woman who was lying down had raised her thick gray eyebrows.

"A person can experience a lot, still it's only a drop in the ocean," she said.

Marketa Shapirova could see the other old woman's face as if through a fog. She knew her husband had gone. She didn't want him to resent her, the way you resent people who have nothing left to give you anymore. It takes the greatest amount of strength to get along and put up with someone you no longer love, she thought to herself. When things get difficult. At the time of death, we're cruel to each other.

A person's worst enemy isn't the one he kills, but the one whose happiness he takes away.

She hung on to two phrases the other old woman had been saying: *they came* and *they didn't come*. Both of them knew it had been a long time since anybody had come around who didn't have a specific reason for it. Not even the delousing doctor with his black net gloves had passed by within the last few months.

"There's just a handful of us." She looked up at the sky. The world looked beautiful. But it wasn't.

"I don't envy anybody anything," said the second old woman. "Except when they can bend over and turn around and straighten up again."

Everything and everybody was preparing them to die. Like a bottle of perfume which has evaporated, even though the bottle has been tightly corked. Something happens and the perfume isn't what it used to be. Until you've crossed the borderline of childhood, you never think of death as something which has to do with graying, thinning hair, with gaps in your teeth, tender gums and aching joints, stiff bones and sores.

"What is it that makes everything fall apart?" whispered Marketa Shapirova. Then she realized that she was going to die without a single German soldier even having to fire a shot.

And someday the one who had caused it all to begin with would be dead too. What wouldn't be dead, though, would be the urge to destroy—or the spirit behind this urge, which used to remind her of poison. How come everything people want and strive for runs aground and is wrecked?

It was a long time ago when she'd first come to grips with loneliness. She'd been ten years old and had had to play by herself. Later, it was all bound up with all the different ways in which Aaron Shapiro had been selfish. And her own selfishness, too. But it had been a long time since she'd thought of how a man is selfish. Of what he expected of her sometimes, and what did not give her as much pleasure as he thought it did. Then later, he got tired of her without even saying so. The nights he came home late.

The moment. A strange feeling, waiting for someone who

might come. The way the other old woman's children's children sometimes came to visit.

She thought about bread. Then she thought of honey. She imagined a slice of bread and butter and golden drops of honey on it. A glass of cold milk. Then she visualized the way her hair had looked when she'd been young. Finally, she called back the faces of her children who were somewhere in the east. Dead. So this is *the moment,* she thought to herself. She felt very much like a tree that's rotting away. Like a river flowing into the sea and losing itself there. Like a cloud before it turns into rain, to drops of water too numerous to be counted. Are we what we are, and, at the same time, because of that, have we already stopped being it without having become anything else yet?

Like a fire that's burned itself out, a river when it flows away, or an extinguished star. After winter, spring comes, but not the other way around. And all of it was true, she said to herself. I was right.

"It's a long time since I've heard a rooster crow," she whispered.

Subconsciously, Marketa Shapirova began to sense that all things were either false or foolish. *The moment.* Like taking off a dress, beautiful or threadbare. I'm naked, she said to herself. And I'm alone. There was no pride that it was Friday, and there were none of the candles she used to light.

It all unwound hazily before Marketa Shapirova's eyes— life carved out of the kernel, without even the thinnest shell. Life—some ancient extinct womanhood.

Now and then she thought about her body. The body of an old person is like an icy ocean out of which large and small icebergs poke their sharp peaks. The icebergs are the pains no one knows about. Not just soul pain which takes in grief and loneliness. Real, physical pain in the joints and bones when you breathe.

Pain gives itself away at night by outcries that can't be suppressed, or groans that push their way out of the chest and through the lips, because sometimes the pain is too great or goes on too long.

Usually nobody spoke of those things anymore, so the frigid ocean and its icebergs were like an arctic sea at night, full of things which can't be seen even above the water's surface.

But sometimes there were quiet tears or a loud catch in the throat for no apparent reason. Old people know there's always a reason for such tears, though; the reasons are many. Colliding with such an iceberg isn't dangerous. Its sharpness and coldness are only inward. They melt on the outside, melt like smoke, reminding us only of what used to be. Not like the ship that sank so long ago, the ship with the lovely name, like the name of an ocean grave. The steamship named after a Greek god.

It was like one of those icebergs or like that ship on the ocean's floor. Better forget we've even got a body.

She wanted to think about what was most important, the thing that guided her, about what she wanted to believe in. Don't harm animals, don't harm yourself, take no one's life. That was certainly difficult, but who said it would be easy? For a long time she'd felt like a sinking ship. For too long, perhaps.

"I thought the cat got your tongue," said the other old woman.

Marketa Shapirova half-opened her eyes and blinked. "I'm giving you an awful lot of trouble."

"Don't exaggerate," Leonie Markusova said. "When we can't do what we want, we've got to do what we can, as the saying goes. People are as smart as animals. They say when you can't go up, try going down! And when you don't know what to do, you've got to find out. They also say that whoever doesn't outlast what's evil, won't live to see things get better." After a while she went on: "I don't like the dark. I hope you're warmly dressed. The wind gets in even under the covers. Can't you feel the draft from the floor? You know what I keep dreaming about more and more these days? Bathing for hours in warm water. I fill the tub to the brim. Then I go to sleep in a nice clean bed. Isn't that silly?"

Marketa Shapirova was thinking of how *the moment* had begun to fill with weariness. For forty years, you might say. Aaron Shapiro had forgotten about it forty years before. All that's left are rocks and ocean, she thought to herself. Light is left, and darkness. The war's like a skin you crawl inside of

83

to keep warm. And suffocate.

They're gassing people in Poland. They don't even need to bother with gas here, she thought to herself. In Germany and Poland, they shoot them. It's not necessary here.

As long as there's light, Marketa Shapirova thought to herself. It creeps across the walls like bedbugs swollen with blood. The young women are complaining about how many soldiers have raped them. Nobody rapes old women.

The young people were grumbling, too, about all the dances and parties they were missing. All the schools they had to leave. The past looks lovely and important only when the present is miserable, the here and now, and when the future looks unclear or even dismal. When does a person cling to the future? When things are going right? That's why it doesn't help to remind people that they ought to forget about the past. It isn't something you can forget about when somebody tells you to, any more than you can order somebody to love. It's just one of those things. The past can be stimulation as well as prison. And it can be a third thing, too, something each of us sees in his own way.

The moment, she murmured to herself.

"I don't like this kind of weather, I'll tell you that," declared Leonie Markusova.

Marketa Shapirova opened her eyes and closed them again so she wouldn't have to talk. Trees don't ask questions when a storm is coming. They're blown over or they rot away, no matter how deep their roots go. Rocks crumble too, and lakes and rivers dry up. What was once an ocean is dry land now. There are gardens and fields where a desert used to be, and deserts in place of fields and gardens. So it goes, over and over again. And in between, there's the person and *the moment*, wandering along between the end and the beginning. Killing is the key to explaining man and life. We're born into a world where one simply kills. And, in inexplicable ways, killing brings with it the killing of those who kill. But it's not quite the same.

Nothing lasts forever—no one person and none of the things he's created. Not even the most finely woven dress, or the stoutest stone house, or chair and table made of oak. But we don't realize that for a long time or we don't want to know. Hope is something we can construct from nothing, just like God, and we don't even notice when hope begins to lose its probability. Nobody and nothing resembles something which hasn't been here before. Even though it looked different. And it'll all happen again.

It's what comes in between that we can influence.

At one time, it was said that either love or justice determine a man. The wise and the foolish disputed which was foremost. That wasn't all there was to it, of course. What about the other way around? The old language came back to her, the one used in prayers. We can be as modest as we like, but we're always the center of our own world.

The moment. The moment. The moment.

She knew exactly. When you abandon everything you can believe in, you're abandoning yourself. As if you've never existed. But that takes a long time.

Once again she remembered that amorphous anniversary, neither fish nor fowl . . . four times ten years. Nothing but a zero left at the end. A cancellation of everything and everybody. She could feel Leonie Markusova watching her.

When Aaron Shapiro had begun to deteriorate (and he was failing fast), he too stopped believing they'd ever get out of this. That was when he had begun to grow away from her and they never got close again. We exist, he said, we still exist, although the one whose very name I can't bring myself to utter wants nothing more than for us *not* to exist. We've even lost what we thought we had won. He was probably already afraid at that time, concealing his fear with a smile, like when he concluded a good business deal, fearful his truth was really just a wish. He wasn't even allowed to go into a shop to buy flowers. In Nuremburg, the Great Reich had adopted laws that had made them prisoners even before they went to jail.

Her vision took in her brother too. Artur Morgenstern. He came to their wedding forty years ago. And here they'd met again. He said the fortress town was punishment for the profligacy which had spread since the destruction of the Temple, eating into Jewish heads wherever they were to be found.

Did that profligacy afflict children and old people, though?

It'll become a burden for them when it's too late, Artur Morgenstern had said. Not really a burden, even. Just pangs of conscience, which don't leap like sparks from one fire to another. They are transmitted from one generation to another, maybe even bypassing one to flicker up in another.

The moment. Just one branch of the family is perishing, Artur Morgenstern said. The most beautiful and most steadfast. "We're good at weeping," he concluded. "Maybe it's a good thing we do it so well. Yet not entirely."

Even with her eyes closed, Marketa Shapirova could see the torn and desolate green wallpaper. But no sparks can spring out of ashes. All the wind can glean from ashes is more ash.

Leonie Markusova heard fragments of words from the other room where the men were praying. "*...And God made two great lights...to rule the day and the lesser light to rule the night. He made the stars also...and [this] was the fourth day.*"

Marketa Shapirova was remembering the sounds of the birds she'd once heard in the fields. You could hear them far and wide. Those sounds had brought to mind words like *distance, shame, afterwards . . . The moment.* One bright midday she'd even heard a skylark sing. She remembered how peaceful she'd felt, as if she herself were a wheatfield which would soon give birth to bread.

Suddenly a pain shot through her body. Like labor pains. Like the pain of her own birth. It was a good thing her mother wasn't here, that she couldn't be her own mother. From their transport, everybody's mother had been gassed last September in the east. It was a good thing, too, that her own children weren't here either. They'd been gassed somewhere in Poland two years ago last March.

The skylark's song, the fields and meadows and forest — these were some of the best things. A clear sunny day, bread and butter and salt — the joy of being alive. All that was left now was *the moment.* But it wasn't quite all. She could almost sense the bridge between the two. She remembered a dream she'd had in her mother's womb. Now she no longer needed an explanation for her inexplicable anxieties and strange fears. There was no longer any bitterness left in her.

The dream had been as white as her wedding gown, as white as the halo around the sun when you see it in the morning, before the snow drowns it in whiteness, in white flakes, like a message being sifted into her aching joints. Is *the moment* white?

She could still feel the world and life within her, but it was like wine now, in her skin and the violet blotches of impetigo.

It warmed her to recall that dream of being inside her mother's belly. Being born is a warm experience. *The moment. The moment. The moment.*

"We're like stunned fish," the second old woman remarked suddenly. I can say that long before *the moment* came, I'd already lumped everything into my prayers, Marketa Shapirova thought to herself. There probably aren't any prayers like that anymore, prayers that cover everything—hunger, food, desolation. Darkness, frost, snow gusts of wind, and both faces of loneliness which we take turns in welcoming and rejecting.

In everything there is an invisible judge and prosecutor, a secret joy, a long-gone, gentle expectation which came back to her like an echo. *The moment.*

He needn't have gone on so far ahead of me, Marketa Shapirova thought to herself. She could almost see her brother, standing there in front of her. He could have advised her now. He probably saw the world in quite a different light. For many people, we're just the clink of coins in the pocket, less than a drop of water—dirt to be swept away with brooms of fire. For only a few are we sunshine in the heart. Why haven't we ever been able to think about others in the same way as they think about us?

She could see her brother now as he had stood there when he was alive, slightly bent, as if he were looking for something on the ground, lost in the overcoat and suit which were too big for him, wearing that crumpled, wide-brimmed hat.

She could see herself, too, as she'd stood once in front of the bathroom mirror naked. It was all gone now. First it had grown old and wrinkled, then finally disappeared entirely.

The difference, which had been the cause of it all, seemed petty and ridiculous. Nobody had ever redeemed it yet.

Otherwise, things would look different than they do.

Life can't be any better than the person is, after all. The whole world is like a great, clouded mirror, and underneath the part we think we know, quite different things are hidden.

Her brother's bushy eyebrows. The hat made of fox fur, the gift of a rabbi in a Warsaw suburb. Looking back, she thought admiringly of her brother. While he was alive, he submitted to all the rules and regulations of his faith as one submits to weakness or temptation. At first he thought the Germans would be afraid. The Germans weren't afraid of anything. Exactly the opposite was true: *they* were the ones who were afraid of the Germans.

Or was it something else the Germans feared? She herself was a practical, earthbound person, less observant than her brother. She ate everything, even if it contained blood, which holds the souls of animals. She had spoiled her stomach with soup made from extracts, with ersatz German honey and butter and meat, with gravies made from ersatz lentils, but only after Artur Morgenstern chose to starve to death rather than eat food he considered unclean.

The moment. The moment. The moment. Life. Before her closed eyes Artur Morgenstern and Aaron Shapiro began to merge into a fuzzy tangle. She could see them in a dimming, almond-tinted glow. Where are they? My God, where is everybody, all the ones who used to be here? She remembered sitting under a pear tree in the courtyard last year while a few youngsters yanked off the unripe fruit to prove how strong they were.

In her mind's eye, Marketa Shapirova could see a treadmill with a squirrel running inside. A double wheel with silver spokes. White sunshine. The faster the wheel turned, the harder the furry little animal inside kept running. The spokes flashed by faster and faster until the difference between the spokes and the light vanished. The circle was impenetrable.

Nothing, nothing, nothing. And that includes my anniversary, too. So far, she'd still had enough strength left to save a piece of bread for Aaron Shapiro for Friday. Yesterday she'd eaten the bread herself. *The moment.* Evening, night and morning, forty years ago. Strange how all that was left of it was one single night, forty years ago. The touch of hands, face against face, dead memory of a young body.

Marketa Shapirova could hear the sound of a river flowing. There was an old columbarium for urns from the crematorium behind the fortress. Every six months, a special squad of Jewish or Communist prisoners dumped the ashes of the recent dead into the river. A lot of ashes had flowed down to the sea by now, but the level of the ocean hadn't risen by one single millimeter.

Someone said the columbarium was being used now for storing potatoes. *The moment.* Books about the brave, the innocent, the honest. She heard mice. Snow slid off the roof and fell into the courtyard with a soft thud.

I'm a wave in that river, she said to herself. And this is *my moment.*

Aaron Shapiro, she called out silently, *come back. Hurry if you still want to find me here. You know how I hate mice. I'm terrified of mice and Germans. I'm not afraid of you anymore or even of myself. My life, Aaron Shapiro. I've never been unfaithful to you. I simply wasn't very close. But that wasn't my fault or yours. And I was only unfaithful to you in my thoughts. One time, at a party, a strange man kissed me on the lips. Sometimes I kept you waiting and held you off when you were very close to me. I didn't want you to be close and I don't know why. This is the moment, now. Closed doors—not those you opened for me whenever I was with you.*

Do you remember, Aaron, that German emigrant from Berlin who came to see us in our old apartment in Prague in 1936? He didn't want the charity we offered him to be more than we could afford. So we wouldn't think ours was the only well where he could quench his thirst. He didn't want us to feel toward him like rich people feel toward the poor, fearful of easing their poverty with their own money. We were simply frightened by his fear. People are frightened by other people who are unhappy. He knew nobody can understand until they accumulate first-hand experience themselves. He had blue eyes. He was so embarrassed. How many emigrants have felt embarrassed since then—as if they were the first to have had to leave someplace where they would have preferred to stay? Leaving a home, a school, a house, and finally a country. Then there were those dreams, Aaron. Do you know the ones I mean?

I watched the sun set, although my eyes were closed, Aaron. It's a circle. I've come back to the beginning. The moment.

Never leave me alone in the evening anymore, Aaron Shapiro. All of you that's with me is your name. My forehead's on fire. Put your hand on me.

She groped for the thermometer. She knew she was alone now. Dimly, she put the thermometer under her arm, poking her hands through the rags in which she was dressed. She tried to guess how long two minutes lasted.

She could see a tangle of fire before her eyes. *The moment.* Fever. Mice paws. Cold. Fear. A feeling of sinfulness, of disappointment, guilt, and loneliness. *The moment. The moment.*

She tried to raise the glass tube to her eyes. She couldn't see anything but snow. Every day, she realized vaguely, there's one infinitesimal bit more of the silvery stuff. More of it meant a smaller fragment of life.

Aaron Shapiro, she called out silently. A flame had lodged inside her temples. She could hardly feel her body anymore. That is, she wasn't aware of it as pain. It was as if her body weren't hers at all, as if it had nothing to do with her. It's burning itself into me, Aaron.

She rolled over on her side. The thermometer slipped out of her hand. It fell and broke. She banged her head on the floor. She no longer dreamed, even secretly, of starting life all over again. She wouldn't have wanted to.

The wind blew in gusts of snow. I won't need doors anymore, she said to herself. I won't need shoes, either.

"Aaron," she whispered inaudibly.

And then, "Who's to blame for it all? At least I haven't killed anybody. If life means whether you kill or don't kill, then I was one of those who didn't."

There was the rose that Aaron Shapiro had bought for her that time, the rose he'd been unable to buy himself because the Great Reich didn't allow people like him to enter a flower shop. Cold snow and mice again. Her fingers stretched as though she were feeling around the floor for the thermometer. A gust of snowflakes touched her hand and settled in between her fingers.

"Aaron Shapiro," Leonie Markusova called into the room where the service was going on. It was musty, and since those people had died of typhus in there last year, it reeked of old disinfectant. Leonie Markusova had never been in there before.

She stood shivering in the doorway without her coat, which she had put over Marketa Shapirova. She wore only a dress with no buttons on top, and under her shawl, it was obvious she had no underwear.

She was trembling all over and her teeth were chattering.

He looked over at her. "Women aren't allowed in here, don't you know that?"

The man conducting the service came from Germany. Since dusk, he'd already mixed up the Friday evening prayer with the Book of Ecclesiastes and he kept repeating, *". . . of every tree of the garden thou mayest eat freely . . ."* and *"In the beginning God created the heavens and the earth . . ."*

There was something in his eyes which was quite the opposite of what he was saying as he recited the verses about how it all began.

"I came because of your wife, for heaven's sake," said Leonie Markusova.

Aaron Shapiro stared at the floor, droning on about offerings of food, about devotion and strength, quiet nights and fruitful days, of gathering strength, of rest, of laws, of sturdiness of body and strength of soul.

He turned toward the cantor, muttering his prayer feverishly, feeling Leonie Markusova's eyes on him.

After a few words he went back to imagining the soups he'd been thinking about before, a catalogue of all the Swiss soups they used to buy.

"You'd better go see her," Leonie Markusova said.

"I must finish this prayer."

"It's the Sabbath," the cantor spoke up, "so we must not complain."

"All right, I'm coming," said Aaron Shapiro.

Suddenly, for the first time, he thought about the Feast of Gladness. At other times he had recalled the Feast of Lights. But now it was all eclipsed by a hungry yearning for soup, the Swiss ones he'd been thinking about or any other kind, made out of dogs or cats or mice. In his mind's eye, he saw a kettle full of piping hot soup.

"Marketa isn't any better," said the second old woman.

"Today a person's better off being a little grey mouse," the old man grumbled to himself. "The tiniest mouse there is. He makes himself as small and unobtrusive as possible so nobody even notices him."

Behind them they could hear the cantor, intoning in his raspy voice. Then he was drowned out by the wind.

"I think she's taken a turn for the worse," said Leonie Markusova.

All at once everything came back to him—the things he'd been running away from when he'd gone to the other room. He had tried to bear up, like when he'd realized there was no point in drawing far-reaching conclusions about his fate. It was only in the beginning that he'd been convinced his decline and fall paralleled the world's decline and fall. Or that the extinction of everything and everybody went along with his own extermination. It was only at first that he was sure things couldn't go on that way, that something would have to happen. That was before he discovered that nothing would.

He went out of the room, ducking his head and shielding his face from the snow. For a moment, he felt the way he used to when he was on his way home. But it didn't add anything to what he knew. At first he'd been homesick for the streets he used to walk along, for places he used to go, people he knew. That filled his days and nights. There were so many people, so many places. But gradually, like old skin, it all shriveled away and no longer seemed to be so alive . . . their apartment, the house, things. After a year of the inactivity to which he'd been condemned, even remembering seemed unreal. It had all evaporated, like a whisper.

Now he could hear the cantor's voice again, and it sounded as if he'd been talking to God the whole time, addressing him as if he were an unfaithful mistress. He spoke accusingly: "Look how devoted I've been to you—how we've trusted each other! All the things we've looked forward to!" That whole afternoon and evening, it sounded as though the cantor's mistress had become a whore. "I lied to life and life lied to me." It was all the crippled yearning that had broken down here.

As if it had come out of the fog, fear, and hunger, or from the apathy these had produced, for the first time in his life he asked himself a question—through he probably wasn't the first one to ask it. What had God done before he created the world and what would he do afterwards? It was just one of those things which no longer had anything to do with him. He was just as unconcerned as when the cantor said that the worst sin of all is the crime of pride. He had a hunger which consumed him the way fire feeds on itself. He shivered with cold. Hunger and cold were like two walls with no room for anything else in between but loneliness, in which a man is a stranger even to himself. The things which had been uncertain before—like prayers for his wife's recovery—were becoming even more indefinite, something like distance, fog, nothingness.

"She's in a bad way. You ought to stay with her," the old woman said.

He let her go ahead. By now my hunger couldn't even be satisfied by soup made from my own blood, he said to himself. He remembered being with Marketa once in a French restaurant and ordering veal marengo, the classic French-Italian recipe created for Napoleon, as the waiter insisted. Tender pieces of veal simmered with tomatoes, pearl onions, ripe olives, and fresh mushrooms, folded in a crêpe, and served with a spinach soufflé and green salad.

"We can't just leave her like this," said Leonie Markusova.

"What do you mean, 'like this'?"

The wind dashed snowflakes into his face and they clung to

93

his beard. They were big flakes and they did not melt. The house was completely white.

The other old woman watched Aaron Shapiro sink gratefully onto his wife's mattress to rest a bit.

Aaron Shapiro saw the broken thermometer on the floor. Beads of bluish mercury and splinters of glass. The mattress was thin and worn and smelled of ammonia. The straw was very old.

"Marketa," he said. "I'm here—I'm with you now."

The snow gave off enough light so he could see how swollen her eyelids were. He could imagine the swirl of visions growing dimmer and dwindling behind them. He was almost annoyed to see she wasn't dead yet, and he was ashamed of himself. That wasn't what he'd wanted. He waited to see whether his voice would get through to her.

If I were in her place, I'd try to make it easier, he thought to himself. The snow made the room look lighter and the snowflakes, as they fell, made him think for a moment that her eyelids trembled.

"Can you hear me?" he asked his wife.

He noticed the other old woman watching him.

"Raise her head a bit," she suggested. "Does she have a fever?"

"I don't know. She doesn't feel hot."

"It's a shame," she said abruptly.

"It's dark," he said. "I can't see a thing."

As the wind shifted, it brought back the cantor's quavering voice. *"In the beginning God created the heavens and the earth . . ."* It sounded like both a path and a maze, like remembering and forgetting. *"In the beginning God created the heavens and the earth...and God saw that it was good..."*

"If they do come, send them for the doctor right away."

"You think she can hear me?" he wondered.

"The nearest doctor is in the Hamburg Caserne."

"I'm afraid she can't hear me."

"Why wouldn't she hear you? Marketa Shapirova!"

"What did she have to say?"

"I had a few things to say myself," the other old woman retorted. "Or do you think I have no voice left or what?"

"Maybe she hears me and doesn't feel like answering."

"Try again in a little while. That's what I did."

Aaron Shapiro looked at her. Then he tried again. "Marketa! If you can hear me, but you're too sick to answer, just nod."

Her nearness felt different than it had when he'd left her earlier that evening.

Later, the light took on a different color as it was reflected by the snow. Around ten o'clock, ersatz coffee made from acorns was brought over from the Hamburg Caserne where the working women were housed. He lifted the coffee mug to his wife's lips, holding his hand under her head.

"Drink some of this," she said.

The other old woman drained her cup in a single draft while it was still hot. Aaron Shapiro spilled coffee over his wife's chest and down the front of Leonie Markusova's coat.

"There, that's right," he said.

"Is she drinking it?" the other old woman asked. She took back her coat. Then she lay down.

Aaron Shapiro could hear three different kinds of doubt in her voice.

"It's still snowing," she said. It was coming down in heavy flakes. "It's snowing as if it's never going to stop." After a while, she went on. "I'm surprised they brought us the coffee. This weather would have been a good excuse not to."

When he looked over at her, he realized she was still waiting for them to come.

"She'll drink it when she feels like it," he said after a while.

"Let's hope so," said the other old woman.

"You'll drink it when you feel like it, won't you?" he said to his wife.

"Maybe she feels more like sleeping than drinking," suggested Leonie Markusova.

"That's possible," he agreed.

"It wore her out, talking."

"I can imagine."

"What time do you suppose it is?"

"I have no idea. Ten o'clock? Eleven. Two."

"Do you think it'll go on snowing all night?"

"Do you intend to wait up all night and see?"

"I can't sleep anyway."

His arms were numb and he was afraid to move. The coffee had made a puddle on the floor. It would have been fairer if they'd killed us, he thought to himself. We don't mean anything to our friends anymore, and our enemies don't even notice. He could tell the other old woman wasn't sleeping either.

"Youth is nothing but a false paradise," he said. He couldn't understand how it happened that kindness turns into cruelty, the way happiness becomes unhappiness, and life turns into death.

"What makes you think it's so?"

"It smells terrible in here," he went on. "Do we all stink so much now?" He stretched out slowly at his wife's side.

"Be glad you can still notice it, at least," the other old woman said. Then, after a while she added, "It's a funny light, isn't it?"

"Good night," he murmured to no one in particular.

"Good night," the other old woman replied.

"Good night, Marketa," he added.

"Good night," repeated the other old woman.

For a little while, Aaron Shapiro thought the sound of the wind and the snow outside was his wife's wheezing. And Leonie Markusova's breathing. Quietly he sipped his cold coffee, leaving just a bit in the bottom of the cup.

"Good night," he said again into the darkness, just to confuse the other old woman in case she wasn't asleep yet. He spread his topcoat over his wife.

"Is she finally asleep?" whispered the other old woman. Her voice gave her away. She was fearful she would have to spend another night like the night before.

"Can't you sleep?" Aaron Shapiro asked her.

"I don't want to," Leonie Markusova told him.

"Maybe she's dreaming about the people she was happy with," he went on.

"Where do you suppose they are? What's become of everybody?"

He felt a sharp pain in his anus, as though his whole body was forcing itself through with a hollow, searing pressure. "What's the matter?" asked Leonie Markusova. "It's ridiculous the way it goes on snowing. What will we do? Where can we take shelter? Where can we go?"

Just as he was dozing off, he heard footsteps and voices.

"I've been waiting for you to come," the other old woman said. Her voice had a different ring to it than when she'd been complaining about the snow.

Two girls had slipped into the room.

"You came over here in all this snow?" the old woman marveled.

"It'll be over within fourteen days," the second girl said.

"You came in this weather?" the old woman murmured contentedly.

"Apparently they have some secret weapon. They won somewhere in a town between some river and the steppes. Half the world's fighting against them by now. Even India."

"You know where that is?" the first girl asked.

"I think so," the other old woman replied. She had no idea.

"It may all be over sooner than we think. In a week or two."

"Can you stop in at the Hamburg Caserne?"

"It can wait till morning," Aaron Shapiro said.

"What for?" the old woman demanded.

"I'll tell her your news," Aaron Shapiro added.

Then they were alone again.

"People are only human," the other old woman said. "They kill and steal and lie, but sometimes they surprise you."

She was silent for a while. "It's probably going to snow forever. By morning we'll all be snowed in."

Everything smelled. Old underwear, old skin, old sweat.

Even after a few hours Aaron Shapiro could tell she hadn't fallen asleep yet. She probably had a horror of the dead. The hours dragged on. She finally dozed off towards morning. He envied her sleep. For some things, our lives are too short, for others, too long.

"Marketa," he whispered.

He knew he'd changed because of what he believed in and what he'd stopped believing in, and by what, through indifference, was no longer even an echo of what it used to be. But he couldn't help it that it wasn't what it used to be. But probably nothing was. He could not find a trace of relief on her face.

Then he whispered to her, "Can you hear me?"

"I'm with you," he said at last.

Inwardly he wondered why it wasn't true. He touched the dead woman's forehead as if he wanted to see if his wife was still alive.

He wondered whether he had lost the last small fragment of the heaven he dreamed about in secret.

Guiltily, he realized that above all, he was sorry for himself. I envy the living and the dead. I envy the living their life, the dead their death. I also envy the portions of my own past which have already perished. And I don't have in me the kind of shame which could reverse it.

Marketa Shapirova's body was as cold as wax. Her long gray and black hair was the only thing about her that was still alive and growing. She did not move, even when he drew as close to her as he used to. He ran his bony fingers across her face, over the fathomless wrinkles, like the crevasses of every age and every battle, feeling how rough and dry the skin was. He waited for a while. Not a single tear came.

He left her eyes open until the morning.

The heavy dark snow went on falling.

Beginning and End

Jiri had noticed it, along with everybody else, as soon as they arrived. One corner of the ceiling of the one-story building was dark and sagging, a cobweb of wire and scaly plaster. It looked as though there would soon be a hole or at least that it would leak and rust when it began to rain. Or maybe it would simply collapse.

"It probably isn't rotten," he said.

"Bacteria, gentlemen," redheaded Richard observed, "are already teeming through the space between heaven and earth." He moved into the bottom bunk ahead of Jiri. He knew where the roof was rickety, like everybody else.

"Stop that," repeated the man who'd been saying "Big deal" when they were trying to figure out the camp's standing and had ranked it among the better ones. Red tidied his bunk. No matter how often they were moved around, he always went to the trouble to make a little piece of the camp homey, even if only for one night. After all, he said, a camp is kind of a home, too. In a way.

Red changed the subject. "This guy was all right until he found a letter from his mother to her lover. *'I dread his breath close to me, his penis, which revolts me as passionately as I adore yours. I dread these lies I'm living. How can I bring up children this way?'* This is what I call an innocent, naive world," he said. It was one of Red's many little stories.

At Jiri's side stood a shortsighted boy who was rather round-shouldered. He couldn't see well, but he didn't wear glasses. Hardly anyone who had come from Poland wore glasses. One experience had been enough for them. In Birkenau, everybody who didn't take off his glasses in time went up the chimney. And then—as Red added—each of them rode off on his own little cloud. Like in a bus. Sometimes Red spoke of stars instead of clouds.

Jiri studied the wires sticking out of the ceiling. The short-sighted one peered at the wires too.

Red Richard's pants were held up by a piece of strap from a German rifle. During their move from Poland to Germany, he had worn it right next to his body. It was made of ox hide and it had a little pouch attached to it, which he'd mended with glue. He didn't have to carry cyanide around in a wad of cotton in his ear anymore.

Tidily, Red removed his jacket. He took out some thumbtacks wrapped in a piece of paper. He folded the paper and put it away again. It was a letter he'd carried around with him for a year and a half.

He pushed a thumbtack carefully into the foot of his bunk and hung his jacket on it. He rolled up his pants into a pillow and placed them at the foot of his bunk.

"From now on, this is my sovereign territory," he announced.

He smoothed his shirt. They knew how proud he was of his one gram of poison.

"You're awfully elegant," said Red's neighbor, the man with the rough voice. They all knew why he said it, too. He thought Red would share it with him.

It was getting dark. The hillside had been a pleasant green. Pine trees, spruce, and birch grew here. There was that strange, aloof kind of gentleness about the place that you find in nature. And it wasn't the first time Jiri had read into it things whose answers had been lost. As the sun set, the hillside first turned red and then began to darken. The shadows elongated and the field in front of the barracks, the building itself, and the sky, all turned cold. This is the way the world cools off each day, before tomorrow becomes another day.

"I don't like people who make such a production of saying their prayers, as if they're telling me, 'Hey, look how good I am and how we're being wronged!' Or as if they want to insure themselves, like 'If anybody's going to survive, at least *we prayed*!' "

102

Red adjusted his shorts.

"I can see how those Hungarian and Polish Jews, who've been claiming God's a hunk of dead sweet wood, are going to try to revive him. Like those beautiful Australian swimmers giving mouth-to-mouth resuscitation when somebody drowns."

"What do you mean by that?" asked the man with the saucepan.

"I'm talking about how some people treat God like a luxury, something that only goes with good conditions. About how God'll start convalescing just as soon as the Hungarian rabbis start getting their strength back again."

Immediately he added: "Have you ever heard of those Japanese kamikaze pilots? The ones who fly those planes that are also torpedoes and time bombs? How they take off, headed right for an enemy ship or moving target, and smash themselves to smithereens, target and all?"

"Maybe somebody else is still going to come," said the man holding an empty saucepan by the window.

In Poland someone had told him that in Germany prisoners are fed twice a day, sometimes five hundred, but at least three hundred calories. He kept one foot in his bottom bunk so nobody else could take it. Finally he placed his pan at the edge of the bunk and lay down. This wasn't the first time he'd been fooled. That can happen despite a lot of experience to the contrary, because it's always better to believe in some things than not to.

"This camp's like the planet Neptune," said redheaded Richard. "You see, Neptune was never sighted with any of the earlier telescopes, like the other stars, but somebody figured it must be there. Some Frenchman, followed Mr. Newton's crazy theory. And then some German actually did discover it. He saw this little dot in the sky, and, lo and behold, it was Neptune! And me, in Birkenau, I used to dream about a camp like this one, where you just worked and they didn't gas people. At first I just imagined it, then I really found it. A new planet. *Meuslowitz bei Leipzig Aussenkomando Buchenwald.* My lovely little planet, where at least they don't gas people."

And then he said, "I can see already that if things go on

this way, we'll leave here in a parlor car. I already know what to order for dessert with expresso coffee. Strawberry Crepe Supreme—luscious fresh strawberries, with sour cream or whipped cream, and brown sugar. Waiter, please!''

"What happened to that fellow's mother?" asked the man with the saucepan to change the topic. He was lying down too, already. He had his saucepan with him, like a lover.

"She'd tell him, 'You're stepping out on me, aren't you, darling? Come on, 'fess up!' And he'd say, 'Look, imagine two apple trees and one gardener. Which tree should he tend: the one with the sweet apples or the one whose fruit is tart and tasteless? You know what I mean?' She did. "Except you're no gardener,' she said. 'You're a whore-chaser. And don't expect me to play along.' ''

Nobody had anything to say to that. It looked as though Red Richard had finally run out of ammunition. They were in a new camp, and in addition it was in German territory. New possibilities had opened for them, all tempered by the usual uncertainties. Besides, none of the German officials had come to check, which wasn't the only thing that contributed to their uneasiness. They knew it was the silence that had set him off. Sometimes just talking was enough. A short while ago they'd heard some Polish women singing. Then there was the din of the chemical and munitions plants. There must be a kennel somewhere in the middle of the hill, now fading into darkness, because now and then, dogs barked. They knew what kind of dogs those were.

But there was the excitment of change, which was like a curtain, but you couldn't see what was behind it yet. Twice during the afternoon, enemy formations had flown over the camp. They were accompanied from the ground by two sixty-second and four fifteen-second sirens.

Until that time, they had stood out in front of the barracks, and the only thing the German guards ordered them to do was to look at the ground during the air raid, not up at the sky. Whoever looked up would be shot. During an air raid, looking at the sky was, the guard said, *"Strengstens verboten!"* The order was a threat; there above the thin clouds, the plans were a first encouraging sign, flying out of range of the local anti-aircraft fire. Red knew they were B-17's,

Flying Fortresses, which could fly farther than anybody had ever dreamed was possible. It was like touching another world which was still unvanquished. And the fact that they were in Germany, and not in Poland anymore, meant something tco, even though they didn't know how to evaluate it yet.

Jiri pondered the changes. He watched as darkness slowly fell. He thought about two things most. Both of them were connected with Germany. In the freight car which had brought them here, a nineteen-year-old soldier had been guarding them, and this soldier told them what was on his mind because he couldn't find anybody but prisoners to talk to. He'd been present when the transports came from Hungary, twenty-one days and nights, one after another. And now he was on his way home to his parents on leave, and he knew that if he told his mother or his father or his grandparents even a fraction of what he'd seen, they'd think he'd gone out of his mind. But the soldier was afraid it wasn't madness. And he was scared that when he had to go back, he'd really go out of his mind, or he wouldn't, which he considered to be even worse. He spoke of suicide, and Jiri told him what he'd heard from Jewish war veterans, that the best way is to stick a loaded revolver in your mouth, but to be sure, it's best to fill the barrel with water first. And then there was the lieutenant who'd brought them here and turned them over to the guards. He hadn't yelled at them once the whole way from the station.

"Hasn't it been quiet?" Red asked suddenly. "I always get suspicious when it's so quiet. I'd just as soon erase days like this from the calendar."

Red told the story he'd heard from an Argentinian Jew who'd been in the Brazilian wholesale coffee business in Prague before the war. "When God made man," he said, "he took some clay, patted it into shape, and stuck it in the oven. When he took it out, he saw he hadn't made a very good job of it; he hadn't left it in the oven long enough. So he put it back in again. When he took it out again, he saw he'd left it in there too long. So he tried a third time. Finally he succeeded. That was how he made the first Jew."

"Don't you know any better stories about ovens?" demanded the man with the saucepan.

"Just that I'm starting to get ovens mixed up with heaven," Red said.

Even those who were still standing around or saying their prayers began to get undressed. It was possible they'd forgotten that their real camp life began only in the morning. Probably.

Jiri decided to take his clothes off too. That was when Red Richard cautiously lit a candle. Red had dozens of habits which made him look like one of the chosen who had survived until now. *Now* was a candle. When Jiri was naked he could feel Red looking at him.

"Actually, you do have quite a nice white body. And that thing of yours happens to be young and white too. Women are going to enjoy doing it to you."

Jiri hung his clothes over the edge of the bunk to air out for a while. He'd worn them for the past two weeks. He looked down over his body and felt his bones, running his hands over his skin.

"Some women love to do it," Red went on. "It's just about the gentlest thing they can do with it. But you mustn't expect them to do it too often. Or just not *that* way. But every good lioness will do that for you, to the very end."

Jiri didn't say anything.

Red grinned. "Life's worthwhile as long as a woman can do that to me," he said. And then he said, "Now the only thing is to survive. But once I survive, then the quality of the life I lead will be important. You know what I mean?"

It was peaceful and quiet all around. It reminded them of just how short a time the ground flak had tried to hit the foreign planes. Women insurgents from Warsaw lived in the next barracks. Red had found that out.

Jiri rather enjoyed it when Red talked about women. There was a tantalizing mystery that Red was close to, here and in Poland. But even Jiri had his own two experiences, and both of them correspond to what Red had said. When he'd worked at the dividing machine in a munitions factory, a splinter of metal had flown into his eye. The little German corporal took him to the factory doctor, a woman who refused to treat him, saying it wasn't her duty to look after the prisoners. Besides that, she told the guard, the eye was badly infected and nothing could be done without an operation anyway. To show the guard, she made him sit down on a stool and turned a bright light on Jiri's throbbing eye. The corporal put another worker on his machine and took him back to the barracks. Jiri knew what it meant to go blind in a camp. The guard stopped in front of the infirmary. There was nobody there but an untrained Russian nurse's aide. The corporal asked where she was from. She told him she had been captured when the German army approached the besieged city by Lake Ladoga. *"Ach Ja, Petersburg,"* said the corporal. She talked with the guard as if she wished her words could kill him. In the meantime, she boiled a scalpel and removed the splinter from his eye. Afterwards, they'd killed that Russian girl.

"A person ought to enjoy himself before he's exterminated," Red concluded.

And then: "Doesn't it seem almost ridiculous that they'll kill you in any case, even if you have some peaceful occupation like a traveling salesman in leather and dry goods? Or that death has so many faces; in the end, you get exterminated, whether it's in a war, by mistake, in an accident, by starvation, by a bullet, or in a train wreck, with gas or germs. But you can always count on it."

He warmed his hands in front of the candle flame for a while, and then he blew it out and pinched the wick so it wouldn't smoke.

Nobody had to answer that.

Jiri looked out the window. They were just at the edge of the hillside. Judging by their barracks and the barracks of the Polish women, this must be a new camp.

He thought of how they had been brought here from the railroad station that afternoon by a gaunt lieutenant in an SS field uniform, with the two lightning bolts and a skull emblem on his cap. The lieutenant's teeth were bared and it looked as though he were grinning, but he wasn't. His jaw was crooked and scarred; probably malaria.

On the way from the station, each of them had tried to map the route in his own memory—it might come in handy someday, you never knew.

Red sighed, as if he were forced to interrupt his monologue.

"Money's nice," he said, "but you can never feel close to

107

it. You can't love it like you can love a woman."

Then he added: "Try caressing it and then wait for it to caress you back. Try buying something with it on a desert island."

Jiri crawled up on his bunk and stretched out. Red lay on the bottom, the nearsighted boy in the middle. Jiri tried not to notice the rotting ceiling. He was chewing on a straw. It was strange, tearing off a blade of dry grass in Poland and to be chewing it still in Germany. Sometimes, he'd bite off a little piece and grind it slowly between his teeth, as though he didn't want to part with it. He wondered how long he could make it last.

He didn't understand that SS man in the green cap with the visor who had brought them here and left immediately. He hadn't shouted at them once, all the way from the railroad station. Red was busy trying to find the most comfortable position.

"We aren't exactly satisfied with the food here either, Lieutenant. I was spoiled at home. Until my fifteenth birthday, my father and mother were divorced, but then they remarried each other. My uncle was famous for his high-quality smoked herring."

That reminded him of the story of his Polish uncle who fell in love with a rabbi's daughter, with whom a corporal of the Polish cavalry was also in love. The corporal challenged his uncle to a duel, while the rabbi's beautiful daughter looked on, enchanted, thrilled that because of her these two young men would suffer at least a nosebleed. "They agreed to meet on the following day at sunrise in a grove of fir trees. But that same evening, Uncle thought it over. With his pistol money, he bought steerage passage on the SS Batory and later became the smartest grocery store owner on the island of Manhattan. When I last heard of him, Colonel, he'd framed her letters in gold. She started writing to him when her corporal gave her a disease. Our people are always moving up in this country, even if otherwise there's a shortage of rope. But I'd like to point out that a few people do get very nervous when they don't have a rational home life, like some of the people I know. Some individuals would still be quite at home in the jungle, sir."

They didn't know what to expect, even though they saw for themselves what was missing. There usually weren't gas chambers in labor camps. The crematoriums were too small, too.

"Did you notice that SS man was wearing gloves all the time?" demanded the skeptic, whom the other men had nicknamed Golden Eyes.

"He probably had his hands shot up in Africa," Red Richard stated promptly. "Around Tripoli or in the Sahara. Or maybe someplace that isn't even on the map."

Nobody had anything to say, so Red decided he might as well go on talking. "We've got the right to file a lawsuit with the International Railroad Stations Court, which now occupies the building of the former League of Nations in Geneva. It's swamp fever. Every three days, tremendous attacks of fever. Imagine that impertinent protozoon moving in on your red blood corpuscles as if they were a dormitory and then destroying them."

"Yackety-yak," the rough voice spoke up. They couldn't turn Red Richard off, but maybe they didn't want to.

Jiri was only listening with half an ear now. He could see the lieutenant's gaunt face. Those green eyes he'd tried to read. What kind of person was he, what could one expect from him?

"Maybe he's a decent guy," he said.

"How can you say such a thing?" asked the man with the saucepan.

"He laughed at me," said Jiri.

"It's chills, I tell you," insisted Red.

"We have no proof and nobody ever will have," observed Golden Eyes.

"What evidence do you have?" a voice asked harshly.

"What evidence *don't* you have?" asked someone in a gentle voice.

"He'd be one of our ninety million," Richard replied.

"I wish at least somebody would behave a little better," Jiri said.

"You're still a greenhorn Jew and not just because you got stuck with the worst bunk," declared Red. "A gentleman in uniform like that can only be decent six feet under, to put it politely and objectively. Absolutely under the turf."

"He hasn't yelled at us yet," Jiri pointed out.

"He's still going to have a few opportunities, kid," said the skeptic.

"Anyway," said Jiri.

The darkness thickened. Jiri wondered what kind of person the man in the SS cap was, how he would probably behave. Not just because he hadn't yelled at them, but because that was not, after all, normal here.

Here, air raids would probably be the worst part. The order not to look up. An order like that is quite welcome.

For the first time in his life he wished he could be sure about this one person, at least, even though he was only one out of ninety million. He knew it was ridiculous, the longer he thought about it. But it would be a kind of breakthrough. He knew what it would mean if this one single person were to be the exception to an infallible truth.

"Can you sweeten with salt and salt with sugar?" Red called in his direction.

Jiri stretched out and put his hands under his head. He observed the texture of the hole in the ceiling. The cracked roof above him reminded him once more of the gaunt, sallow face of that guy with malaria.

Jiri wondered what would happen if he smiled at that malarial face. It's just high spirits, Jiri reminded himself. Things better not talked of. Better to keep quiet. But he wished somebody would help him make up his mind what kind of person the officer was and how he would treat them.

"Is it comfortable up there?" called the nearsighted boy.

"It's all right," Jiri told him.

"I wish somebody would explain to me why, of all things, a person is always inclined to impress his own enemies," mused Red.

"If you want to, you can lie down here with me," offered the nearsighted boy.

"Actually, I have nothing against fags personally," declared Red Richard. "I don't object to bald heads or flatfoots and deviants; as long as nobody is trying to rape me, I like practically everybody. Humanity would become extinct if everybody was a pansy, and quicker than Papa Himmler plans it."

It was quiet again. Jiri had never experienced this kind of silence.

"Even the best of them can only be good under two well-weighed tons of dirt," redheaded Richard voiced Jiri's thoughts.

"Our kind of people have to be smart. We've got to start thinking things over right now: what is, what was, and what will be; where did it start and where is it going? And everybody is everybody else's referee, even for ourselves."

"For me, they're dead, even if they're still alive," said the rough voice.

"I don't agree," Red answered promptly. "One thing I'm not sure about is how many of them and which ones we are going to allow to run loose around the world. Or whether I won't swiftly and diligently prepare graves for all of them with nice turf cushions."

They'd all prefer to be far away from here, Jiri thought to himself. Yet he was still wondering whether he ought to risk smiling at the malarial skull-face. He liked listening to the redhead's blabber. The mysteries of how it was going to be when the war ended, of what was on their minds now. It was what they were all waiting for, but they couldn't imagine it. Somebody will come to the camp gate and grab the latch.

"Hi there, fellas! Well, it's all over. Other dances are in style now. You're lucky you lived through it. Pick up your marbles and clear out of here and make room for others. Just go, as far as your legs can carry you. We're going to raze this place to the ground."

An American Tommy or a Russian Ivan or some "rassig" Jewish face in an Allied uniform. Who knows?

The moon came out. The silhouettes of the fence, the hillside, and the watchtowers were visible. The wind carried the sound of dogs barking.

Jiri was almost glad no one replied to Red's last remark. Even though he usually waited for these replies. He just could not imagine what it could possibly be like, just as he could not imagine so many other things. Maybe I'll have to sock that malarial skull-face. But he would feel a lot better if he could be sure of what was a real smile and what was a grimace.

We are insects to them, lice, or something worse. And it's

been that way for three years. But like everything else this too contained a bit of paradox.

"Somebody ought to go out and have a look around," said the rough voice.

"I agree, for a change," answered Red Richard.

"Why should we just sit and wait for nothing?" said the rough voice.

Jiri knew it upset him to think about revenge. That was the strongest yearning that was left, after the urge to eat one's fill, or take a bath. It took the edge off all the talk about women which Red relished so much. But even that was only possible when they weren't getting knocked around or when they weren't absolutely famished. When hunger was bad enough, it consumed everything else. But just a mouthful was all they needed—a bite of bread or a piece of sugar beet—and then they started thinking about getting back at them again. Everybody was waging his private war with Germany. Their loathing had a thousand faces. And it was only when a person's true thoughts fell away, that things began to fall apart. But despite everything, loathing had already killed a lot of people, Jiri thought to himself, and it would still kill a lot more. But there were also a thousand faces to letting oneself be killed, too. And, in addition to witnesses who could tell about it, there were countless other people who could no longer speak about it.

And now they were in Germany and the question was whether they were right to regard all Germans in exactly the same way. Sometimes during the night they would talk about revenge and hope they would miss the most brutal part of it, so that they would not repeat what should not be repeated. Even Red and the nearsighted boy were like little kids who think that it is sufficient to shut their eyes in order to obliterate what they cannot then see. It wasn't just cowardice that made so many of them wish it could happen without them, especially the man with the rough voice for whom "Germany had ceased to exist." He even pronounced it with a small "g."

"I can go out and have a look around if you want me to," Jiri said.

"I'll go with you," offered the nearsighted boy.

"You can't see worth a damn, there's no point," Red told him.

"I can see in the dark like a wildcat, if you want to know," said the boy.

"All my earthly possessions," said Red, stroking his belt.

It was warm outside. The wind from the hillside smelled of resin and green leaves. The reek of chemicals rolled from the factory. All munitions plants stink like that, Jiri thought.

Now they could figure out roughly the position of the camp and of the small town. The camp was concealed from the north by a gently sloping, wooded hill. The white trunks of the birch trees were thin, like famished women. They were something firm and tender in them. Outside, beside the barbed wire, there was a splintered wooden propeller, probably from some small American plane that had been shot down nearby. The propeller and the other pieces reminded them both of the afternoon's raid.

It was kind of a mirage: the thirsty man in the desert who quenches his thirst with an image of cold water. It's only a dream of water. This had been the nature of their thoughts many times before. They were like men who were finished but don't fully realize it. Knowing it makes it come sooner.

That accident with the steel splinter in the eye had happened at Auschwitz-Birkenau, in the *Buna Werke* where he and the nearsighted kid used to work.

All I'm after is to feel what it's like to be that German, he said to himself. It's clear to me why I want to.

"Sometimes they have fighter planes with plywood sides to make them lighter," said the shortsighted boy.

From the south, you could see the town. Houses and church steeples and fences were silhouetted in the moonlight and starlight. They figured it must have a population of several tens of thousands. They were always making calculations as if everything depended on it.

The factory was working two shifts, and now and then a light flashed as if someone were adjusting blackout curtains. Then everything was drowned in darkness again.

In the moonlight, a church spire stabbed the sky. It was a handsome Catholic church with a cross on top. The name of the town was Meuslowitz. The nearest big town was Leipzig.

113

"We can use that propeller for firewood," said Nearsighted. "It would be a pity to leave it here," he added. There were kennels beside the powder magazine. The dogs were barking. That reminded them of hunger. Hunger made Jiri afraid and fear reminded him of something else too. It was all connected. The women's barracks were not far and they could hug its shadow. They could both stay in the shadow.

"I can see Red getting back to Prague XII and heading straight for the post office, saying, 'Mr. Postmaster, I'm back again. Isn't there some registered mail here for me?' "

Nearsighted was whispering and in his whispers there was a soft chuckle. It was a nice evening. They felt good. Jiri's tension eased. It's worth risking things for a little bit of freedom, he thought. It gets impossible otherwise.

"There'll be a lot of that after the war," whispered the shortsighted boy.

"That's still a long way off," Jiri replied.

He realized it was seething inside the boy too, ready to boil over, like in himself. The sky was clear and silent, full of stars.

"It's a beautiful evening," said the nearsighted boy.

"I don't think there's any sense in talking so much about it yet," observed Jiri.

"I think it's Friday," said Nearsighted.

"You're right, like that kid this afternoon when he said he felt God in his breast," said Jiri. "He thought it was because they hadn't yet managed to kill his conscience."

"Let's hope they won't kill it along with him," said Nearsighted.

"I think that can wait," said Jiri.

The shortsighted one didn't answer.

"Are you hungry?" Jiri asked him. "If there are Italians and Frenchmen here besides us and the women from Warsaw, we'll really have a great time in the factory."

"I hope we go to the tool room to work," said Nearsighted.

Then they noticed there was someone standing on the other side of the barbed wire.

"Do you think there's electricity in it?" asked Jiri.

"You'd better not try."

114

Jiri whistled softly. It was one of the Polish women. Her profile was turned to the moonlight, which made her shoulder appear to be made of silver. She was about twenty. She was dressed in a potato sack and smelled of potatoes. Nearsighted took a few steps forward.

"Where do they hand out the food around here?" he asked.

She understood him well. Her hair was short, blond, and bristly. She looked at them a long time before she answered. They told her where they had come from and how many they were. They learned that there were about two thousand women in the camp and that most of them worked at the ramp unloading steel sheets for the munitions factory. They were watched by female guards with Alsatian dogs. Those Catholic songs came from the barracks where she was.

"Not in the evening anymore," she replied in Polish. "They only hand it out at noon. And in the evening, it's just for the night shift so they won't get hungry at work and start stealing."

She pointed into the darkness with her forefingers. Then she said she had been in the sewers. Neither Jiri nor the near-sighted kid understood what she meant by that.

"Just once," she repeated. Then she smiled and stepped back, as though she were afraid of them after all.

The church steeple she'd been gazing at was silvery from the front and dark on the other side. The Polish girl paused a few steps away from them. She seemed to be crying. But when they looked at her, she smiled. They could see her white teeth and the gaps where her teeth were missing. She backed away into the darkness. They passed her barracks and went back to their own.

"What did she say?" asked Red.

"It's like everywhere else. You get fed just once a day," Jiri answered.

"So there are young girls here," sighed Red.

"You know, it's nice and warm out," said the nearsighted boy.

"Was she pretty?" Red was interested.

"I couldn't see very well, but she looked all right," he replied. "She was smiling and crying."

"Women do that, it makes them beautiful."

"Well, go on and open the door then, if it's warm outside," suggested the saucepan man.

"Don't make a draft for me here," said the man by the door.

Suddenly they stopped. There was no sound, inside, outside, or anywhere else. The silence pressed in on every side, as if there were no factories here, no town, nothing but forests. They waited for Red Richard to break the silence. Red was exhausted now; he too was silent.

"Red?" the saucepan man called out.

"Would you believe it, I finally feel like sleeping?" Red yawned.

"This is quite a small camp for such a big factory," Jiri observed. "With two twelve-hour shifts."

"Their barracks is as big as ours," said the nearsighted boy.

"Lieutenant, it would almost pay to have a cafe or canteen, with the number of people we have here," said redheaded Richard finally. "Those rebellious ladies from the east can form a choir with us. Or just a room with a few tables."

"A whorehouse, you mean?"

"No, just a couple tables and chairs where people can sit around and talk and listen to nice dance music."

"What are you going to call your new cafe?" asked the rough voice.

"Chez Theodor Herzl or the Leipzig Cafe. What's the difference? Honolulu Bar, Bar America, Dusseldorf Coffee House, Latrine Cafe. It doesn't matter."

"You really don't need anybody but yourself," declared the saucepan man.

"Nobody can ever manage all by himself," Red stated sadly.

"My mother used to say you should be fair in your judgments of other people," said Red.

"Once when we were building air-raid shelters back in Theresienstadt, we beat up a Jewish boy because he made it very clear to us that he was more German than anybody else," said Jiri. "We let him exercise his muscles with a shovel and pick for a couple extra hours, so he'd get it out of his system. His dad was *Oberscharführer* Kleindienst, personal chauffeur of some big wheel in General Daluege's staff in Prague. When they were taking a shower, one of his chauffeur buddies noticed that he was circumcised. So overnight, they crossed him off the list of supermen and sent him straight to *Theresienbad*."

"I was afraid he wanted to prove something else," said Red. "If you know what I mean."

"No, I don't, to tell you the truth," Jiri admitted.

"That reminds me of a lot of things, and most of them were beautiful," said Red, and then he fell silent again.

And like a mist, the unknown, the thing they felt so intimately, still remained. The yesterday which repeats itself over and over again.

Jiri didn't know whether the present was what kept bringing back nightmares, or whether it was those old nightmares that were responsible for their presence here.

He knew that it was only among the people he was with now that he could feel less alone than he had ever felt, each of his own, as though he were approaching the moment when it would be better to touch the wires or to put an end to his own quest for himself by the kind of suicide that was offered him.

Those were the moments when many of them had wanted to die. All they wanted was for it to happen quickly and painlessly with a strong jolt of electricity into the wires, because sometimes there wasn't much. Or a good dose of *cyklon b*, because sometimes the Germans were being frugal, and instead of the customary five minutes, people choked and strangled for more than half an hour. Sometimes it took as long as three hours.

It was a thick web of loneliness, fear, and apathy in which you could discern a wish not to live. As they used to dream of sunny streets where people walked free and unafraid, or of children at play, of men and women in love, these dreams were suddenly confronted now with other dreams where the most beautiful thing was to die.

But now Red and the others were silent, as though they'd grown tired of listening to their own words.

Everything Red wanted to hear was expressed again in silence.

Jiri tossed restlessly in his bunk. They could hear him roll-

117

ing around in search of a better position. They all knew what for. Nobody had any idea of what time it was. The flickers of light in the factory probably meant it was only ten o'clock and the shifts were changing.

"You know what Alexander of Macedonia said when they asked him why he was crying? He'd already conquered the whole world and he was grieving because he had nothing left to conquer," redheaded Richard said.

"You must be awfully well-read, Red," said Jiri.

"Not really," grunted Red Richard. It was worming its way into his brain as insistently as silence was into Jiri's skull. "I heard about it last week at Auschwitz-Birkenau when we were out on the *Appelplatz.*"

"My ankles swell and my ears ring when I stand up for a long time," put in the man with the saucepan. "My skin feels tight, as if my chest and my legs and arms and head had all grown bigger and my skin'd shrunk, the thing that holds it all together. Like a balloon pumped full of air. And my heart thumps like I'd been running. When I have to stand too long, I see movies I've never even seen in front of my eyes. Movies I'll probably never see."

"It's all the same to me, when I've got to stand for a long time," the shortsighted boy contributed. "I couldn't care less by now."

"Does the water rush into your legs from the rest of your body?" asked the man with the saucepan.

"Actually, the last time I really felt in my element was in Birkenau," Red went on. "There was this rabbi from Transylvania, a heretic and mystic, who asked another heretic-mystic whether a chicken's still kosher after it's swallowed a pin. And how many worlds God made and discarded before he created this perfect work. They used to talk about the sperm of people that have already perished and are stored away somewhere in Switzerland. And that the story of Frankenstein was written by that English lady after a visit to Prague. Apparently, she was influenced by the story of the Golem, who was invented by Rabbi Löw. And that he never got to be the chief rabbi of Prague. Those two rabbis looked at the smoke coming out of the chimney and pondered whether it was really smoke or the difference between truth and lies. Or between wrong and right. One of the rabbis claimed the world began as a ball which exploded and went on sputtering. That's how it's all going to end anyway, he said. The other one was imagining how they were going to blow up along with everything they were talking about. That was their last selection. They went up the chimney, along with the story the first rabbi had told: God let it be known that the seed that was supposed to bring forth a child to a certain Jewish woman would turn out to be the righteous one who would fix everything as soon as it had grown. So the devil complained that it was unfair to him. To which God replies that he shouldn't worry: that there's another seed—of his man—in another lady. The catch is that the second one'll look just as trustworthy as the first; so, besides the two of them nobody else in the world will be able to tell. Good, huh? Get it?''

"Didn't they say that man is greater than God?" asked the man with the saucepan. "And that creation and destruction are like German food from the same pot?"

"No, they just said that two kings can't wear one crown. And that a king's not a king until everybody recognizes him as such," Red went on. "When they looked up at the chimney and at the smoke, they were convinced that fire isn't what it makes of other things, but what it is. When you throw wood on a fire, it turns black. Put a piece of tin in the fire and it gets red. Iron whitens. It was terribly important for them to find out for themselves that fire mainly heats. Understand? Next to them, I had the feeling that it wasn't just the Germans who were trying to drive us back into the caves."

"Don't you know some other joke? Even an old one," suggested the man with the saucepan.

Jiri touched the ceiling, trying to feel where the dark stain started. He thought about the Polish girls and about the watchtower and the church steeple. That brought him back to the lieutenant with the malarial jaw and the grimace which could be a portion of a smile.

He looked through the window at the stars. A lot of people will want to go back to where they came from. The names of many countries and many towns where people used to live before everything blew up like an overheated boiler came to mind. As if it had had to happen sooner or later. But things would probably never be the way they used to be, before they'd gone away. It would be nice if it were as easy as finding the key to a door which had always been slammed shut. Some of them would go to America, or to Australia, somewhere far away where no one knew them and where they too knew nobody who could remind them of anything else. Perhaps they would be more impatient than other people—or quite the opposite. He could imagine how it would be. They'll have had a different education than other people, but who can tell whether, in the future, it will turn out to have been any worse? A few of the survivors will be somewhat deranged, although nobody will ever be able to tell. They'll be deranged in the sense that their madness will be like an invisible bridge spanning the distance between what was and what is yet to be. But maybe even those who were far away when all this happened will go mad later, Jiri thought to himself, after it's all over. They'll become a little deranged, too, because they weren't part of it and because, in a certain sense, they'll be envious.

For almost ten minutes, he imagined how he would explain to those who fortunately hadn't been present. He looked for words and phrases and stories to tell them about it and he knew he probably wouldn't be able to find any. And silence explains nothing. Maybe there would be songs about it. It would be wonderful if there were to be at least one good, true song about it. A song about how the end came before the beginning, and how no one—literally no one (not even those who used to find an explanation for everything in prayer)—had known about it.

Everything pushes its way to the surface more easily at night, Jiri thought. But what he thought about most was the shaved-headed kid in uniform with his short, energetic strides and a way of looking at you which neither threatened nor made any promises. He could think about him for hours. Nobody said a word.

Suddenly there was a roaring noise in the darkness. At first it was faint, no more than a strong wind. Then it resembled a breeze running along the tops of the tall grass, like breath before it becomes a voice.

They knew what was happening before anyone said a

120

word. It sounded different from the two afternoon air raids. The silence was like a time bomb. Murmurs ran through the room. You could hear the men shifting around in their bunks. The little one and his people were suddenly praying. There were no sirens to be heard. It was as if the flak were crouching with them in the darkness. They were B-17's. Hundreds or thousands of motors at an inaccessible altitude. To Jiri, they meant something between what was and what will be.

Then the voice of the engines began to sound like the sea or a sandstorm; then came a crashing of rocks and a soft buzz like when a mosquito flies into your ear. But this was just the beginning.

The aircraft came from unknown bases. They had crossed the ocean, a continent perhaps, and certainly many cities. They'd passed beyond German anti-aircraft stations, that torn net of defense. The activity of thousands and thousands of unknown people lay behind this raid. It was like a gift which brings destruction, as if their destruction could be a gift.

As I've observed the best death is the quickest one, Jiri said to himself, as if he were building a bulwark of words between himself and the engines above. He was ashamed of his fear, but proud to be on the side of those unknown men above flying the machines. There was no relief in knowing that the nearsighted kid and the redhead and those who were praying all felt the same.

He was still afraid, like an animal driven into a trap, although the knowledge that the trap will be destroyed along with him mingled with the satisfaction of feeling that there was somebody stronger than the Germans. Well, this was Germany—the third air raid in one day.

"Let them," Red said again. And then in a voice that almost seemed to crouch, he added: "I think we ought to attract them somehow. Maybe people have a kind of magnet inside. Or else they transmit a secret code on unknown wave lengths. Maybe we're all like time bombs that haven't gone off yet and nobody in the world knows what makes them tick, not even us. But inside, something goes on ticking away even if you can't always hear it."

121

"Aw, you're just talking," said the man with the saucepan.

"You've got to figure it out for yourself," Red insisted. "Now they're going to start rolling it out like when my mother used to roll out the dough to make apple strudel."

Sirens began to scream in the town below, along with the bark of anti-aircraft guns. Something had obviously gone wrong on the ground. The factory sirens joined in the chorus at short intervals. The top emergency alarm.

"Where do you suppose they're going to?" wondered the shortsighted boy.

"Just you wait. As soon as things quiet down, I'll phone the General Staff," Red answered. "Quite enjoyable night life you have, Lieutenant," he rambled on. "I'm beginning to like it here so much I'll recommend it to the others."

There was silence for a while before he added: "The Germans, the Jews. It's not dead. It'll never be dead. It'll only look like it's dead. But maybe it will be dead one day, like a dried sea bed or a crumbled rock formation. But as long as there's some sort of half-naked man, with a coat or skirt of bulrushes or grass, it won't be dead."

"Wouldn't you rather keep your mouth shut now?" said the rough voice nervously.

"Why now?"

"Because somebody might suddenly come in here and understand you," the rough voice explained.

"Yea, the lieutenant intends to visit us at just this moment," said Red.

"Don't worry," said Jiri. "If a bomb fell in here, we wouldn't even have time to run to the latrine."

He was driving out everything that had been accumulating inside him with the roaring of engines, with the flash of searchlights that began to comb the sky. Every bomb that falls here will solve a lot of things, he thought, including the mystery of the guy in the green cap and the leer that looked like a smile. He reminded himself that this was not the first time. Everyone of them died like this every day. Many times a day, every night.

"Maybe they're just flying over," suggested the nearsighted boy.

"There's a powder magazine on the other side of the hill," said the saucepan man. "I noticed it along the way."

"The Germans are really strange and funny people," Red observed. "Some of their great leader's girlfriends apparently committed suicide. He liked to have them pee on his head." Sometimes he talked about the great leader's peculiar desires and tastes where women were concerned. It turned their stomachs.

The roaring was right above their heads now. It filled the room with a force they could only perceive, not alter.

The roaring grew so loud that it seemed to be packing itself solidly into all the space that was left between the planes and the ground.

"The German sky has become English or American," said the shortsighted kid.

"It'd have been worse if the American or English sky were German," said Red. "But maybe not for us yet."

Then the roaring grew, as though the center of the formation of planes had drawn into a tight dense circle. It would have been like an eclipse of the sun, if it hadn't been night.

"I'd like to be far enough along to be able to tell jokes about gas chambers," Red remarked. "I'd like to be with the people who'll be telling them. For instance: 'That amusing figure skating double pirouette, the Bergen-Belsen. Or the triple Freiberg-Mauthausen-Buchenwald.' "

No one laughed.

And then he added: "It's just those bastards who wish every day was a pile of shit they could flush down the toilet. No excitement, no inspiration, a gray existence. No rewards or punishment. For them, people without blue eyes and blond hair are an infectious disease, incapable of appreciating or creating something beautiful. Who else would want to do what they do, spend their time flushing everything down the john, one day after another in darkness, cold, and boredom? One night after another, their whole life."

"Directly over us," whispered the shortsighted boy.

"Just imagine if you'd been born a few parallels west, you'd be flying up there now, a kind of cousin of mine," said Red.

"What happened with that fellow when he found out his

123

mother had been unfaithful to his dad?'' Golden Eyes asked nervously.

"She discovered he was cheating on her because, all of a sudden, he started wearing clean underwear every day,'' Red replied in an altered tone.

"But maybe the boy just read it somewhere.''

The redhead tried to recollect what she had written: *"Then in the morning we'd make love, but it will never happen. It would be too wonderful. You would be the mechanic of my trembling.* And her son read that letter.''

"You didn't happen to be that boy?'' asked the man with the saucepan.

There were thousands and thousands of planes. The heavens thundered. It was as though somebody were rolling thousands of oil drums across the sky. Even the earth was rumbling, making it seem as if it were about to open up and swallow itself. It was like an earthquake, bigger than the whole earth, yet hidden inside its own nucleus and just as inexplicable.

"They've been right above us for too long,'' put in the nearsighted boy. "There are too many of them.''

"A lot more things are still good,'' said Red Richard quietly. "Internal combustion engines were perfected back in 1926. Light metals and alloys. George Gershwin who was born in 1898, just like my mother. Some ideas, but there are plenty of those; the problem is that they never materialize.''

He had hardly finished his sentence when the first explosion came. The window shattered. Everything collapsed along with it. It must have struck very close. The wood and walls mingled with earth. The roaring of the planes filled the void of sound as the noise of the explosion and falling debris diminished, and then it too began to fade away. The earth was again enveloped in the now muffled sound of bombs falling in the distance.

"What happened?'' asked the nearsighted boy.

"That was close,'' said the man with the saucepan.

"It fell around here,'' said Golden Eyes.

"As long as you can hear it, it hasn't hit you,'' said the skeptic.

"It exploded in the woods,'' said the nearsighted boy.

"There'll be a nice crater left," observed the man with the rough voice.

"They're flying away," said the nearsighted boy.

"After the war they can use that crater as a garbage dump for the ones who move in here after us," suggested the rough voice.

"Jiri?" asked the nearsighted boy looking up at the ceiling. "Are you still alive?"

"More or less," Jiri answered. "It's over."

"Does anybody have a match?" Red called out finally.

"If *you* don't have something, nobody has," Golden Eyes replied. It was obvious he was thinking of something else.

"I had some in my jacket pocket," said the nearsighted boy. "Does anybody know where my jacket is?" His voice sounded strange.

"I don't know anything. I'm almost dead," Red said.

Jiri touched the ceiling. The roaring had lessened, like a huge net somewhere in the distance, drawn high above them. Jiri felt around cautiously to determine how far he could move. Then he checked to make sure that he still had all his limbs and that he could still sit up. He ran his hand through the web of wires in the roof. They were still intact.

He looked up at the plaster that clung to the wires. The wooden walls hadn't survived the explosion. Where the ceiling ceased to offer any protection, the starry sky began. The tongues of the searchlights were no longer there. Anti-aircraft fire rained up from earth, as though the gunners wanted at least to use up the prescribed amount of ammunition.

"My leg's broken," groaned Red Richard.

"Where are you anyway?" asked Jiri.

"It took me along with my bunk," Red said.

"That's unlikely because I'm right above you."

"It's no joke," said Red.

"How can you tell?"

"I swear."

"Where are you?"

"Jump down, but not on top of me."

"I can't," said Jiri.

"There's a plank digging into my leg, come on, don't be a bastard!" said Richard. Then he added: "I've got a letter in

125

there with an address to write to." And at the end: "Pass me the belt, at least."

Jiri lowered himself from his bunk. Then he saw what had happened. The bunks were held together by bits of wood and wire and were wedged among the broken floorboards and debris. Red lay on the ground. Jiri understood that the thing Red had in the little pouch on his belt was better than being sent away, supposedly to the hospital.

"I can't lift it by myself," said Jiri after a moment. "It's heavy. The whole building's lying on you."

"That's me all over," Red grunted. "The whole damn house has to fall on me." It didn't sound funny, but Red was trying.

He touched Jiri's elbow. It was so dark that the short-sighted boy had to bend low to see where Richard was and where the beam was that lay on his leg.

"Grab it in the middle," Jiri told the nearsighted boy. "We've got to raise it about half a meter, that is above the knee. Then we'll take two steps to the left. Put it down when I tell you, right?"

"Hurry up," Red urged.

Finally they lifted the beam. When the walls collapsed, the room had been cut in two. The men were separated now and could communicate only by shouting. Outside, they could hear the Polish women singing in their barracks. It was one of those sweet Polish hymns. Suddenly it stopped. Then they heard the dogs barking and whining.

"At last!" Richard groaned. "My leg's crushed."

"It's not over yet," the saucepan man declared.

"I'm going to lose that leg," Richard went on softly. "I've been in good health for too long, considering we're in Germany. It's not a good country."

"You'll survive," the saucepan man reassured him.

"I knew it as soon as we got here," Richard went on.

"Don't you have the feeling those planes are coming back?" the shortsighted kid asked.

"They're going to wipe out Leipzig," Richard said. "Then they'll wipe us out. I'll be through with it."

Four searchlights were switched on above the camp. Suddenly they could see everything in bluish clarity—the woods, the little town, the church, the factory, where the camp was and where the factory building started. The searchlights came nearer. They were like trees on fire, burning and falling slowly to earth, as if attached to small parachutes. They looked like branches of fir trees on fire, their ashy needles falling.

The explosions ceased. The planes began to disappear again into the night.

"That's the end," Jiri said.

"They did a good job," said the man with the saucepan.

"I'm dying," said Red.

The sirens now changed their volume and rhythm. The air raid was over. They could imagine how things looked outside. They heard the ambulances and fire trucks rushing around. The air was torn with the barking of the German police dogs. The night was filled with sound. Everything was still functioning. There seemed to be a lot going on outside. They felt a part of all that activity and at the same time isolated from it.

"Their planes are supposed to have wooden bodies so they can fly with a load of the biggest bombs there are and not get hit," said the nearsighted boy. "Wooden bodies and Rolls Royce engines."

"Nobody has it," said Red. "Please don't trample me, at least."

Jiri handed Red his jacket and pants, but not the belt. That he kept. To be on the safe side, Jiri carefully clambered up on his bunk.

"I'll lie down beside you for a little while," said the nearsighted boy.

"If you want to," Jiri moved over.

"It's cold at night," said the boy.

"What time is it?"

"What does it matter?"

"Is it warmer like that?"

"Absolutely."

Jiri thought about Red Richard who didn't want to bother them with his pain, and how he'd taken away even the mouthful that could have helped him, that capsule hidden in his belt. They'll know what to do in the morning. Keeping your pain to yourself means a lot more than sharing your joy, Jiri decided. Then, once more, he thought of the man with the leering face.

The nearsighted boy pressed closer to him. They lay there under the stained square of ceiling which was the only thing that had resisted the air pressure, thanks to the web of wires. And who knows what else?

Briefly, Jiri recalled the kennels where a Nazi flag was flying when they'd arrived that afternoon. He could still see the officer who'd brought them here without yelling at them once. Then, as he chewed his straw, it seemed that the stalk of grass contained more than some distant peace.

"What do you think's wrong with your leg?" asked the rough voice.

"It's a nasty fracture, but the splintering is probably the worst part of it."

"Could you manage to stand on the other leg in the morning?"

They all understood what he meant.

"I'd rather stay seated as long as I can," Richard replied.

He howled like a dog during the night several times and asked the others to forgive him.

"Don't excuse yourself," said Jiri.

"I hope it'll be morning soon," whispered Red. "Excuse me for having been born."

But there was still a long time until dawn. The night was full of feverish, distant voices. There was just a hint of light, a smudge of haze in the distance. Jiri was waiting for the sun to come up. He tried to estimate how much energy he could use until then without being utterly exhausted in the morning. He could not sleep because he kept thinking of all the things which, as Red Richard said, happen only once...things you can't lose twice. He pressed his hands to his belly. For an answer to everything, Jiri looked toward where dawn was promising to appear. But even there, he knew there was no answer.

Suddenly he heard Richard trying to sit up.

"Stand up!" he said in a tense, cracked whisper.

Jiri saw the gleam of flashlights and a sheen of helmets. He jumped down from his bunk, the nearsighted boy after him.

128

"Do you have any dead or wounded here?" asked an SS officer.

"I've got a broken leg," Richard told him quietly.

"We need one man quick," said the officer. Richard looked down.

"Well then, who?" the officer in the helmet asked more sharply. He spilled a semicircle of weak light over them.

"Me," Jiri replied. He stepped forward because he didn't want the man in the helmet to get any other ideas.

"Don't you want to get dressed?" asked the officer.

"I'm dressed already, it's all right," said Jiri.

The officer didn't ask more.

They moved to the place where the door had been before and went through the grove of trees along the hillside. The bombs had ripped open the second circle of wire fences and destroyed the watchtowers.

The grass was wet with dew. The woods were thin. The bark of the birch trees was peeling and the beeches looked old and solid, though not as supple. But they still looked like trees in the morning do, fragile, but strong. Hazelnut and blackberry bushes grew close to the earth and there were cranberry and huckleberry plants among the moss. The taller trees cast shadows. The approaching dawn was invisible as they crawled up the hillside because the woods had grown thicker. Jiri hadn't been in a forest for three years.

The tall officer was silent the whole way. He took long strides and glanced back now and then to see if Jiri was keeping up with him. Higher up there were clearings in the woods with patches of last year's heather.

"You're going to collect our dead," the tall officer said finally.

"All right," Jiri replied.

"Take a swig of this first," said the officer and handed him a field flask of rum.

"Thanks," said Jiri. He pretended to take a drink, but he just wet his tongue, holding it so the liquid wouldn't trickle down his throat.

"We're only people, made of skin and bones," said the officer. Jiri wiped his lips.

"Start at this end," said the officer. He adjusted his helmet

129

as if it were a cap, up from his face. "Fifty paces north from here." He gestured toward the hilltop with his hand and chin. "My men are digging pits there. Drag over everything you find."

Again, he indicated the direction with his extinguished flashlight and took back the flask.

"Then you can go back to your barracks by yourself."

"O.K."

"Then you'll get your reward."

"I understand."

"I hope you've got good nerves and a strong stomach."

For safety's sake, Jiri simply nodded.

"This is Germany. I keep my word," said the officer.

It was only after the officer had gone that Jiri realized what he was supposed to do. He watched him leave. He didn't even turn around. It was difficult to concentrate on the task ahead of him and not to think of his barracks where Red Richard, the nearsighted kid, and even the praying guys had probably crossed him off their list.

Jiri tried to collect the bodies without looking at them or thinking about what it was he was collecting or even about the fact that this was maybe the last thing he'd do in his life. These woods had been the retreat, then, for those voices they'd heard shouting, people who couldn't find room in the concrete bunkers built into the hillside further down the slope. And it's probably a nice big bunker, Jiri figured. But only for those who got there in time.

He could taste the rum on the roof of his mouth. The rim and the neck of the tin flask. The place Red was talking about, where elephants go to die, he said to himself. Trees turned upside down in the bottom of a snake pit. Red's broken and crushed leg. That gram of cyanide which, if he had only had it on him, he could have dropped into the officer's rum.

The bomb had fallen into these woods just missing their barracks with the reinforced concrete ceiling. The things nobody can ever predict. The trees loomed into the morning sky, broken and charred. Some lay flat.

He could hear birds singing, but when he looked around, he saw none. Suddenly he was glad it wasn't quite daylight yet. As for all those many German promises, rarely kept even when officers made them, he did not feel like thinking of them. But regardless of his preferences, wishes, and fears, daybreak was coming. The light was growing stronger and brighter.

There was a kind of emptiness around him once the officer had left him, and Jiri started the job. He told himself each time that it was only a boot or a button or a glove, a cap, a sleeve, just *something*. He went from tree to tree, from bush to bush, from trunk to trunk. He stumbled into the lair of some animal which wasn't there anymore.

He kept telling himself that this was an *it*. He didn't allow himself to admit what he knew, that these were parts of something which might have looked the way he looked himself. Then he stopped bothering about being all covered with blood. He tried to dig up in himself a revulsion for the people who had been killed here and lay around now, ripped apart and scattered into pieces which nobody could ever put together again. As if they hadn't been alive just last night. The other side of their existence was very far and very near at the same time. He told himselff repeatedly that this was *their* business, that he just landed in it the way people like him had been landing in such situations during the past few years. It was not just that no one had ever asked his opinion about anything. He had nothing to do with it except that he was supposed to clean up. *Because this wasn't his fault.*

The more he thought about Red, the more thoughts came into his head. In Birkenau, Red had escorted his twin brothers to the showers because he couldn't stand the idea of German doctors performing experiments on them. It wasn't hard to imagine what they'd have to look forward to afterwards. He didn't want them to be castrated. So day after day, he talked to them, convincing them that going into the showers wasn't really the worst thing that could happen to them. He was afraid the Germans would maim them. So he thought that convincing them to go voluntarily was the best thing he could do for them. All they knew was that when he came to Birkenau and found the two of them still alive, he'd asked them where their parents were. Smiling, they told him they'd "gone up the chimney." They probably smiled because they didn't think he'd believe them at first. They also knew why it was sometimes better to go up the chimney than to stay in Birkenau.

And if it had been the other way around, they would have gone with Red, just as afterwards he went with them to the selection—because a person simply couldn't win at every selection. They would have given him advice, as he did with them, to be careful about cold water, so he wouldn't catch a cold when he went outside afterwards and get pneumonia. As if all three of them didn't know that in Birkenau there was no "after the showers." This shower game and all the talk about *afterwards* was something they had played even with themselves. Everybody knew why. For three days afterwards, Red wouldn't speak to anybody.

What he said next carved itself into Jiri's memory. He understood why Red was so afraid they'd maim him. That letter he always carried around with him represented the past, vanished like a phantom, and Red was scared he'd never be able to piece it back together with his future. But it was all part of the game which Red played with himself, that there still *was* some kind of a future. And that, as long as he still lived, it was one link in an unending chain. It was for the other side of his hope that he kept that gram of poison. He had the feeling that Red was the other side of the forest. The thing he was collecting. It was only later that he realized that he too was part of the other side—on this side.

There was always something else, this *something else,* the way they lived and which was part of the inscription on the gates which read: *Eine Laus dein Tod Jedem das seine.*

His back, arms, and head began to ache.

He didn't even want to think about whether he was glad this had happened to those around him because that reminded him of Red Richard's wounded leg and what that was bound to lead to.

He did what the officer told him. He couldn't measure time. He knew that whatever reward he might get (it was real rum he'd been offered) he'd give to the nearsighted kid. All of it. Or to Red Richard. Let them divide it up.

Suddenly he stopped. He straightened slowly. And he knew clearly then what had happened and what was to be.

He'd been feeling chilly, but now he began to shiver and

the chills grew worse. Goose pimples broke out. Again he realized that there were things which would never be the way he wanted them to be—those two layers of which existence is composed, according to Red Richard.

He focused his eyes on a birch tree draped with rags. He looked at the lonely, slender trees at the edge of the clearing. All he saw were branches, jagged and swollen by the splinters of the bomb, and then *those things.*

Those things which still looked clean and tidy. The green collar of a coat and silver tabs, a scrap of sleeve, a pants leg, and all of it full of *what* had been there before. At the level of his face, a cap swayed in the early morning breeze. A cap with a dark visor and underneath it, *something* he recognized though he'd seen the lieutenant only once and briefly. He knew he couldn't be mistaken. *That* was *it. It* belonged to the skinny fellow who had escorted them from the station. There it was, with *its* crippled malarial jaw, the immobile, convulsive fragment of a smile.

And Jiri suddenly realized that it wasn't a smile and it wasn't a grimace of grief; it wasn't anything at all. He knew now that he'd never discover what was behind that grimacing face, what kind of man he'd been. Whether he would have slapped him back if he had smiled.

At the same time, he knew it wasn't just *that.* And also that he probably never would do what he'd been planning to do sometime in the future. Richard the Redhead had said in the train that, sometimes when danger has passed, an enemy is something different. But not even Richard was always right about everything. He knew that nobody should ever do it unless he's sure of what that grimacing face in the cap was really like. Or *wasn't.*

There was silence all around, except for a murmuring like trees sighing in the wind now and then, as though a squirrel were running from one tree trunk to another. The trees were swaying in the wind, fresh, peaceful, and alive. That was a different kind of life, and the man was envious. On the other side of the hill, the sound of German voices rose, the men, women, and children who hadn't made it into the shelter that had been built just for them.

The ones who kill and the ones who are killed, thought Jiri.

133

It makes a difference, being able to die only once, but only afterwards.

He began wondering how long he'd have to stay there. Picking up corpses and bits of human beings and flesh and clothing was all a part of warfare, just like working in a munitions factory or on the ramps. Like the women in the clean-up crews in Birkenau. After new transports arrived from Holland, Denmark, Hungary, or from the Czech or Moravian Protectorate, they had to wash down the walls to get rid of the remains of babies whom soldiers had dashed against the walls like tennis balls.

It was strange that the Germans weren't interested in baby clothes, even though they were quality woolen stuff—red, pink, and blue swaddling clothes, pillows, and quilts.

The women swept out the boxcars, picking up the tassled caps and pacifiers, the rattles and toys.

These babies, the ones smashed to a pulp against the walls of the crematorium, or even here in the sweet-smelling forest, weren't the only things Jiri thought about. When he did a job like this, he always thought about the living. The living were the ones who had to bear it. Inside the living, images were accumulating which you'd prefer to erase, if you only could. But there was even a difference in that.

He tried to think about strawberries growing in the woods, and blackberries, and about how you can squeeze them to make juice that's redder than blood. He'd rather envied the trees and moss.

It too was something a bit different.

And suddenly he realized he wasn't afraid of blood or of smearing his hands and clothes and soul with blood. Suddenly he knew that he wasn't frightened anymore, that life would never be the way it was before all this. And this disturbed him, rather that encouraged him. As if he knew that everything, literally everything that happens to a person, can never be wiped away again as if it had never happened.

He tried to find out from the movements of the trees and from their soft voices what it was that made them, alive or dead, different from human beings. He looked up, as if searching for justice in the crowns of the trees, as if it could be somewhere, even when everyone had been killed.

He heard the birds again. They were singing, but he couldn't see them. He heard human voices, arguing in German.

Jiri leaned against a tree, five paces away, his back turned to the last birch tree. He rubbed his lips against the bark that hung in moist, thin strips from the shattered edges of the broken trunk. It was smooth and mute and almost clean.

The sun drank up the remnants of the night.

Michael and the Other Boy with the Dagger

I

Every time Michael had to stand there, he looked so angry. He was vaguely conscious of the old man's hoarse voice. He could tell he had it in for him again. Michael was standing in line with forty-five other prisoners, and there were five more rows of men behind them—two hundred and twenty-five hairless heads covered with crumpled cloth caps. He kept his hands in his pockets and shuffled his feet. He'd found a pigeon feather that morning. He was careful with it, and had wedged it into his pocket so it wouldn't fall through the hole.

Michael didn't budge. *On the reservation, the last scion of Vinnetou, the Red-skinned Gentleman, recalls the vanished glories of bygone days. Four hunters on white horses with red and white lances and bows and arrows and guns.*

"Michael, did you hear what I'm telling you?"

Michael didn't bother to reply. The old man's voice sounded like earth moldering away, old soil drying up and crumbling into dust.

"Do you think you might be able to stand up just a little straighter? And take your hands out of your pockets?"

"You want me to freeze?"

"For God's sake," said the old man.

Michael knew he wasn't lined up right. He knew the old man didn't dare pick on anybody else. He couldn't pick on anybody. *The vanished glories of bygone days. Furs you can lie on, other hides and furs to walk on and still others to cover yourself with.*

Michael suddenly bared his stained rodent teeth at the old man and wiped his nose with the back of his hand. When he managed to get under the old man's skin, he felt alive again, as though he weren't a total flop.

"Have you decided you want to be tonight's scapegoat?" asked the old man.

Michael calmly licked the index finger of his right hand, the one with the broken nail. His tongue probed the wound. *Everything is starting to fester for me.* He'd cut himself on a wire. In the wintertime, when there was a snowfall, even the crows got electrocuted.

Michael swallowed. But the thing with the sweet taste, the yellow stuff mingled with blood that he sucked out of his finger, didn't happen for the sake of crow's meat roasted on a shovel over the coals in the barracks stove. He'd hung a foot wrapping over a wire to dry.

"Nobody ever makes us a present of this rubble," said the old man. "We'd always be within easy reach."

That morning Manitou had watched the assembly line of the factory go off to the happy hunting grounds, along with the night shift crew and dozens of Italian black ants and German white ants who hadn't made it to the shelters in time. And the Jewish red ants who weren't allowed into the shelters under any circumstances.

By afternoon they'd have a rough idea of how many white, blond ants were left in the rubble, how many ants dressed in green and brown uniforms and how many black and red ants. Then the *hajot*. Black ants weren't allowed in until the very last minute, and then only if there was enough room. When the bombs started dropping between heaven and earth, the red ants could sizzle in their own juice right on the spot so they wouldn't get any idea of rejoicing over an air raid.

The old man's voice broke into his thoughts again. Michael raised his little bird face, covered with mud and freckles.

II

"Attention!" bawled the old man. *"Mützen ab!"*

Michael whipped off his cap. The count came to two hundred and twenty-five men. The old man began with the words, "dirty Jew," as if it were a title. Then instead of a name, a number which was tattooed on the forearm. "Two hundred and twenty-five dirty Jews, sir," he concluded.

"Precisely," said the officer.

The officer looked around and stopped some five paces from the old man, who turned away so he wouldn't have to face him directly.

So *Herr Obersturmführer* hasn't gotten it in the neck yet, Michael thought to himself. He's skinned through this time too.

"Two hundred and twenty-five men plus one," repeated the old man.

The colonel drew a sheet of paper from the wide cuff of his coat-sleeve. He compared the figure with the roll call. One of his eyes was made of green glass. That was why they called him Eyeball. The white, the pupil, and the iris of each eye was different, but you could never be sure which eye was which. Michael wanted to find out which eye was living and which was dead.

"At ease," said the colonel.

"Mützen auf," the old man ordered.

All two hundred and twenty-five men—along with the old man—put on their caps.

"You're going to have to clean up this rubble," announced the colonel. "No more shifts. Everybody has to work. You'll get additional help on the spot."

"Yes, sir."

"The quicker you get the job done, the sooner you go back to one shift. The better you work, the more willing I'll be to consider letting the Italian deserters help you unload the cement and rolled steel from the trains."

"Yes, sir."

"Trains can't wait."

"No, sir."

"And nobody should fuss around too much with rubble."

"Yes, *Herr Obersturmführer.*

The colonel surveyed them with his live eye.

"Attention!"

"*Mützen ab!*" shrilled the old man.

"*Scheise!*" Eyeball bellowed suddenly. "If what I'm telling you strikes somebody as funny, well..." But he didn't finish his sentence. He strode rapidly along the front row.

The old man gulped. He turned white. His skin shriveled and his eyes narrowed. He stared fixedly at the *Obersturmführer.*

"He who laughs last, laughs in German," declared the colonel. "I hope you haven't forgotten that. You can ask your *Jahve* to remind you, if you need to."

"Yes, *Herr Obersturmführer.*"

"How long have you been here?" the officer demanded.

"Five years, *Herr Obersturmführer.*"

Michael didn't move a muscle. Nobody did. *The vanished glories of bygone days.* Our *Führer* needn't have done us this honor, Michael thought to himself. He wasn't the only one who was thinking the same thing. He wouldn't ask for more than a pair of wooden clogs. He had to wrap up his left foot in rags each morning to replace the shoe he'd lost.

"How many are there of you?" asked the officer.

"Including children, sir?"

"Do you multiply overnight, perhaps? Am I supposed to think you give birth through this hole?" Eyeball pointed to his buttocks. "What I want from you is work, work, and more work. How many of you are unable to work?"

"We're all quite able, *Herr Obersturmführer.*"

"Take your shovels with you then. At ease!"

"Yes, sir. But we haven't got any shovels, sir. *Mützen auf!*" the old man said.

He knew he'd made a mistake immediately.

"We never got any shovels, *Herr Obersturmführer.* They don't give us shovels, sir. We've never had any picks or shovels or things like that here, *Herr Obersturmführer.*"

"Come here!" Eyeball ordered. "So you haven't got any shovels, you say?"

"We've never been allowed to take shovels into the camp, *Herr Obersturmführer*. Things like that aren't allowed here, sir."

The old man bowed his head and took off his cap although he hadn't been told to.

"Come here!" Eyeball repeated. "Right over here, where I'm pointing."

The old man stepped up to the spot to which the colonel was pointing.

"Do you want to get undressed?"

Three shots rang out in quick succession. The old man tottered forward, as though he couldn't believe it. He staggered backwards as if he wanted to run away but couldn't, so he crumpled to the ground with shock and wonder in his eyes.

Michael could feel the other two hundred and twenty-four men freeze. He stared squarely into the colonel's eyes, trying to figure out which of them was real. The old man lay there on the ground. They ought to put something under his head at least, Michael thought to himself. Or cover him with something. He wished Eyeball would appoint somebody to substitute for the old man. The irises of both eyes looked exactly the same now.

That brought him back to wondering what he always wondered when they killed somebody. Each person has more than one life in him. You've simply got to split up your life into little pieces. Each piece. The little pieces never come together entirely so that they can all be destroyed together. The old man took a long time to die. Poor guy, Michael kept saying to himself. Poor old guy.

"You there, at the end!" cried Eyeball. "Take him away. Throw him into the latrine. I'm not going to ask for favors much longer. You there, the one at the end of the row. I hope you understand me?"

Michael was the first to step forward.

"Can you carry him by yourself?"

"I've carried lots of people already," Michael said.

"Where?"

"In the infirmary block and to the crematorium. I've carried even heavier people."

Michael focused on the thought that each of us has three lives: childhood, maturity, and old age. First you're scared that you won't get something, then that you'll lose what you've already got. Poor old guy. Poor little old fellow.

He wished he could find a way to make the old man more comfortable. As if it mattered. Fear was always what had annoyed him most about the old man. Just because he was scared, the old man would infect him with it, too.

"I hope you haven't strained yourself," said Eyeball in a jocular tone. "What sort of work have you been doing?"

"I carry sheet metal on the ramp and I load coal and cement."

"Are they making smaller sacks these days?"

"I can carry ninety pounds on each shoulder."

"How far?"

"Yesterday it was between fifty and eighty meters."

Michael waited for Eyeball's orders to approach the old man before he died. It wasn't over yet. The old man wasn't dead yet. Michael began to be nervous. He was afraid the officer would notice how nervous he was.

"Why are you gaping at me like that? Haven't you ever seen an *Obersturmführer*? Well, what are you waiting for? You expect him to fart in his pants or what? I'm too good a shot for that. It all depends on you, whether or not we stay friends."

"He's still alive," he lied to the colonel.

"Where's he hit?"

"In the shoulder. One bullet went in just above the heart. The third at the side. You can see for yourself," Michael went on lying.

He spoke humbly, in the way the colonel disliked and yet expected. For a few seconds, Michael thought he heard soft, snoring sounds coming from the old man's gullet.

"Move aside," ordered the colonel. "A little bit of life into this dying."

He squinted. The colonel kicked him. Michael ducked, then tumbled backwards, legs in the air. He rolled over so he could spring to his feet before the colonel started shooting. The German fired four shots, deafening Michael. He could count them, so he hadn't been hit.

"Take him over to the latrine," commanded the *Obersturm-führer*. "On the double!"

Michael stood up. He watched the colonel reload his pistol and stick it back in its holster. Looking like a scared bird, Michael reached into his pocket, took out the pigeon feather and dropped it on the old man's body.

Two prisoners at the end of the row and two others behind them picked up the old man's body. The colonel watched them with his good eye. They carried him to a wooden shed with a tarpaper roof at the edge of the camp, opposite the infirmary and next to the laundry. With his good eye the German was looking for someone else to do the roll call.

The colonel was satisfied with himself. He had superbly demonstrated the worthlessness of this little bunch, these two hundred and twenty-five men. A flock of ants. The rubble, the bomb debris rose up into the heights, while the prisoners bearing the body of the old man with the hoarse voice and the rest of them sank back into the muck.

"Get undressed in the meantime," Eyeball said. "You've got twenty-five seconds. Put on your caps!"

Facing the officer with his hands in his pockets, their naked-ness looked even more naked because they were wearing caps.

III

Later in the afternoon, chilled to the bone, they were told to get dressed again. They were given forty-five seconds, but they did it in twenty.

A pudgy little man in civilian clothes appeared at the camp gate. He had a big round swastika badge stuck like a cookie on his lapel.

It was a log gate. Even before the little man led them off to the bomb site, Michael was trying not to think about the ditch full of quicklime under the wooden roof where....

He thought of the moment when Eyeball was reloading his pistol. The thought shaped itself into a wish that, instead of the hoarse old man, it had been the colonel with the green eye lying there next to the latrine wall. He'd have all five lines of forty-five men go there.

143

The back of the factory tract had been hit hardest. Broken pipes and twisted wires, chunks of cement and shattered machinery were piled as high as the second floor.

Now I've begun my life in these ruins, Michael said to himself.

The pudgy little man was saying, "I don't care what your origin is or where you come from. All I care about is how you work. That's the way we'll understand each other."

"Divide up into groups of tens and fives," he went on. "The last five will work singly. Some of the bombs are timed and some haven't exploded yet, but they will as soon as we start cleaning up. Call our people. The ones in the green field jackets are the sappers and that's what they're here for."

He eyed Michael. "You skip up there," he told him, pointing to what was left of the big long hall on the second floor. A steel ladder with its rungs dangling loose led up there. "Stack up the bricks there. You don't need to go all the way up to where the roof's caved in."

White, blond and blue-eyed ants are the most peculiar ants there are, Michael decided. A cold wind was blowing.

Michael looked around, wondering what he could strip from the first German corpse. The lathes looked like shattered cannons. The big gears resembled great burnt out clocks.

For a while Michael watched the swarms of Italian black ants and Jewish red ants. The white ants would soon pull themselves together. They will rebuild the factory in a couple of days. That's what those white ants expect of us. He'd have them lying in the bottom of the latrine, too, next to Old Man number 60363. Then he'd shovel quicklime over them. It'd eat out their lungs and their eyes and their ears and their livers and they'd stink too, the way latrines stink. And for a couple seconds before they drowned in the stinking filth, he'd hope they were conscious.

He didn't touch a brick for the first twenty minutes.

Two *Wehrmacht* soldiers were chatting under the fire escape that had been torn loose by the force of the explosion. They were swapping stories about how, during air raids, the burned, wounded old folks, mothers, and children would jump from the flaming upper stories of their homes. And about what panic and poor organization make people do.

The first one was talking about how he'd circumnavigated the globe in a submarine and who the captain was and who he was related to. They sailed so far out into the Atlantic that he thought they were going to attack North America. When they wanted to submerge off Crete, they went down a critical five centimeters and almost didn't come up again. The only country he ever really saw was Albania. Suddenly they stopped talking.

A wind had risen. It whistled among the bricks and rubble and broken steel and iron, mingling with voices talking and giving orders and other noises. It's a world of my ants and their ants. Most of the ants are inside a fence and have numbers on. It's an accident, what sort of ants you're born among. Every one of us has three lives.

IV

It wasn't until about five o'clock that Michael finally started stacking bricks. He was cold. He had to have something to show for the time, at least.

Michael kept thinking this raid hadn't amounted to very much if they were just stacking bricks and rubble instead of people. He made three piles of debris. The bits that were less than half a brick he threw away. He thought that if the little German came around, he'd like it that way. Suddenly he stopped dead. What he had pulled out looked like a sock. It was a dirty, dusty old sock. He wondered if there weren't a leg under all those bricks. Or a piece of a leg. Or maybe there was a locker around somewhere, like in the dressing room where the workers changed their clothes. He shook it out.

It was a woolen sock. And here I've been wearing a tattered burlap rag around my foot, he thought to himself. Suddenly he forgot everything else. Like an echo, he could hear himself reassuring the officer with the green glass eye and the pudgy little man with the swastika that he had no intention of stealing anything.

He could see the green glass eye in front of him. That strange, inanimate eye with its exaggerated white, looking as if it were made of some algaelike substance. The sock felt good. Suddenly everything felt quiet and empty.

The sock had taken his breath away. He brushed off the dirt. He sat down on a pile of bricks and took off his clog. Nobody must see me, that's the main thing. And who's going to bother to clamber up that broken ladder, through all this mess?

Carefully he unwrapped the bit of burlap. The fabric was ready to fall apart.

He rejoiced at having found the sock and everything that went with it. He was reminded of the Italian workers—the black ants—who had found some German flannel shirts and sweaters in a bombed out warehouse last winter after an air raid and had brought everything back to the barracks with them. They wore the stuff beneath their prison undershirts until spring came, and then they took it all off and burned it.

Michael pulled the sock up as far as it would go. It was a grown man's sock. He stood up and slipped his foot back into the clog. The sock had a hidden smoothness. He admired the way his foot looked. He stood on one leg like a stork.

He forgot all about the old man and what he'd wanted to do. Suddenly he was once more part of the world where people wear socks, where they put underwear on clean bodies and socks on their feet before they put their shoes on. He didn't even notice the cold wind anymore or the whirling dust that stung the cheeks and feet and hands. Anything that was left bare.

He could see himself walking down the street on a windy, wintry day like today, and as he walked along beside his father, his hands were stuck deep into the warm pockets of his winter coat.

Father asked him if he'd like to have some roasted chestnuts.

Then they went home. Mother was cross because they were late. Steam rose from serving dishes on the table. Dad had planned a treat for later that afternoon. Magic lantern slides.

They pulled down the window shades.

When Michael shut his eyes, it seemed almost as dark now as it had been that Sunday when they had seen the lantern slides. He'd known this kind of darkness one other time. It was in Poland on the night of October twenty-eighth. Or twenty-ninth. The night was thick with smoke.

Something else came to him from somewhere. It was his mother's voice. She'd been carefully hidden the whole time. I didn't go up the chimney at all, she said.

He let her wear the sock for a while. She was just as tall as he was. Afterwards, they all sat down to supper around the kitchen table.

I'll keep the sock on as long as I'm stacking bricks. But only to find the other sock.

V

There was a loud crack and a rattle of plaster. Suddenly he saw a German boy from the Hitler Youth clean-up squad sliding down the rubble that had been heaped up under the caved-in roof. There was nothing to break his fall to the ground floor. Michael knew nothing could keep the boy's body from sliding down the avalanche of plaster. And if he weren't killed by the time he hit the cement floor, he'd be impaled on the sharp blades of the machines.

The slide of broken plaster reached Michael first. He braced himself so the hurtling body wouldn't drag him along with it. Jagged bricks and the edge of something metallic struck his shin.

Michael held out his arms as if he were trying to get his balance. Then he felt the impact of another body against his chest. Instinctively, the other body molded itself to him. They slipped and fell and chunks of plaster showered down with them.

The German boy scrambled up and spat. He rubbed his eyes and ears and nose. He had a dagger stuck in his belt and he was wearing a dirty shirt and torn black corduroy pants.

"Look what they've done, the filthy swine!"

His forehead and knees and elbows were bleeding.

"What are you doing here?" he demanded.

"What do you think?" Michael replied.

"Where do you belong? What division are you from? This is our section."

147

"I'm from the Jewish group. Your *Führer* assigned today's little chores to us."

"I saw you from up there. You've been looting."

The *hajot* looked at Michael's hands and pockets and then at the way he stood there in his rags, covered with the dust he'd raised in his fall.

"Come with me!"

"I only take orders from one kind of person," Michael refused.

It had only taken a second for him to clutch that strange body so he wouldn't be killed.

"It's going to take your people a hundred years to put things back together again," Michael said. "You can tell your father that. Or your mother."

He started to get nervous. He knew exactly when he began to get that nervous. "You're as close to being a corpse as I am."

There'd been no point telling the officer they'd never had any shovels, Michael decided. He spat, as if he were saying goodbye to his second and third lives. As if they were feeding themselves with shovels.

Their eyes met and held fast. It lasted longer than it took for the *hajot's* division to come and go.

"I hope you don't think you scared me with your crazy talk," the *hajot* said.

"It doesn't matter as long as it's just talk," Michael answered slowly. "Unless they've killed all your folks—father, mother, sister. Everybody."

The German boy turned and limped to the ladder.

To begin with Michael took off the sock. He began to wrap the piece of burlap rag around his foot and ankle again. He shivered.

The German boy stood in the middle of the rubble.

"Hey..." he said suddenly.

"What?" Michael shouted back. He started to get nervous again. He was terribly cold, like when they didn't let him sleep.

The German boy limped over to the ladder. Michael glanced down at his foot now wrapped in burlap again. The sock lay on a pile of bricks. There must be a corpse around here somewhere still wearing the other sock. Maybe it was a female corpse. But that was unimportant. Feet and hands. Fingers and lips. Breast. Ears and fingers.

Michael didn't see the German boy start down the ladder. He didn't see him fall.

He could hear the noise as it echoed from the other side of the shattered hall, but he couldn't see anything. It was a long way down and the ladder collapsed quickly. He could piece it all together from the sounds. It took only a few seconds.

Michael stayed where he was.

VI

Darkness came quickly. The signals began again. Whistles—three long and three short. The people down there looked like ants. The rubble had been tidied up.

The sun was setting. It was a wintry sunset above the outlines of the shattered assembly plant of the munitions factory, above the crippled town. The sunset was like a dying bird looking for its nest. It was the way some days die, as if there were blood and heartbeats and a strange anxiety in every splinter and shard of time, everything we have inside us and which we look for in each other.

The pearly light that came with twilight flooded the space between the sky and earth. It drowned the submarine ranges of hills where the white, blond, blue-eyed ants and the funny little black ants and the starved, watchful, always sleepy red ants lived their three lives or uninterrupted single life. They looked like they were one single species, washed in that watery light.

It was that invisible water; it had a weight which made it impossible to pull away. They were all there, shoulder to shoulder, including the old man with the hoarse voice. *And suddenly, right in front of him, lay the land transformed by age-old dreams. He wrapped the warm white fur around him and walked across other skins and hides and lay down on another robe of fur.*

It hardly mattered to him anymore that he wasn't going to find the other sock.

Who knows what will happen tonight or tomorrow morning? Before more freight trains start coming and going. It was cold. The scream of German ambulances cut through the last of the short sirens, signaling that it was time to go back to camp. Michael went slowly.

The tall grass rippled across the broad prairie. The wind whispered and chanted and made no threats. Michael had a pearl-handled rifle in his holster and, under his saddle, a strong white horse. The sun years and moon years that the hoarse old man used to talk about. His horse was strong and spirited. His name was Michael. The land, where there was sun and warmth and people lived as most of them had lived before, lay in front of him. A cloud of dust rose silently in the distance and settled slowly. And the wind brought with it from afar the promise of a wonderful life.

The Last Day of the Fire

Chick was sitting on a three-legged cobbler's stool daubed with dried resin. He was looking at the old man. So this is my granddad Emil. And I'm his grandson. My mother was his daughter, he's his mother's son and so on, back into the inscrutable past. Mother Sonya, Grandmother Theresa.

"It's late," the old man said.

"What makes you say that?" Chick asked.

He could never quite understand why older people look back so much, as if the world had begun elsewhere, before they came along. By now, though, he could imagine why they didn't want to look ahead.

"You want my shirt?" asked the old man.

"Mine's enough, thanks."

"The sewers must be swarming with rats."

"I hope you don't feel like talking about rats. Sure, the sewers are full of them. But the Germans don't go down there. They're more scared of the sewers than of fire and contagious diseases. It'd be stupid for them to go into the sewers. But they're dumb if they don't."

He looked over at the old man who couldn't see him. We belong to each other, he thought.

"Frame houses are the worst, the kinds with wooden floors and rafters and attics," Chick said. "Or those old dirt floor shacks made out of homemade bricks. Most of them are held together with wooden laths or poles. Sometimes I can imagine a forest on fire."

Now and then he thought about food and about water.

153

Once, someone had told him about a meal of several courses, starting with soup and big chunks of roast beef that covered a whole plate and boiled potatoes with melted butter.

"I wish people would burn as easily as trees do," the old man replied.

Chick made up his mind not to answer.

"The hope killed them," said the old man. "It killed the very best of them. And hopelessness straightened out the very best of us."

Well then, so my mother, Sonya, was his daughter, Chick reminded himself. Mother wasn't with them anymore. They'd picked her up on the street last year and shipped her to Treblinka. They thought there were factories there. Like here. Father went after her in February. By that time they knew where he was going.

The word even got back here about which camps were the end stations—like Kulmhof-Chelmno, east of Poznan, or Belzec, which was some hundred kilometers from Lublin, or Majdanek on the outskirts of Lublin and Sobibor, forty kilometers south of Brest Litovsk.

Chick was cleaning his fingernails with a stick. The old man wrinkled his nose as he sniffed the smell of the singed streets and houses. When he inhaled, it sounded like someone raking leaves. Occasionally he turned his head toward the high wall which divided them from the city outside. The old man's nostrils, thick with hair, distended.

"We lived a decent and beautiful life," the old man said. "Maybe it's our innocence that irritates those who hate us so much and makes them kill us and burn us and hang us. It was a wonderful life because we lived in peace with ourselves. But we were always in the minority."

"Where's the difference?"

"It cheered us and encouraged us that we knew how to live so we could survive. But the spirit of those who have already died has passed into the lives of those who aren't born yet. But this is the end of the road now, at least for us."

"You mean for both of us?" Chick teased him.

"Who knows whether somebody will ever find out what became of us? Who knows whether somebody will still be left to weep for us?"

God forbid I should look like him someday, Chick said to himself, observing the skin of the old man's neck and face and forehead. But, fortunately, this is not my biggest problem.

There were gray hairs on his chest. The backs of his hands and his neck were like a crocodile's skin. His shirt was open. His untrimmed hair, the hair of an old man, was thinning at the temples and lay limply across his scalp, like old twine. When he wasn't talking, his lips made the boy think of a broken safety pin. At the beginning the old man had prayed. His prayers were mild and angry both, modest and full of pathos, and sometimes, without his realizing it, they sounded funny and majestic just as he did when he was at his best. But now he hadn't prayed for twenty days.

II

"The fire's been burning for twenty-one days," the old man declared.

"I'm surprised you still bother to keep count."

"Since the day he was born."

"Hitler, you mean?"

"I don't want to say the name."

"You're going off your rocker," said Chick.

Chick had already seen plenty of old people burned alive. Instead of extinguishing the fire, the wind made it burn even brighter. Whenever anybody tried to put it out by dousing it with whatever water was still left, he went up in flames like kindling.

Women and children burned fastest. That was odd, because they were all nothing but skin and bones, men and old folks just as much as the women and children.

Chick spat. People are as different when they're dead as when they're alive. Except for the ways in which death doesn't differentiate. But some people are lucky when they're alive and some are lucky too in the way the fire catches up with them. Or a bullet. You could adjust to it, even when nobody wanted to. Sometimes when the patrols picked up somebody, they simply backed him against the flames and shot him so he'd burn on the spot, as soon as he fell.

He spat again. He only wanted the best for the old man. And the best was what was fastest. Or whatever was his own decision. He doesn't expect me to do it for him, does he?

"I've never seen the ocean," said Chick. He imagined water. It was pleasant and unreal, imagining.

The old man lifted his head, and Chick suddenly wondered how he was going to die.

"I'd never have thought that someone who teaches people how to sing would have had the chance to see so much of the world," added Chick, getting off the subject of water. He didn't want to annoy the old man anymore, although he used to enjoy teasing and annoying him.

The old man's lips tightened, then they parted as if he wanted to say something. From his expression you could never tell whether he was smiling or just the opposite.

"I taught others and that's how I taught myself," he said.

His mouth looks like a flytrap, Chick thought. But all he can catch are ashes.

"Your mother was a beautiful woman," the old man stated suddenly.

Chicked raised his head. They were back where the old man wanted to be—with the Levy-Cohen clan. The old man kept going back to something which had perhaps been the beginning of it all, as if it were evaporating in front of his eyes.

"She had eyes like pearls. And she walked like a dancer. When your mother was nineteen years old and went to a party, the boys got dizzy."

"She had short legs and was gray all over. Even her skin turned gray. She said you'd beaten her when she was a little girl. Maybe she was pretty like you say when she was young."

"I remember your father on his wedding day—he was the happiest man that walked the earth."

"I wish I had your worries," said Chick.

"He was the happiest man that ever walked this earth the day he got married and that morning when you were born.

156

Wherever you looked there were vases of roses. It was in the spring."

Chick realized the old man's memory was failing. For a long time he hadn't known when he was born and when certain things had happened. Sometimes he couldn't remember the days of the week and he'd have to start counting from the first day of the Uprising. Sometimes he had a hard time remembering his wife's name and his children's names. But there was a lot he did remember. He knew the names of all the days of the week since the fire started.

Again Chick wondered how the old man was going to die. Where did everything come from and where was it going? Chick wriggled uncomfortably, like somebody with an itch. He wondered what had made the old man think about his mother.

"What's wrong?"

"Fleas," Chick answered. "The last time I washed my shirt was the day before yesterday."

"Roses," said the old man. He scratched his shoulders. The hair on his temples was a yellowish white. Ashes lay among the hairs.

Chick was silent.

It was as if the old man were already saying goodbye. Or as if he could no longer believe that it had missed them again.

He thought about how the best of them, who at that very minute were being driven out of the bunkers by gas and fire, had perhaps already written themselves off in their own minds. It was over.

"We all wanted the same thing," the old man went on. "To have a good job and know that somebody and something would go on here after we'd gone."

"You're getting soft in head, that's all," said Chick. "If you're so anxious to leave something behind, why didn't you plant some trees? Trees always live longer than people do."

"Come over here and let me pat your head."

"Big thrill..." said Chick.

He was thinking how sometimes women carried grenades under their skirts and, when a patrol caught them, they'd blow everything up, including themselves. He didn't make any move towards the old man. He said it to the old man.

157

"I just want to hold your hand."

"I'm O.K. where I am. Want something?"

"Just to have you a little closer."

"We both stink to high heaven." Chick chuckled. He made a point of laughing a little bit too long and too loud before the moment slipped away.

"You're from a priestly clan. The Levy-Cohens. Your mother Sonya and I and my father Leo and my grandfather Ferdinand and great-grandfather Joseph. Far, far back."

Chick stopped scratching. From the window to the south, he looked across one bombsight to another, an almost levelled field of ruins which were still smoldering. In the distance an infantryman was spreading fire with a flamethrower. The old man couldn't see it. But he felt its hot gasp. It occurred to him that he hadn't heard the old man sing for a long time, although usually, not so long ago, the worse things got, the more he sang.

III

That afternoon, heat and ash fell in waves over the whole city. Firemen and special divisions of the Polish police, armed with manual and engine-driven firehoses, drove the fire and ashes back inside the wall. Nobody had ever seen anything like it.

Steam rolled out of the sewers like the smoke from the factories behind the ghetto. The thickest smoke rolled from those factories which had been directly hit.

After lunch it rained for a little while. The fire brigades outside the wall took a rest.

But it didn't rain enough to put out any fires, or even for them to quench their thirst. It was just a few drops, enough so you could hold out your hand and lick them off.

"Lots of people drown in the sewers," Chick said.

It was the rats he was thinking of. Rats grew fat on the freshly drowned bodies, although they didn't turn up their noses at those who had been drowned or strangled by the smoke some time ago. It's almost easier to defend yourself against people than against rats. But rats never meant any of things Chick had been thinking about earlier, and despite the revulsion he felt, the sewers represented both the world of rats and the world of people—people who allowed themselves (or were forced to) be herded into the sewers to join the rats or those who did the herding. They were acting on behalf of the rats. The rats were doing fine. For them, the more, the merrier. But he never told the old man about the rats and he was uncomfortable whenever the subject was brought up.

"Don't you ever pray anymore?" asked Chick.

"We're fighting back now," the old man said. "Self-defense is man's first and last responsibility. Defending yourself is more important than praying."

Some of the rats in the sewer must be as big as little rabbits by now, Chick thought. The fire never went into the sewers. On the outside, where the sewers opened, German patrols had set up booby traps so that, while the eye might glimpse the sky or the river or a field, the hand or foot would trip an automatic switch. These German inventions were reliable. But *their* inventions were almost as reliable.

Sometimes young people sent the older ones ahead to clear the way for them, and, other times, the oldest ones went voluntarily to face the booby traps.

Chick watched the fire. In its own peculiar way, it jumped from house to house, sometimes from one window to another or from one roof to the next. It skipped over certain streets or houses and kept coming back to others. For a while it disappeared entirely, then leaped up once more. One fire flared as another died down. Others merged into one and then split up into smaller blazes. Again he tried to imagine the burning forest.

He could never figure out why, except that it was because of the wind and whatever material was burning. Most of the houses caught fire and burned down during the night. Fires got worse then. Some of the fires only began to smolder as day was breaking.

"Is it true there's a lot of stealing going on?" the old man asked.

"Not everywhere. Usually it's only where everything's already burned down."

Chick noted a few isolated explosions. He knew that if the shells fell on them, it would be over quickly. Looters from the Polish side were interested in the gold teeth of the corpses and such things.

Only the best people can survive, Chick decided. And the luckiest and strongest rats.

"Must think they'll find gold here," the old man said. "Without gold, you can live. Without bread, it's worse."

"Mother sewed this velveteen patch on the knee of my pants," Chick mused. "Corduroy wears better than velveteen, though."

He looked out at the fire and wondered what to do about the old man. The walls of the room were sweating with the heat. The plaster cracked and flaked like the crust on freshly baked bread. But he didn't want to think of food right now. He licked his parched lips. To kill the old man meant destroying everything that made him suffer too, together with how much worse that suffering might be when Chick was gone. Under the circumstances, killing the old man was the kindest thing he could do for him. He cleaned his eyes and nose with the rag of his jacket.

Heaps of rubble were all there was left of some blocks. The devastated streets were full of echoes. He was quite aware that he mustn't leave the old man here at the mercy of the fire. And that he mustn't let him fall into the hands of the Germans. All he had to do was figure out what to do about it.

He thought of his mother and father. It was a good thing his parents weren't there anymore. If the hope that they were going from worse to better hadn't killed them, being *here* would have. Although getting killed here meant *not letting* yourself be killed. The old man was right. Hope can be a damned messy business, he thought to himself. There's nothing worse than false hopes. A person can let himself be lured into hell that way. Hopelessness is much better. Hopelessness puts a stone in your hand, at least, if not a dagger or a bomb. When someone has nothing left to hope for, then at least he is sure of it. If somebody doesn't like it, let him take a running jump! And I'd be the first one to jump, I guess. Because I don't like it.

IV

"Is there anything that could still save us?" asked the old man.

"It's hard to tell which one of us is dirtier. We stink. Just like the Germans say we do. I've almost got more dirt and fleas than skin."

"Rain would save and drown us too. I wouldn't mind a cloudburst and some floods."

"Can you eat that? Can you stick your hands inside and warm them when it's cold and rainy? Can you shoot it out of a gun?"

"Their burns don't hurt me," the old man continued.

"I'll put the keg outside to catch a bit of water in case it starts to rain after I leave." When the old man said nothing he went on. "Rain would foul up their plans for them."

He reached up and prodded at the ceiling with his stick, inspecting it. Then he absent-mindedly kicked the keg of dirty rain water they'd used for washing up until the second week after the fire started. The wooden sides were dry and shrunken and it smelled musty, which took away your thirst.

He looked up at the ceiling again, then at the old man. He saw it wouldn't be difficult to make it fall. Once and for all. He calculated the thickness of the ceiling. The old man wouldn't suffer long under a load like that. He knew right away it was a good idea. I'll make a neat job of it, he said to himself.

The old man was silent. Chick was concentrating on the ceiling. He looked for the reinforcements embedded in the plaster.

"Remember how sometimes I used to crawl in bed with Mother on Sunday mornings?" Chick asked suddenly.

"I remember in Prague how the women used to sing in the synagogue," the old man answered. "I can remember everything."

"When a person remembers something that's happened to him once, is it like living it over a second time?"

"As much as saying you exist twice when you look at yourself in a mirror," the old man told him.

161

"Or like when people remember something that's happened, it becomes eternal?"

"Only as long as you know *how* to remember," the old man said.

"That's what I wanted to know," Chick said.

"What's the matter with you?"

"Something's been biting me. Something bites me all the time, even though I've washed my shirt and pants. My shoes are full of mud. I feel sticky all over."

"Rome burned down when Nero was emperor. It was a big city, too. He went crazy and set fire to all the houses and then he watched the ashes fly. Herostratus burned down the Temple of Diana in Ephesus so nobody would ever forget his name. It never was our world. It was always theirs. We had nothing to do with it."

"Maybe we're small fry, too, in comparison with those who went before us. But I wish just once we could be in the shoes of the people who think up and organize such lovely spectacles. Not just always in the spectators' seats. I guess lots of people are going to remember this major general, too."

"Are the bites bad?"

"I probably have sweet blood."

Chick looked up at the ceiling. He could picture Rome, a strange city full of temples and water streaming off blazing roofs. Then he pictured a carafe of clear, cool water on a table full of all the food the old man had talked about before.

"Are you still here?" demanded the old man.

"Can't you hear me?"

"I hear you when you talk, but not when you don't."

"I've been thinking about old Blumentritt who used to live here before we moved in. Too many of those jumpers were in a hurry. You don't have to worry, though. I won't let that happen to you."

The old man stiffened in surprise.

"It's just as bad to let them kill you as it is to burn."

"The worst is that first second, before the flames swallow you up. You don't even know about the rest of it. Apparently it's like when an airplane crashes. I'm telling you," Chick reassured him, "you don't have to be scared."

162

"I wish I knew where you're going," the old man said suddenly. His cheeks dropped over toothless jaws. "Don't come back for me," he added.

Nervously, Chick spat.

"Mila Street's burnt down and Nizka's gone. It's as though the city's on a grill, the way they used to roast mutton. It's starving to death and dying of thirst. It won't last much longer. Not as long as it's taken already." The old man's voice came in a sizzling hiss, as though it were already on fire.

"Go down into the sewers," he said. "Don't come back for me. Go east or west. Leave me here. I've learned how to guess what's going on around me. If worse comes to worst, I'll jump."

"Forget it," said Chick wearily. But it occurred to him that in many ways he really was a lot like the old man. It was a silly idea, but it sustained him for a while. He couldn't keep on torturing himself with thoughts of water and food.

The roof above their heads held up what was left of the upper stories of the house and the roof.

"Babies aren't being born anymore, wells are poisoned, bakers' ovens have turned cold. Even the rainbow is on fire. It's disabled, just like me. Its eyes have been burned out, too. And it's deaf because its ears have been clogged with ashes." The old man coughed for a long time, as if the ashes were choking him.

"A sick horse couldn't have said it any better," Chick observed.

"The wind's turning against us," the old man said. "Only those who fight ought to eat."

"Eat *what*?"

"Things will never be what they used to be. Those were the best times—when we were all together. There's only one place where we'll still be together, but that'd be a shame for you. I won't mind one bit, staying here by myself for a couple of days."

The first thing he'd have to do was put the old man and his chair under the middle rafter which held up what was left of the roof. Then drag the water keg closer.

163

"After a while I'll go out and look around for something to eat and drink," Chick said.

If he climbed up and stamped his foot hard, the rafter and the whole floor would fall right on top of the old man. But then he'd fall, too. The rafter was enough.

"Before you go, I'd like to hear a few of those things that were in the first declaration," the old man said.

"The part about how we'll all go down in defeat, but the Nazis won't get a single drop of our blood for nothing? Or how it tells you to take a knife in your hands or an ax or a piece of metal?"

"Yes. *No more defenselessness! Barricade your homes! Be sly and deceitful, don't be afraid of using any trick! Let them try to take us! Let every mother turn into a lioness to defend her young! Away with panic and doubt! Away with the spirit of slavery! Whoever fights for his life can save it!"*

He remembered a lot of it, but he didn't remember it absolutely accurately; and maybe he didn't remember all of it. He had that instead of prayers.

If the old man's lucky, the rafter and the floor will fall at the same time, Chick thought to himself.

"Yes," said the old man. "And then the part where they say we've been like sheep, but it was no sin to be that way, and now it's more of an art to stay alive, when people are trying to take your life away from you—or that way!"

"Or how, if we're supposed to perish, then let's do it with firm and avenging hands on the triggers of our guns and the handles of our daggers—so they will not tremble even with our last thoughts."

Chick drew in a deep breath.

"And now we must destroy the enemy by attacking him at the gates, out of the ruins, from the underground labyrinths, from the gutted buildings, making him pay with a sea of blood," said the old man.

Chick knew exactly what the old man wanted to hear. Some things are hard to remember, other things even harder to forget.

"As we move down the road to our death, we must be like blazing torches, destroying as many of our enemies as we can

164

on the way, serving as a signal that rivers of our blood will mingle and stain the rivers of their blood."

He'd read it all to the old man dozens of times during the last twenty-one days. And Germans only lied.

"I hear a siren," the old man said.

"I'll make it as easy as I can for you," said Chick. "I'll drag your chair into the middle of the room. You'll have that big rafter right above your head. It looks like a jagged splinter. It still holds but if somebody pulled at it—even a little bit—it would fall. Then the whole roof will probably cave in."

"I get the idea," the old man said after a while. "Now?"

"Now I'll just move you a little bit, because I've got to go out," Chick repeated. "You decide for yourself about the rest of it. But only after I've gone."

Chick leaned against the chair. The old man was hunched over, propped on the scorched arm of the old chair. Its crimson upholstery was ripped. It must have been a handsome Italian chair once.

"I get the idea," the old man repeated after he'd moved into the middle of the room.

"I don't quite get it myself," Chick said.

"You'll be blessed, child."

"Who's going to bless me? You've already cursed everything and everybody."

A cloud of dust and ashes floated down around the chair.

"If you don't want to, just sit right here and nothing will happen to you," Chick said.

"Fine," the old man agreed, "You're leaving now?"

Then he felt the friction of skin against skin. Chick always did that when he went out. It was as if the grandson were brushing dust or mud off his face or his breast.

"I'll give it a try," the old man said.

"Be careful, though. As long as you're sitting down nothing can happen."

"Don't come back again," the old man told him as he eased himself back into the armchair.

The old man had big ears, like floppy, wrinkled telephone receivers.

Then Chick left without a word.

165

V

Suddenly the old man felt alone. Like a rickety ship deserted on the open sea, encircled by darkness and waves and swirling water he couldn't see.

An idea had been going around in the old man's head during the past few days about people long extinct, people he'd only read about, like the light of dead stars, of all the people whose glory had grown as great as the shadow they cast when they faced the sun, who thought they were greater than the sun itself. And they had perished, despite their glory, because they hadn't understood the message that had been born one day.

He and his people would perish, too, because they had understood.

Among the strange sounds which came from far and near, a voice that had seemed remote when he was alone drew closer.

He could feel bits of ashes settling on his skin. He sniffed to get the ashes out of his nose.

He thought of how he had lived through the twenty-one days of the fire, ever since the day, on the birthday of the one who was master of the life of every Jew, a band of forty thousand plucked up the courage to fight back after three times a hundred thousand of his Jewish brethren had been slaughtered.

He wondered what it would be like when everyone was dead. Was it all a mistake somebody had committed ages ago, or was it part of a single destiny which began somewhere and would end, as everything human must end? Would all this be forgotten like all failures punished by defeat?

How far would it reach? How long would the children of today's children remember this? Will there ever be children in the world anymore?

He kept very quiet so the patrol wouldn't know he was there. Before nightfall he heard isolated screams and shouting. But he couldn't tell whether they were battle cries or calls of the dying. He could imagine men and women, their bodies on fire, running like burning torches toward the German soldiers to stab them with their knives or pieces of sharp metal, unless they were stopped first by German bayonets or bullets or flamethrowers.

He tried to figure out what it was that had breathed strength into the weak and revealed the weakness of the strong. He wished he knew where his grandson Joseph was, the boy known as Chick Levy-Cohen.

His throat tightened at the feeling of brotherhood there would be once this war was over—if anybody survived. He wished he could reach out and touch all the tailors and slave laborers from the munitions dumps and war plants, the brush-makers and tinkers, bakers and streetpavers, all those who had banded together to tell the rest of the world, *Look how we died when we found out who was against us!*

He knew at that moment what it was he used to depend on, the way he was depending on the rafter now. It had once been the best of what he felt. And it had retreated before the dependability of the rafter.

He thought about the device his grandson had rigged up for him. His eyes stared opaquely into space. He could not see things that were to be seen, but he saw other things which were invisible. He could hear the walls of houses as they cracked, buckled, and crumbled. It happened slowly and you could hear it happening. Some of the houses survived when a shell struck them, even though their inhabitants didn't. But a few hours later, the house suddenly collapsed, although nothing had touched it since. It was as if it wanted to bury its dead under its rubble twice, a hundred times, on into infinity.

A shell whistled, fell, and exploded some five houses down the street. He breathed in the sudden, hot smell of explosives, the brain and body of the bombs, the dust from broken stones and wood and wool. He clutched at the arms of the chair and groped along the floor with the soles of his shoes to get his bearings in case he decided to stand up.

He knew that if he took a careless step he might fall into the very depths of the house. Come and go, fall deep or wait for a touch overhead. Among all the different sounds, he could distinguish between the ones that were important and those which weren't. The second shell didn't come. He felt a bond between all the living and dead and with those twenty-one days he had survived.

VI

"I see the rafter's shifted just a little," Chick said when he returned. "Things have been pretty lively here, I see."

"You shouldn't have come back."

"A shell, was it?"

"One, about a block away," the old man answered.

"We're still lucky."

"Aren't you tired?"

"Not really."

"You've got a good nature," said the old man. "You were born with it."

Chick dragged the old man and his armchair back to the wall again. There were new burns on his face and hands, along with the old ones.

It was almost dark. The only light that came in was from the fires, and this light had its own peculiar strength and weakness. The sky was clear again, as it had been for several days. Maybe the world on the other side of those walls is lovely now, Chick thought. Maybe the fog doesn't cover everything. Maybe it's been melted by the fire.

The reflections of the fire lit up the sky as if there were a carnival going on somewhere, far away and very near. Somewhere they could never go, though.

Maybe the soldiers are celebrating something, he thought.

From under his shirt, Chick pulled a small loaf of Polish bread. The old man fingered it.

"Bread," he said.

"Without water."

"Where've you been?"

"Go ahead and eat."

"Can't you tell me where you've been?"

You could hear the old man's jaws crack as he bit off the bread and mashed it between his gums. He looked terrifying, covered with soot and ashes, starving and wild with thirst, weak, but still strong enough to eat. Chick started to eat, too. He kicked the side of the barrel, and he rubbed his singed left eyelid. He had no eyebrows or eyelashes anymore. Mother would probably have been glad if she could have seen the two of us here together eating bread, he thought.

"Are you going to sleep now?" the old man asked him.

The Junkers flew over in the middle of the night. They dropped two loads of bombs on the burning desert of rock and debris. The night turned bright with new fires, old ones swelled, and those which had been smoldering revived. The old man couldn't see it. His extinguished eyes were fixed on the place where Chick lay, next to the wall. He couldn't sleep.

The boy didn't even wake up during the raid.

The old man listened to the night noises after the planes departed. He turned his face to the wind that was blowing through the window. He couldn't see the bright lights of the airplanes that didn't have to worry about anti-aircraft fire here. He didn't even see the radar lights blinking on the Junker's underbellies and wings and rudders. Like red-eyed fish.

The old man listened to the silence and to his grandson's breathing.

Chick woke up at daybreak, tired after his night's sleep.

"You should have waked me up a long time ago." He rubbed his eyes.

During the last few days, he'd been having awful dreams. But some lovely ones, too. Sometimes he dreamed about great, strong, beautiful ships which would take him far away from here. One of the ships was called the *Majestic*. It was as if those ships were living beings. They talked to him about their voyages and ports of call and about the stars, just the way he talked to them. Sometimes they talked about lands where there was no war going on. He imagined a country like that and how people lived there, even when he was awake. But it wasn't painful for him. He knew the old man's memories were painful and he wanted to avoid that for himself. But as long as he was awake, those dreams seemed sillier and sillier. Those were strange night-secrets, that the dreams which seemed beautiful in the dark still felt that way at daybreak. Or else he dreamed he heard a lovely song. The song was he, the old man himself, and all the people he'd ever known and who were no more. He also dreamed of victory, the day when each one of them would take on a thousand Germans—not like it was in reality. Just the opposite.

169

"You were tossing around and yelling something about getting another bottle. Were you thirsty?" the old man asked. "What are you going to do now?"

Chick was smearing red paint over his eyelids and forehead, throat, and chest. He wound an old hiking sock around his head. He looked as though he'd been wounded.

"Towards morning you were mumbling something about tigers and bottles," the old man told him. "Ah, my little boy."

"Don't call me boy. It makes me feel like a sissy."

Chick touched the sock-bandage to make sure it held fast. "You haven't slept for twenty-two nights. Where does that get you? You going soft in the head or what?"

The boy's skin was thin, almost translucent. The paint protected him against the wind, but it didn't let his skin breathe, either. Coats of old paint were covered by a coat of new.

"What good is it to anybody when you don't sleep, I'd like to know? You're not helping me. Or yourself, either."

"You looked like a little baby girl when you were born."

"A Levy-Cohen. Don't start in on that again!"

"Will you move me over into the middle of the room again?"

"Sure."

"I know where you go when you go out. How many of them have you taken care of by now?"

Surprised, Chick looked quickly into the old man's blank eyes.

"Two," he said.

"They'll raise monuments to you for every one of them you get."

"Aw, skip it."

"Are those the bottles full of kerosene, like the ones Fink, the shoemaker, was talking about?"

"Why do you ask when you already know?"

"I know as well as you do that before they could begin, they had to get rid of whoever was old and corrupt. Even a blind man finally sees everything, if he lives long enough, as the saying goes. How do you do it?"

"I lie on the sidewalk like a corpse, my head limp, my eyes blank. When a tank comes along, I wait until it passes; then I

170

jump up, lift the cover of the turret, set a match to the bottle, and throw it in. A Molotov cocktail. The hydraulics are in the turret.''

''Hydraulics,'' the old man murmured. Like he was talking about a dream or a lovely song which can never be forgotten.

Chick wiped his nose on his sleeve. Then he pulled the old man and the armchair into the middle of the room.

''Is it true that somebody who believes but behaves like a beast goes to hell, and somebody who *doesn't* believe but behaves decently goes to heaven?'' asked Chick.

''I know what's *not* true,'' the old man replied. ''I know what hasn't even been written down yet.''

''Don't panic,'' Chick said once more.

''I'll wait,'' the old man said. ''I'll stay here as long as I can. I'll stay right here until I die. Even if everything gets covered with ashes and all the buildings and streets disappear, I'll stay here along with everything that disappears.''

VII

On his way to the sewers Chick tried to imagine how the German commander must look. He recalled the old resentment he used to feel toward the old man. It wasn't hate anymore, although it wasn't love yet. Who knows what it was? He'd been right when he said that with time, everything changes—the big things get smaller and the smaller things disappear entirely. It doesn't take long to get used to new things and to forget how it used to be. Although you probably never forget entirely.

He went down into the sewer between Svatojirska and Bonifraterska Streets, which were Aryan. He was looking for bottles. He figured that overhead, Saska Gardens or Krashinsky Park were smoldering. There were still signs in the sewers indicating street intersections. He was scared of rats, large or small, skinny or fat. They were gray and fleet and looked like cats sometimes. The worst was when one of them ran across his hand or foot or even brushed against his face when the tunnel narrowed and he had to crawl on his belly.

Two hours later, he was glad when an old man, who was guarding one of the exits, showed him how to get out.

Killing is a kind of pleasure, too. When you kill, you don't allow somebody else to get the jump on you by killing you first. He never thought he could kill somebody as casually as tying his shoes. For Chick, killing had begun to mean what light meant. They'd learned within the last three weeks.

He felt the granite cobblestones under his feet. He began to tense up as he always did before he was getting ready to go into action.

The first tank appeared from the ruins of Karmelitska Street, coming from Novolipka. It was rolling past the old Toebens and Schultz factories. I'm not going to run away from you, and I hope you're not going to run away from me either, Chick thought to himself.

He could hear the difference between the noise the motor made and the rumble of the treads. It loomed in front of him so suddenly that it took his breath away, choking him with the dust it raised.

He saw the tongue of flame as it leaped out from the other side of the tank, licking up the sidewalk and the street and the houses as high as the third floor.

Even before the air began to shudder, he could hear the hiss and sizzle and see the shimmering orange glare.

A blue violet flame ruffled into orange and the fire shot out at him before he knew what was happening. First it touched him with its molten fingers, then it blinded him, taking his breath and voice away and stopping his heart. It was only afterwards that the flames caught and consumed him. All there was on the sidewalk was the smear of soot and ashes left from his body.

VIII

The old man called Emil Cohen—a member of the Levy-Cohen clan on his mother's and his father's side—waited. By now, we've lost our ambition to prove something to ourselves. We have nothing to prove anymore. Nobody knows we exist. Nobody knows anything. And nobody asks anybody how it all could have happened.

The sun turned pale. He couldn't see, but he could feel it sinking into a gray and crimson trench of mist, torn by the wind and veiled by soot and ashes. For a few seconds, he thought he knew the very moment when the sun went out. He was cold. But at the same time, he felt like singing, as if the thing he had captured inside him were more than just a sudden throb. It was like a mother giving birth to a child, like when that miraculous, lovely spark strikes between a man and a woman. His lips quivered as if he were praying. But he wasn't. "They're dying and burning," he whispered. "They're dying and burning. There's no more water, no more food. Only fires. Ashes. We have no ammunition. No guns. How long does it take to die of thirst?" He wanted to call out to someone, "Come, before we all perish and burn. Come, before it's too late for the very last of us and for you too! Do you hear me? Can anybody hear me?" But he knew, of course, that no one could hear him. "In a few hours, maybe, we'll be dead. We'll all be burned and dead."

Everybody who forgives, perishes, he thought. Only those who don't, survive.

But he no longer asked himself which was more important, forgiving or hope, and which to choose. We're dying, just like we've always died, only with small interludes of peace and quiet. Why are things that way? Dying, dying, dying, and yet that long echo of past life. What price must a person pay just to survive?

But he knew he'd never get an answer. Nobody ever had. There were just those moments of tranquility, those happy interludes between one catastrophe and the next, when people didn't have to look into themselves so profoundly and ask questions to which there had never been any answers and perhaps never would be.

Yet at the same time, he knew that such an answer does exist inside every person, even if it dies with him, and that, in a way, it never dies.

The old man inhaled deeply and smelled the acrid streets and houses. He could feel the fire on his leathery old hide and in his nostrils as clearly as if he were seeing it with his own eyes. The song he whispered had no words. It was just a voice. It rang with the fate he shared with so many others. He

173

didn't worry any longer about attracting the attention of the German patrols. In his whispering there were the voices of all the people who had lost families, possessions, and finally life. And there were also the fears for all who wondered what would be, what would happen to them where the transports went, where they would go, how the war would end, and what would happen to the world.

Would the world go on turning from the sun toward the sea and from the sea toward night, from night toward mountains, and from the mountains toward people, regardless of how many people died? He didn't know how many there were. Just that there were a lot. And that there were going to be more. A lot more.

The old man couldn't weep because he had no eyes. He knew his grandson Joseph would not come back this time—the last of the Levy-Cohen clan, the kid called Chick. He could feel that to live and to die meant an eternity made up of people who were and the people who are yet to be, that eternity which is only *now* joining life with everything beyond life. He knew now what it was. The dead are the best in what they give to the world at this moment. Because nothing is worth more than life. It's all over. This is the end. For us, it's all over now.

His song made no sound and his voice was like the wind blowing one dying flame into two, then four, and so on, kindling infinite fires. At the same time, it sounded like water being poured over the fires, putting them out. Like a breath before it becomes a voice. The old man forgot he was over eighty. For a few seconds, he had the impression that the whole world was rocking under his feet. But he could see that nothing had changed. Nothing had happened that hadn't happened before.

He could feel the strongest desire of all—the yearning to survive—seeping out of him. It had once been strong enough to get them this far. He was trying to alter in his mind the greatest thing he believed in, as if he'd come to a point beyond which it was easy to understand in what conditions the opposite of life is more than life itself.

Then he thought he felt the first tongues of flame licking at the wall on the side where a window used to be. It was like stepping into a swiftly flowing stream. His coat began to burn. He could still imagine where Zamenhof Street was located, and Nizka Avenue.

Then he lifted his arms and took a step forward. And he touched the rafter above his head, gripping it firmly with both hands.

Black Lion

A tattered red flag hung over the doorway of the house on the corner. The right wing of the old town hall had been hit by tank shells about four o'clock the afternoon before. Smoke was still rolling from its tower.

The German-owned watch shop in the building on the corner of Parizska Boulevard had been looted.

The boy called Black Lion only needed to glance at the bullet-pocked plaster of the house and at the shop to know where they'd *been*. When his eyes slid down the shattered face of the building and fixed on the two men from the Revolutionary Guard, he knew where they still *were*. He hitched up his pants.

"Come on!" he nodded to the two boys who were with him and looked back to make sure they were coming.

"What's in there?" asked the first.

They ducked inside behind Black Lion, the boy with the shaggy mane. It was chilly in the hallway. The walls were paneled shoulder high with shiny brown marble and white cherubs.

The shorter of the two guards looked around. "Get out of here!" he told them sharply.

"These two kids just came back from a concentration camp," explained the shaggy one. "They'd like to see a little action too."

"Go on, scram," the man with the Revolutionary Guard armband repeated. "This isn't a theater performance. It's not for little kids."

He looked back. His taller companion didn't even notice as

they all rushed up the stairs together.

"Aw, let's forget it," said the smaller of the two youngsters, the one called Tiny.

"Are you sure it's going to be worth it?" asked the second, the one called Curly (although his head was shaved).

"This'll be a sight to see," said Black Lion. "I wouldn't miss it for the world. It may turn out to be a real spectacle."

When he got to the landing between the second and third floors, the shorter man, whose RG armband had slipped to his wrist, looked back and saw Black Lion dashing up the stairs.

"Get out of here!" he bellowed. "How many times do you have to be told?"

"We'll keep an eye on things for you here on the stairs," Black Lion volunteered. Tiny and Curly slowed down, hesitating.

The two men from the Revolutionary Guard stopped in front of a double door painted gray green and covered with stickers. Two curved serpents with flashing green tongues coiled on each side of the door.

The name plate had been removed from under the doorbell. The tall RG pressed the button. He pushed it twice, then twice more quickly.

Cautiously, Black Lion moved up to the next floor.

"What're you still hanging around here for?" growled the smaller of the two men. "Get out of here or else." He ran his hand over his pistol. Both men were carrying revolvers with wide German Army straps made of pale cowhide.

"These two boys are from a concentration camp," Black Lion repeated. "They'd like to see a little action too. That's only fair."

The tall one eyed him sharply. The bushy-haired boy's eyes were sunken and his face was gaunt.

Both armed men had equipment seized from Afrika Korps stocks during the first few days of the Uprising. The shorter of the two spat into a corner, next to the door that led to the attic.

"What're we going to do here, anyway?" whispered Tiny.

"Maybe you'll get a chance to give them a kick in the ass," Black Lion told him.

He spoke softly. They looked up at the door of the apartment. Some of Black Lion's tension had rubbed off on them. The building had a familiar, musty smell, the kind old buildings have.

"Maybe we can squeeze some food out of them," suggested Curly.

The smaller guard overheard. "Are you hungry?"

"I told you where they came from," said Black Lion. "They've been staying in our house. They escaped on the way from Buchenwald to Dachau. My dad's hidden them in the laundry of our building for four weeks. They've been on the run for over two months."

Curly grinned at the smaller guard. "We're not exactly hungry," he explained. "You might say we've got an appetite."

"Justice comes first," Black Lion said.

The tall one kicked the door. "All right, come on, how about it?" he yelled. It echoed through the building. "Are you going to open up?"

Black Lion tensed. He peered at the door, waiting to see what he expected to see, what he wanted to show the other two boys. He wished he could get through that gray green wood. He drew a deep breath.

The door made a hollow sound when it was kicked. Tiny looked down to see how deep the elevator shaft was.

Standing behind the Revolutionary Guards, Curly noticed how well-dressed and well-equipped they were.

"Justice," murmured Black Lion. "We're in luck."

"Come on!" echoed the shorter RG. He looked around at the two boys who were watching curiously and at the shaggy-maned youngster who was mumbling something about justice.

"They ought to have opened the door by now, that's for sure," Tiny observed.

Then he turned to the shaggy one. "When somebody hammered on the door like that at the camp barracks and if we were at the other end, they usually didn't give us this much time," he explained. "We really had to move."

"Kick the ventilator, why don't you?" Curly suggested.

The tall one turned around. "Keep your good advice to yourselves! We'll handle this."

"I'll look after things," Black Lion spoke up promptly.

"Leave it to me." He went over to the door and kicked it without a word, then put his shoulder against it to see how strong it was. The hinges split. Something cracked inside the lock. Black Lion felt pain shoot through his toes and shoulder.

The tall one moved his right hand away from the door. In his left, he held a German Army pistol. Just then, the door opened.

A woman in an apron stood in the doorway. She looked frightened. She was pale with big dark rings under her eyes as if she hadn't slept or eaten or had any fresh air for at least a week. She was trembling.

"What is it you want?" she asked in broken Czech.

"Grellova?" the tall one demanded curtly.

The woman nodded. The tall man pushed her aside, holding his pistol. The two men with the RG armbands stepped inside. The tall one gestured to the woman with the muzzle of his gun.

They both looked to see if there was anybody behind the woman, and it was almost as if they were trying to shield her. The short one tried to close the door. Black Lion quickly stuck in his foot. The shorter guard didn't do anything. He wanted to see what the tall one was doing.

Black Lion wheeled around. "Quit dragging your feet!" he snapped at Tiny. "Come on! Quick!" The hall of the apartment was dark and stuffy and full of junk—rolled-up carpets, a stepladder, sandbags.

"Where's your husband?" the tall one asked the woman.

"In bed," she answered.

"What's the matter with him?" the short one asked.

"He's had an attack—bad heart," replied the woman.

Tiny lingered in the doorway so he wouldn't have far to go in case he needed to make a quick getaway. Black Lion propped the door open with a coal scuttle. Curly tried to see through the glass-paned door that led into the kitchen from the hall. It was frosted glass. The tall one stepped forward and elbowed his way through the door into the next room.

A gaunt man in striped pyjamas lay there in bed.

The shorter Revolutionary Guard shoved the woman ahead of him.

180

"Why did it take you so long to open the door?" barked the tall one.

The short one nudged his gun into the woman's back. "Well?"

"I wasn't sure whether..." she answered.

"Were you expecting someone else?"

"No."

"I suppose you don't like it when people come around without letting you know," the tall one said.

Paintings had been removed from the walls. All that was left were faded spots. There was only one, a Madonna, hanging on one of the side walls. It was a spacious room with old German furniture and two windows overlooking the street.

Black Lion sensed something he couldn't put into words, something that was part of what he meant by justice. He was quite sure that what was going to happen next would be the kind of a scene he'd dreamed about. He had no doubt that until yesterday this German woman named Grellova, who was practically wetting her pants in fear now, had been yelling, "Heil, Hitler!" and saluting until her arm ached. He didn't feel sorry for her because her face was so white, as white as if someone had slapped her. Or for the hunched way she was standing. He wasn't sorry for her at all.

The tall one yanked off the quilt. With his pistol, the shorter one motioned the woman toward the bed. The man who lay in bed was unarmed. The tall man lowered his left hand.

Black Lion turned to the two boys. "Nazis," he said. "They'll get what's coming to them now. They're scared shitless. But up until yesterday, they were still shooting at *us*. Up until then, they were ready to gouge out both my eyes. Just yesterday, they'd have gladly tied you like a calf to the turret of a tank and lugged you through the streets until you were full of bullet holes. Sometimes, when they caught one of the rebels, they cut off their..."

"Hmm," mused Tiny.

"They're scared shitless now," Curly agreed.

Tiny figured that, for a German, the woman's voice should have sounded steadier and that the fellow in the bed shouldn't have been trembling so much. He couldn't compare them to the other Germans he'd known. But it occurred to him that the man's pyjamas were striped, like prisoners' uniforms. His were probably made out of better material, though.

The shorter guard felt the quilt. "It's cold, you bastard!" he yelled. "Get up!"

The man scrambled out of bed. He had sharp gray eyes and stubbly chin and cheeks. He hadn't shaved for at least three days. He stood next to the woman. They looked like prisoners of war, which was probably what they wanted to look like. The man was barefoot and he kept shifting from one foot to the other. But he didn't move, and even though his bedroom slippers were within reach, he didn't attempt to put them on.

"Have you got any guns?" demanded the tall one.

"Don't lie!" barked the shorter. "Or else..."

"We haven't got any," the woman said quickly. "We've never had any weapons here."

The man's chin trembled. He couldn't speak.

"What did you do with them?" asked the tall one.

"We never had any weapons," the woman insisted.

"We..." the man began.

There were two gas mask cases on the china cupboard. There were sandbags and fire axes in the corners of the room.

Black Lion watched the faces of the man and woman. She looked even more drained and tired than she had at first. It was a different kind of weariness than the kind that goes with sleeplessness. It was one of the many varieties of fear which they were tasting now—fear of force, fear of helplessness, fear of injustice, as well as of justice and of what they all had in common.

The woman stood beside the man, as if she longed to lean on him. The fellow looked ready to collapse. But he probably hadn't looked like that yesterday, or the day before. There had been shooting on Tuesday from this building, out onto the street. Into the square, too.

The windows were perfect for shooting in any direction.

"Let's see your identity cards," ordered the tall one.

Cautiously, the woman edged to the wardrobe. "We keep them in here," she said and took out her purse and their documents. Her face was the color of ash. Her fingers shook as she turned the key in the wardrobe lock.

182

The tall one pointed to the door with the frosted glass panes. "What's in there?" he said.

"The kitchen," the woman answered. Her words seemed to be sending signals, as if by saying, "kitchen" she meant "please."

"They're really scared," murmured Tiny.

"We know that feeling," Curly added, just as quietly.

"But it's different when *they're* the ones who're scared," Tiny added, and he sounded almost puzzled.

"This is a new one on me," Curly said. "Honest to God, I thought they really *were* stronger than you and me, I honestly did."

The tall one inspected their identity cards as if he were looking for something. He leafed through them from beginning to end and back again.

"Grellova?" he repeated.

"Yes," declared the woman.

"Heinrich Grell?" The man nodded.

"Grell, Heinrich."

The shorter RG kicked open the door into the kitchen. Out rolled the hot stench of scorched wool.

The tall one stuck the I.D. cards into his pocket.

"Something's burning in there," said Black Lion.

"Go take a look," said the tall guard.

"Go on!" urged the shorter.

Black Lion reached the kitchen range in three strides. With his shaggy hair and flattened nose, he did indeed look like a lion in profile.

Tiny and Curly followed. They weren't in such a hurry, though. When Black Lion opened the oven door, smoke poured out into the kitchen. He took a poker and raked out what was left of a German Army uniform. The tarnished silver buttons were still there, and warped epaulets.

"Take a look at this!" announced Black Lion.

Curly looked into a wooden bin. "Coal," he said.

"It's a uniform," Black Lion said.

"Let's see! SS?" demanded Curly.

"Green wool," Tiny observed knowingly. "He wasn't in the air corps, then. It doesn't look like Luftwaffe stuff."

"A big wheel," Curly noted.

"He probably was high-ranking," Black Lion agreed. "The rats!" he went on. "Rats! Rats!" Then he closed the door of the oven.

"Should I run water or something?" Tiny asked.

Black Lion kicked the oven door shut again as the short RG had done. He looked from one to the other. He knew this must be making a big impression on the two boys.

The oven door fell open again. The back of the grate was full of soot from the burned woolen trousers. Scraps of paper lay along the sides. Black Lion wondered what it was they'd been trying to burn. An hour later, they'd have cleaned out the stove and there'd have been nothing left.

"They miscalculated," he said out loud. "Put out what's left of the fire." He picked up the remnants of the uniform and carried it back into the living room on the poker.

"It doesn't say in your I.D. that you're an officer," the tall one remarked.

"I was in the reserves," the man replied.

"Are you or are you not an officer?"

"No... Yes, I was, but I'm retired now," the man stuttered. His eyes blinked rapidly.

"Put up your hands!"

The man raised his hands. The tall one inspected his arm below the elbow. He was looking for the distinguishing tattoo of the SS.

"He had to," said the woman.

"Shut up!" the short guard ordered.

"He had to," she whispered.

"I told you to shut up," the short one snapped. He turned to the man. "Were you a member of the National Socialist Party?"

"We had to be," replied the man, his chin quivering.

"Rank?"

"Colonel."

"What branch?"

"I was just an accountant."

"Let him lie down," the woman said.

"That bed was empty a minute ago," said the short one. Then he turned to the man. "Is this your wife?"

"Yes," answered the man.

184

"Any children?"

"No," the man replied.

"Is there anything you have to tell us?" queried the short one.

"What do you want to know?" the woman asked.

"You just figure out what might interest us."

"I don't know what would interest you," the woman murmured.

The man's chin kept trembling. His eyes shifted from the linoleum on the floor to the Revolutionary Guards, to the three boys, and back to the bed, but he never once looked at his wife.

"Why did you want to burn your uniform?" asked the tall one.

"The war's over," the woman said.

"I'm asking him!"

"The war's over and we lost," the man said finally. "It's over. We don't want to have anything to do with it anymore."

"Somebody was shooting from your windows," burst out the tall guard.

"Not from ours," the man said slowly.

"From this very window, and from that one over there." The tall one pointed.

The shorter RG kept eyeing the windows, then the smoldering wool of the uniform, then glancing back at the man and woman. As if he were looking for something and he didn't know what.

"Who was shooting from here?" the tall one demanded once again.

"It wasn't us," the man retorted promptly.

"He's a sick man," the woman said.

"You can trust us," the man declared.

"He's got a heart condition."

"I've been sick for years," he said.

"We're human beings just like everybody else," pleaded the woman.

"We're innocent," said the man.

"God knows what you're trying to blame us for," the woman went on.

"Sure, we were probably the ones who were doing the shooting from your windows! At our own people," said the tall one.

"It wasn't us," the man with the quivering chin insisted. His pyjamas were too big for him.

"Do you have a medical certificate?" asked the short one.

"No. We burned it," said the man.

The woman kept staring at the picture of the Madonna in its old cracked frame, as if it were a mirror.

That was the first time the man glanced at the woman, and then he noticed what she was looking at.

"So who was it, then, that was doing the shooting?" the tall one demanded, as if he already knew the answer. Or as if he wanted to make sure of something else. "I only ask a question once," he went on. "I don't have to remind you that what you don't tell us, we'll easily find out for ourselves."

"We're not the ones you're looking for," the woman said.

"Who, then?" the short one bellowed suddenly.

"The general's bodyguards," whispered the man in pyjamas.

"Are you one of them?" asked the tall one.

The short RG looked up sharply.

"No," the man answered immediately. "They've already gone. They left yesterday. They came here without asking. They just took over our apartment on orders from above. They didn't even ask us. We couldn't have refused. It was still dark when they went away."

"Who do you think you are?" the tall one demanded. "Who do you think you are?"

"Well?" yelled the short one. "Don't you hear what we asked you?"

"We had nothing to do with them," said the man in pyjamas.

"Otherwise we wouldn't have stayed on here," the woman added.

"Why did you burn your medical certificate?" the small one demanded.

"We wanted to start a new life," the woman said.

"We had nothing to do with them and we were glad when they left," the man insisted.

"That's the truth, we didn't have anything to do with them," the woman said.

"Like with that cold bed, hm, you bastard!"

"We've got some money we put aside for our trip," the woman said.

"A little extra, more than we need..." The man did not finish his sentence.

"What do you mean by that?" asked the shorter Revolutionary Guard.

"A few family jewels," said the man.

"Don't even talk to them," the tall guard told the shorter.

"How many wedding rings do you have? How many gold molars?"

"We haven't got any wedding rings," the man said.

"It's just our personal jewelry," the women went on.

"Don't talk about it with them," the tall one told the other.

"It's our own jewelry, a little bit of gold," the woman repeated.

"Gold from somebody's molars," the short RG persisted.

"Skip it," the tall one told him.

"Things like that don't mean anything to us anymore," the man continued.

"Why did they come to your place in particular? Why did they leave you here?" the tall one asked the man.

He shrugged his shoulders. "I don't know."

"How should we know?" the woman asked softly.

"When did they come?" asked the taller guard.

"I don't remember exactly," replied the man.

"So much has happened during the last forty-eight hours," the woman said.

Black Lion was surprised by the flat, curt tone of the conversation. So this is justice, he said to himself. *Justice*, walking into an apartment where somebody's tracks are being covered up, papers and a uniform burned, a place from whose windows somebody had been shooting. In whose rooms a German general's bodyguards had spent the night.

There were mattresses on the floor behind the drawn window drapes. Like all the other German-occupied apartments, this one had been used until yesterday as a gun emplacement. The muzzles of machine guns and bazookas had poked out between those mattresses and sandbags. They'd had plenty of everything, including rifles and pistols.

"Get over against the wall," snapped the tall one.

It was the wall where the picture hung, next to the window. The man and woman stood side by side, hugging the wall, facing each other.

"You might as well enjoy yourselves and take it out on them," Black Lion said to Tiny. "If you feel like taking it out on somebody. And help yourselves to whatever you think you've got coming to you."

Tiny just looked at him.

"I don't give a shit," he said. All he was thinking about was that they didn't need to stay until it was all over.

The uniform was still smoldering. They noticed that the floor was scarred from when the furniture had been shoved around.

"Face the window!" the tall one ordered.

The man broke into a sweat. Large drops stood out on his neck and forehead.

"You boys go out in the kitchen for a minute," said the smaller of the Revolutionary Guards.

Black Lion went first.

"And close the door behind you!"

"Turn to the window!"

The woman was sweating too. She was as white as a sheet.

Black Lion was the last to leave the room. When, out of the corner of his eye, he saw the man and woman facing the window, he suddenly realized what was going to happen. The three of them stepped over the scraps of uniform. Black Lion left the kitchen door slightly ajar. Cold sweat broke out on his forehead, like on the man's and woman's. He felt a buzzing in his head. Justice. *Justice.* Like climbing a hill. Justice, he said to himself. *Justice.*

So these are Nazis. They'd been members of the Party. And even if they said they *had* to be, they were probably glad they'd *had* to be. Now that would serve them as a shield. And just yesterday, and the day before, they'd been shooting at the insurgents on Parizska Boulevard from both windows. Who knows whom they'd shot before? Nobody *has* to do anything unless he's willing to take the responsibility for it—today, yesterday, and tomorrow. Otherwise, he's not a human being, but a rag and he shouldn't expect to be treated with kid gloves.

He wondered how far it was from the windowsill down to the sidewalk. In his mind's eye, a picture composed itself of cobblestones dug out of the street, of burned fragments and treads from a Nazi tank. All that was left of it was a pile of scrap iron and, beside it, the stains which are all that's left of people. Until the rain washes them away. There had been people who were hit and who then bled to death before anybody could help them, simply because they were in the firing line of these windows. Although it was the last day of the war. Maybe the last hour.

The kitchen window opened on the courtyard. It was the same distance from the ground as the other windows in front. The pavement was all that was different.

"Tiny," he whispered.

"What?"

"Curly?"

"Yeah?"

"They're going to put them on trial in there. And all that goes with it."

"They'll probably go on lying for a while and try to wiggle out of it," said Tiny. "If I were in their shoes, I'd squirm like a worm."

"I hope you two got the message," concluded Black Lion.

"You're white as a sheet," said Curly. "Is there something wrong with you?"

"No."

"Now you're red in the face all of a sudden," Curly went on, peering closely at Black Lion. "What's the matter?"

"Nothing," said the shaggy one. He watched as the two boys rummaged around in the kitchen.

Just thinking about it made him feel feverish. *Justice.* That was what was happening in there.

"Justice," Black Lion muttered again, staring at the boys as if he were trying to remind himself of why they were there.

"Hey, look, we found some food!" said Tiny.

"A jar of apricots," Curly announced. "It hasn't even

189

been opened yet. You want some?"

Black Lion felt a kind of surprise bordering on disappointment. There you go, he thought to himself, gorging yourselves now of all times. But along with disappointment, he also felt a shade of admiration because of the way they'd simply shrugged their shoulders in the laundry room when his father had asked them about where they'd come from, where they'd been, and how they'd got here.

He turned toward the door which was half-open. He could see what was going on in the other room. The two men with the armbands were standing side by side now, feet apart, blocking the doorway in case the man and woman decided to try to make a dash for the stairs. Both their pistols were aimed at the hearts of the man and the woman.

But the man and woman didn't move. They faced the window, their backs to the Revolutionary Guards.

"What do you see when you look down out the window?" asked the taller.

When they did not reply, the smaller yelled, "Well, what d'you see? What do you see down there? Don't act like you're blind!"

"Nothing," the man in pyjamas answered humbly. "Houses," he offered. "The street. People. People. Otherwise nothing in particular. It's all over now. For you, this is peacetime already."

"What do you see down there on the sidewalk?" pressed the taller guard.

"Just let us say our prayers," the woman whispered.

"Speak up—what do you see from the window when you look down at the sidewalk?" the taller one went on, as if everything depended on what they saw.

"What do you see there on the pavement?" He lowered his voice menacingly.

"Don't act like you're deaf, dumb, and blind!" shouted the smaller guard. "Don't act like it's peacetime for us and hell for you! Who's it hell for? Who? You think we're crazy, that it's something that can be forgotten? Forgive and forget? Go ahead, talk—tell us what you see down there, or else."

He moved his gun closer to the woman's back, but he didn't touch her.

"Let us say our prayers," she repeated.

"Do you think we can't prove it?" yelled the smaller guard.

"Wait," the tall one told him.

"We're people just the same as you are," the woman murmured softly. "We're just people."

"See that fellow with the bandaged head standing there by the lamppost? What did he do to you?" asked the taller guard. "Answer my question first, then you." He stepped closer and motioned at the man with his gun, then at the woman.

"What more do you want?" asked the man.

"Answer what I asked you!" Now the tall one began to shout too.

"What do we need their answer for?" whispered the smaller guard. "What for? What good does it do? What difference does it make to what's past?"

"Wait," the tall one repeated.

"I never saw that person before," the man in pyjamas said.

"We don't know anybody around here," the woman added.

"You shot at him!" the tall one said.

"Make them look at those bloodstains on the sidewalk," urged the smaller one. "Tell them that since we're being so patient, they ought to be good enough to at least look at those bloodstains on the sidewalk."

"We had nothing to do with it," said the man.

"We had nothing to do with it," the woman echoed.

"No, we didn't," the man went on.

"No," the woman added.

"I want you to look at those bloodstains," the small one insisted.

"So you don't see anything in particular when you look out the window?" said the tall one.

"Nothing that would have anything to do with me," the woman said.

"You call *that* nothing?" yelled the smaller.

"People," the woman went on.

"For how many days were you shooting up here?" demanded the tall one coldly.

"We didn't do any shooting at all, on my honor as an officer," the man said quietly. "I don't shoot civilians. We're not bandits."

"Does this rag belong to you?" asked the tall one, pointing to what was left of the uniform.

"Yes," the man admitted.

"Where's your pistol?"

"The general's bodyguards disarmed us," said the man.

"What've you been doing?" the tall one asked the woman.

"I was a nurse on the Eastern Front, then in the West. Afterwards I joined my husband who was stationed here." She leaned her hand against the wall and touched the picture of the Madonna, making it crooked.

"We're your prisoners and we expect you to hand us over to the authorities according to the laws which are valid in every civilized country."

"We aren't enough of an authority to suit you?" the smaller guard barked.

"Step over to the window," the tall one said. "One step, no more, no less."

"We didn't shoot at all," the woman insisted softly. "We never did any shooting."

"Did you keep your windows open all during the uprising?" the small one asked.

"Open the window wide," the tall one ordered the man in pyjamas.

"Open the window over on your side too," the small one told the woman.

"One step more," repeated the tall one. "All right." He paused. "Now move a little closer. Right to the window. So your legs are up against the frame. That's it."

"What is it you want?" the woman asked.

"What are you going to do to us?" the man asked.

Black Lion clutched Tiny's shoulder. He leaned against Curly.

"They're going to have to jump," he said. "Justice. In one minute they're going to have to jump."

"We want you to take a good look at what's down there," said the tall one.

"We want you to see it so close that you get spots in front

of your eyes," the shorter one added.

"They'll have to jump," Black Lion went on. "And they'll be squashed like bedbugs. This is justice."

His eyes were glued to their backs. He watched every move the man and woman made and heard every word the Revolutionary Guards said to them. The windows framed the four of them.

"I demand to be put on trial," said the man in pyjamas. "I request a regular court to which I can transmit all my information and all my property."

"Hand us over to your authorities," the woman pleaded.

"Tell them we'll hand them over the quickest way," the smaller Revolutionary Guard said to his companion.

"We'll hand you over all right," the tall one said. "Nobody will be handed over so swiftly and surely."

"We didn't do anything," the woman repeated. "We didn't do anything to anybody. You have no right to do something to us which we haven't deserved."

Then her lips parted as though she'd intended to say something else. But she didn't say it. Her lips contradicted what was in her eyes, which were still watchful and filled with fear.

"We found this uniform here—there was shooting from your window—you haven't answered a single one of our questions: how long you've been here and what went on while your general's bodyguards were here. You even refuse to look at those bloodstains. That blood didn't come from one single person. Just what you can see ought to give even the two of you an idea of what you've been handing out to everybody else so generously. You have one minute. I'll count to sixty."

"I'll count," offered the smaller one.

"Look down there," said the tall one.

The shorter Revolutionary Guard had begun to count and he was already at eight.

The man and woman said nothing.

"Lean out the window and look," the tall one said.

Then, when the smaller one had gotten to twenty, he said. "What color is the pavement?"

"Lean out a little farther," the tall one ordered.

"Oh, my God," the woman choked.

"No," muttered the man.

The back of his pyjamas were soaking wet. So was the back of the woman's dress.

"But we haven't done anything," she murmured. When her husband did not say a word, she went on: "But we didn't do any shooting."

There was sweat in her words, and tears too, but all dried up. No more mumbling, no more choked back screams in the woman's voice.

When she stopped talking, her husband's wheezy breathing became audible. His breath came in sharp jerks. As though he were praying. Or talking to himself, saying the same thing over and over. He no longer looked at his wife, although her eyes clung to him. Both of them stood there, frozen to the spot.

The two, the man and woman, kept staring down at the pavement, at the bloodstains to which the Revolutionary Guards had wanted to draw their attention.

The tall guard let the safety catch click on his pistol. The smaller one did the same.

Black Lion was sweating like the man and woman by the window. From the street came the sounds of people and cars and bells ringing in the distance, fragments of shouts and laughter. Justice was at work now. It had a face of its own, a voice, words, breath, silence, time. It was something you couldn't hold in your hand and yet it could fill a room like some invisible substance, thick enough to cut with a knife. Like not having enough air—or too much. Like the energy everything is full of. Or like fumes when somebody strikes a match.

It was a strange kind of pressure that had to be released.

"They'll get it, they'll get it, even if they hadn't told all the lies they've told already, or if they'd kept their mouths shut even tighter than they have," he said.

And then he whispered, "They're going to have to jump. They're going to have to jump. They'll probably do it together."

He'd been watching the two boys as they opened a jar of apricots. They ruined a fork and spoon doing it.

The man took the woman's hand and held it tight and the woman clung to him.

"I'll tell you when it's over," Black Lion whispered.

A hollow thud came from the next room as the woman fainted and collapsed to the floor.

"She passed out," said Black Lion disappointedly.

The man in pyjamas bent over her.

"You forgot your bad heart," the tall one said.

The man looked away.

"Don't take one more step," the tall one commanded. He glanced at the smaller guard, who stared back at him.

"In a while they'll come and take you away," he said. "In the meantime, we'll look around. Give me the key to everything that's locked up and show me everything that can be opened. Don't try to put anything over on us or conceal some hiding place."

The man shuffled slowly over to the wardrobe where he'd hung his civilian clothes before he'd jumped into bed. He pulled some keys out of a pocket and handed them to the tall guard.

Then he walked over to the picture of the Madonna and took it down. There was a lock set in the wall.

"See if you can bring her around," the tall one told the man. "Get some water," he said to the smaller one.

Then the smaller RG opened the wardrobe. He took his time. Besides the suits and shirts and underwear, there were two big suitcases, a man's and a woman's, both packed and ready to go.

"Where are those two concentration camp kids?" the tall one called.

Black Lion stepped into the room from the kitchen. "Here," he said, pointing through the open door at the two boys.

They stopped eating the apricots.

"Help yourselves to anything you need," the tall one told them.

The wooden rack in the wardrobe sagged with clothes that smelled of mothballs because nobody had worn them for years. There were almost a dozen suits and coats. Tiny bent down carefully, because behind the two suitcases in the bottom of the wardrobe where the shoes were, he saw a knobby sack made out of white linen.

"What's in it?" demanded Curly, who was standing right behind him.

"Sugar," Tiny replied. "Lump sugar."

"How do you know?" wondered Curly.

"Take what you need," the tall one repeated. "And then get the hell out of here."

Tiny took the sack of sugar and straightened up. "This," he said.

Curly made a face. "Grub," he said.

The taller Revolutionary Guard broke into a laugh. "Scram," he said, but in quite a different tone.

The shorter guard grinned.

Black Lion picked up the case with the gas masks and watched the two boys leave ahead of him. They payed no attention to the man and woman. He looked over at the open window.

When the boys got downstairs and out on the sidewalk, they kicked around all the bits of brick and broken plaster they wanted to. After that, just as obliviously, they passed the dark stain on the sidewalk next to the corner where the sewer was. The man with the bandaged head wasn't standing there anymore. The street was full of people different than the ones who had been there before, and in a little while, others would take their place too.

Then, with an unflagging sense of pride, Black Lion took Tiny and Curly home with him. He had an unquestionable feeling that what he had just experienced had been *justice*. But he'd had a different feeling about it when they'd gone into the building than when they'd come out. And suddenly he felt satisfaction that those two people, whom he'd seen for the first time in his life, and probably for the last, hadn't jumped. That they didn't have to jump.

"Come on," he said to the little kid. "Let me give you a hand with that sugar."

Early in the Morning

"Don't you worry about me," the boy said sharply.

"The excitement's all over, if you had the notion anybody's still jumping," the fat man told him.

He knew who he was right away, from his clothes and his face and eyes. He could tell immediately. He'd seen the boy yesterday, tripping over the corpses beside the overturned German machine gun. He was still wearing the same silly, wrinkled blue knickers, an army shirt, and white shoes with big gold buckles.

"You should have been here last night if you wanted to see them jump," the fat man added. The boy must have hurried. Just as he'd hurried yesterday beside that German machine gun.

It was the boy's eyes that were strange—squinting, almost adult eyes whose lashes had been scorched. His eyebrows were singed too, as if a bullet had whizzed past his head. Or as if he'd gotten too close to a fire.

He's really got funny eyes, the man thought to himself. Even the pupils were narrow, as if he regarded everything he saw with suspicion. Those eyes didn't match his delicate, childlike complexion and rosy lips. It was as if someone had carved them out with a knife and left two sharp splinters of steel behind.

"I told you they're not jumping anymore. It looks like it's all over. Now they're just moving along like wind-up toys. Or robots. As if each one of them is somebody else now."

The boy had two long scars on his forehead, as though his skull were coming apart beneath the skin. Or as if someone had beaten him.

Like those kids who, for five or six days, had been going around killing and stealing whatever there was to kill and steal. A fuzz of golden hair showed from under his cloth cap.

"No death-defying leaps today," the fat man continued. "You haven't missed anything."

The boy just eyed him narrowly.

"All the fun and games ended last night," the fat man assured him. "That's all I can tell you. And now nobody else has any business here on this bridge. You might get hurt. Somebody else might get hurt too. I don't want to argue with you."

"I'll stand over here by the guardrail," the boy said.

"You're not standing anywhere, that's what I'm telling you. You got your share yesterday, I can see that."

The boy said nothing.

"All of this—these two bridges, from one end to the other—they're military territory now, see?" The fat man strode off slowly, slapping his gun. It was a new 1944 German machine gun. Reserve cartridges stuck out of his pocket. The gun was slung across his chest, but he was so fat that it hung high.

"I bet I can read your mind," he said. Something warned him he ought to get rid of the boy before there was trouble. "It's your tough luck if you don't believe me when I tell you nobody's jumping anymore. It's all over with."

He peered at the boy suspiciously. "If you're looking for somebody, you picked the wrong bridge. Forget it. Can't you see they're finished, even without your help?"

A brisk morning breeze was blowing. The river was dirty. Next to the suspension bridge, which had been destroyed before the war ended, a temporary wooden bridge had been built, later reinforced with a few extra pillars to support trucks and streetcars. Tanks only risked it when the bridge was empty.

The bridges looked like sisters, side by side.

"Just don't tell me you came here to admire the old bridge or see how much this wooden one can carry," the fat man said. "I wasn't born yesterday."

"Yeah, well, I didn't have to throw up last night the way some people did," the boy recalled.

Yesterday, while the shooting was still going on, the youngster had been standing on the corner of Parizska Boulevard and Jachymov Street, where the barber shop and the beauty parlor were, across the street from the bank and the Sherry Bar. They'd closed the bar on Saturday as soon as the shooting started. Somebody had boarded up the glass doors.

The youngster watched the shooting at close range. It was almost as if he *wanted* a bullet to nick him, if not hit him directly. Or as if he wanted to see whether he was invulnerable. He stayed there until it was all over. As if he were looking for something or somebody. Or as if he found it immensely entertaining.

The rebels finally succeeded in killing a German machine gun crew. The boy was the first to rush forward.

Everybody expected he was going to rob the soldiers or take their guns. But all he did was pick up a glinting cartridge case which lay on the ground beside the empty ammunition belt. He didn't touch the dead German soldiers.

The fact he hadn't robbed them was what saved his life, because as he moved on to give others a chance, a tank standing next to the Law School had opened fire and killed a woman who had been running over to tear the clothes off the gunners.

It blew her into pieces. It tore off her arms and legs as if she'd been a tousled rag doll, and all that was left of her were a few wet scraps of flesh and bone and cloth and shoe leather.

The barber got a piece of shrapnel in his thigh. Half of the bystanders were shot and half were kept as hostages by the Germans. That was when the fat man got sick to his stomach.

Later, for a change, the Sherry Bar had been turned into a prison for captured German soldiers and officers and civilians because there wasn't enough room for them in the textile shop or the anti-aircraft shelter in the building where the funeral parlor was.

The captive German soldiers streaming down the street from the stockyards and across the wooden bridge didn't seem in such bad shape.

A defeated army never looks scary. The rows of men came and went with a disordered kind of regularity, with uneven gaps between, the way water flows from a far-off spring.

That was how the Revolutionary Guard dispatched them from the freight depot and the other railroad stations and highway check points toward a single staging area. According to the fat man's calculations, there must be at least one whole division.

He had to admit that even now, when he saw them as helpless as they were, a shiver ran up his spine—like when he'd gotten sick to his stomach the day before. He could imagine how he'd feel if those soldiers marching along here now were marching in a different way. Fortunately....

He couldn't even say whether they were moving in a more orderly formation than they had been earlier that morning. He hadn't seen the ones who had come through during the night. He'd reported for duty at five o'clock that morning. He hadn't had much sleep during the past five days, so he was a little edgy and, at the same time, proud of himself for his endurance. Anyway, he wanted to be left alone and he didn't want the youngster hanging around.

He could find no trace of softness or humility in that kid's face.

"There's a tavern at the other end of the wooden bridge," he said. "It's called the Fatted Calf and half the town's in there. They'll give you free beer and something to eat. Why don't you go on over?"

The prisoners were straggling along in a more disorderly fashion than at first. The disorder annoyed the fat man for a while, but then he got used to it. With the sloppy way whole units straggled by, drifting apart and intermingling—flyers and engineers, cannoneers and infantry, motorized artillery and flamethrowers. The fear, which each of these soldiers, individually, had inspired only yesterday, evaporated.

Even to look at, a defeated army is a mean and pitiful sight.

To the fat man, there was justice to it and, at the same time, it was unfair. Each soldier was carrying a fragment of shattered prestige which had been trodden into the dust—a bit of the former glory of an army, now defeated, which had come here intending to stay for a thousand years. They were leaving now, so thoroughly despised that it wasn't worth the trouble to do more than prod, look, or pity.

Yet there was something about them, a captured army, that

filled the victors, and those who had helped them to victory, with satisfaction, even though it hadn't been a battlefield surrender.

In some lines, members of almost every branch of the armed forces marched side by side, most of them without belts and some of them barefoot. Some soldiers only had on underwear beneath their coats.

As the morning wore on, it got tedious. The fat man saw that words wouldn't get rid of the youngster. It wasn't hard to imagine what was going on inside his head. It wouldn't be difficult to grab one of the soldiers once they got beyond the stockyards and to take away his belt or coat or trousers.

"I wouldn't mind if they were still jumping, but they aren't," he repeated.

He could think of other possibilities when he looked at the prisoners and at the youngster.

"By now, you can see for yourself they're not jumping. You've been hanging around here long enough already. If you thought they were, you see with your own eyes they're not."

There are some kids like that who don't miss a thing, the fat man decided. They can sniff out everything. Not like hyenas or vultures. Like beasts of prey, they want to catch their prey alive. Yet look at him—those blue eyes and fair hair, that delicate skin. Maybe part of it's curiosity. But that isn't all.

Why? They could be a thousand becauses — or none at all. So many explanations that they were all mixed up with everything else.

On the first day of the uprising, on Saturday at noon the fat man recalled, two youngsters like this one came up to a German soldier who figured they wanted to trade some food for his gun and ammunition. But instead, they tossed a coal sack over his head, and one of them started hitting him with a beer bottle, the other with an iron pipe. The soldier groped around as if he were playing blindman's bluff, while the youngsters talked to him through the sack. They didn't even bother to drag him off into a hallway and finish him up in there. The fat man saw it when all that was left of the beer bottle were splinters of glass.

A woman had screamed as if the soldier were somebody she knew. "You want to kill him?" Then she ran away yelling, "They want to kill him, they want to kill him!"

Nobody stopped them. Nobody called from a window in the next apartment house. Nobody else ran away like the woman did. Nobody told them to stop, that enough was enough.

The boy watched the lines. Each row of prisoners disappeared from sight as the street turned behind the stockyards and ran along the river, so at a distance it looked as though they were marching right into the water. The fat man had it figured out by now how long it took for one column to reach the bridge he was guarding. The boy was still trying to work it out. There must have been at least two thousand prisoners.

"Now you've seen them in all their tarnished glory, so why don't you go on over to the Fatted Calf, how about it?" the fat man suggested. "Why not have a little fun and relaxation?" he asked after a long pause.

As the first soldiers of the new column approached, he stepped forward to keep a closer eye on things. He had no time to worry about the kid now. If any prisoner got too close to the side of the bridge, he only had to yell at him to move into the middle of the roadway.

"Look, we've gotten acquainted now and there's nothing more to say," declared the fat man. "But right now, this is military territory, pure and simple, and I have my orders and my responsibility is not to allow anybody to loiter here."

"I've got as much business here as you have," the boy said.

"What'd you mean, you've got as much business here as me? Are you a member of the Revolutionary Guard? Are you sixteen years old, at least? Where'd you come from, anyway? Why do you keep sticking your hand in the fire? You want to lose it at the very last minute? How come they let you through on the other side? It doesn't look as though you got much sleep last night. All right, look around. You've seen all there is to see, nothing else is going to happen, so get moving, huh, why don't you? I've got just so much patience. If you thought they were jumping, now you've had a chance to see for yourself they're not. It was different last night."

"That isn't why I came. I'm here, though, and I'm staying for a little while. No regulations apply to me."

"I've got to keep a close eye on everything and I don't want any distractions that might cause trouble."

"I'm not in your way, am I?"

"I'm not saying whether you're in my way or not. I'm only telling you I have to have a free hand here, just in case. Don't try to aggravate me, or there'll be trouble."

"I didn't come here to argue. I came to look around. I want to see them go."

"You'll really make me mad if you don't believe me when I tell you they're not jumping and if you try to kid me into believing you're just interested in seeing them go. You can see better from the other side."

"I want to see them up close, that's all," the boy insisted.

Every fifty meters or so, the column of prisoners was escorted by two or three members of the Revolutionary Guard. When the fat man saw them, he just winked or nodded or wagged a finger so it wouldn't look as though they didn't know how to run things in an orderly way.

As far as you could see—towards the stockyards or in the other direction, where the Prime Minister's offices used to be—no more than three guards were to be seen. The soldiers seemed to be marching into captivity all by themselves. As though their last drop of discipline had trickled into this final act of obedience, which resembled the dregs of something else—or its total collapse. Had they softened up or was it just exhaustion? It was as though they were going voluntarily, trying to avoid something they were still afraid of. And as if they were using their helplessness like a shield, for the admiration of their guards, protecting themselves by the fact that there were so many of them going together.

"They're going now like the Jews went before," the fat man remarked.

The youngster didn't react. That was when the fat man understood why the boy had come here.

"Did you ever hear the old story about the fellow who played his pipe and all these rats followed him and behind the rats, there were people from some country where they'd never been able to make good? So they followed the fellow with the pipe into another country where even greater disappointments waited in store for them. And that was the end of the line for them."

"This isn't quite the same thing," said the youngster.

"They look a little more human when they've been beaten," the fat man said.

"How many are there?"

"What do you care? Lots. Half of Schörner's army." The fat man had a big belly, drawn in by a wide German belt from Afrika Corps stocks. Most of his clothing was of German origin.

"Who are you?" he demanded suddenly. "Who are you, anyway?" Then, as if he wanted to give the boy time to answer or to prepare himself in case he got no answer, he went on: "If anybody told you they're still jumping, well, it isn't true, see? They haven't for quite a while, I can tell you that. The last one who jumped did it at daybreak." He eyed the youngster curiously. "I'd like to know who you are."

The boy took off his cap. It was an Italian-style cloth cap, but the fat man knew caps like that were worn in places other than the army.

When he did it, it was obvious that his head had been shaved recently. Then he rolled his sleeve back over his elbow and proudly showed the fat man the tattooed numerals and two letters. A capital C and a small one.

Suddenly the fat man's eyes turned from the numbers on the boy's forearm.

"Hey, what the hell..." he said. "What's going on?"

"Don't you want to shoot him?" the youngster suggested quickly.

The two of them watched as one of the prisoners stepped out of line when his column passed the wooden railing on the other side of the bridge. The man dashed toward them with outstretched arms, jacket flapping and head lowered, as if he were charging them like a bull. The fat man grabbed his machine gun and aimed it at the prisoner.

The man was about twenty paces away. That would have

given the fat man time enough to raise the gun muzzle to the level of his chest and to pull the trigger before he got much closer.

"Let me worry about it," snapped the fat man.

When he was only a few steps away, the prisoner swerved suddenly, scrambling over the railing, and jumping into the water. He just missed one of the cables that dangled from the other bridge. As if he'd wanted to catch it, but failed.

There was a loud splash, as though a bale of cotton had hit the water.

"Well, I guess they're still jumping after all," murmured the fat man.

"Are you going to leave him there in the water?" the youngster asked.

"Is that any of your business?"

"So for God's sake, shoot!" the youngster said. "Or give me your gun. Don't you want to let him have it before he gets away?"

"Son of a bitch, so they're still jumping," mused the fat man.

The circles in the river's surface widened and floated off with the current under the suspension bridge.

"Are you going to let him get away? You're going to let him swim for it?" the boy demanded.

"The ones who jumped last night had a chance, but that guy doesn't."

"Don't you want to kill him and get it over with?"

"Most of the ones who jumped last night just swam away."

"I might've known."

"Where do you suppose you can swim to from here?"

"Kill him before he gets too far!"

"I told you not to get mixed up in this. It's none of your business. Don't you worry."

He raised the machine gun so he could shoot over the railing. He had to pull the strap over his head because his belly got in the way when he tried to aim down over the railing.

"I thought these little performances were over," he said. He readied his gun.

The boy looked on impatiently. None of the other prisoners had moved out of line in the meantime. The columns of men plodded along as though that one prisoner were an exception which had nothing to do with them. Within a few seconds, the unit, to which the prisoner who had just jumped off the bridge belonged, had passed by. Everybody looked straight ahead and kept on going.

"You can't believe everything you hear," the fat man continued. "They're still jumping."

The wind whistled through the steel cables of the suspension bridge and you could hear the water lapping against the riverbank and the heavy tread of the prisoners who had shoes and the creaking of the new timbers in the temporary bridge.

"So they're still doing it. But this is the first one since I've been on duty."

"So what?"

"You keep your nose out of this," the fat man told him.

"Just don't let him get away," the youngster urged.

"Don't you worry."

After a little while, the prisoner surfaced. He had shrewdly tried to swim under the bridge under water, against the current, and that had slowed him down. Then, when nobody could see him, he was going to turn and float down with the current until he reached a safety ladder further down the quay.

"What if everybody decided to do the same thing?"

From the bridge, the fat man was carrying on a long-distance conversation with the prisoner. "Why do you want to make me bloodthirsty? Up until yesterday, I was. But today I'm not anymore. I didn't want to be bloodthirsty today."

"Shoot him!" said the boy.

The fat man turned as though he hadn't heard. "Well, he didn't intend to drown himself, anyway. He just felt like jumping. We're all glad we're alive on this earth, aren't we after all?"

"Kill him," the boy repeated.

"You're kind of impatient."

"No, I'm not."

"You're not very forgiving either, are you?"

"Kill him!" the boy said angrily.

"It's cold, isn't it?" The fat man was talking to the prisoner again. "It's a lot colder than it looks from the road or when the sun's shining like now. It's easy to jump in. It's harder to get out."

He watched as the prisoner struggled to take off the water-logged coat that was dragging him down. He was trying to get his shoes off too.

"So you're my first jumper," the fat man told the prisoner in an almost kindly tone. He aimed the gun awkwardly, shifting it to follow the man's movements in the water. He gave him a chance to start swimming. Then the point of the gun's muzzle halted somewhere about the prisoner's leg. He probably didn't realize he wasn't very deeply submerged as he plunged under the water's surface. Or he got tired and floated up into the current.

"Yesterday, I'd have told you that a smart general would rather lose a battle than lose a war. But today, I'm not so sure."

The fat man shot at the prisoner's thigh. He fired two rounds. The first one was short, as though he were only practicing. The second was longer. The bullets cut through the water as though somebody had underscored a line with two projections. Those were the man's legs in the water now. The echo of the shots filled the hollowness under the bridge, but there were other sounds too.

"He doesn't have anything to escape with now," the fat man said. "Even if he swam to where there are none of our patrols."

"All he can do is swim with his arms now," he went on. "The current'll help him, though. He'll drink his fill of these waters. I wish I knew why they jump. What gets into them? Why is it always bridges they jump off of?"

The fat man looked over at the youngster. "Somebody must have told you they're still jumping." He grinned. "Even if he makes it to shore, he won't have anything to crawl out with and to walk on. I got him in the legs good and proper. He can only make it if he's in the water. Not on shore. Unless one of out soft-hearted folks helps him. Well, now what do you have to say?''

The youngster swallowed hard.

At that moment, the boy was visualizing those people from Budapest, the man whose son was sent into the ovens and who was allowed to accompany him as far as the door to the shower room. But when he wanted to go in too, the guard said no.

Afterwards, the man knelt in the earth. It was muddy after the long October rains. He stayed there for twelve hours, raking the mud with his fingernails, as if he wanted to pull something out by the roots.

That evening, the other prisoners urged him to come to the barracks before he got shot. He wanted to be shot. But when they came a second time to coax him in, he made them promise to gather up stones to defend themselves. He pleaded with them to break at least the few German skulls of that happened to be around.

They formed a circle around him, like a wall, so the German guards wouldn't overhear what he was saying. One of the prisoners slapped his face to silence him. For his own good.

The one who slapped him was the one the guard shot first. Then he fired a path through to the man who was kneeling in the mud.

"Are you saying your prayers or what?"

The man on his knees was silent.

"I'll shoot you too. I'm only human. I'm only flesh and blood too. Nobody's going to play around with me."

So he shot him and asked no more questions. Behind his back, the guard could hear the other prisoners slipping off to the barracks.

"Have you got so little ammunition that you just shot his legs?'' the boy asked, instead of answering the questions he'd been asked.

"You're awfully bloodthirsty. You'd have killed him, wouldn't you?"

"What're you saving your bullets for?"

"That's none of your business," the fat man replied in his kindly way. He shoved a new round of ammunition into the gun.

"Don't make me nervous," he went on. "I don't know why they were still jumping. It's not a question of saving ammunition. We've got plenty of ammunition."

He chuckled disbelievingly. "Who'd have thought it? That they'd still be jumping! And in broad daylight."

The river was dirty as it flowed through the middle of the town. The sun was shining and a breeze blew. A yellow suitcase was floating upside down in the middle of the river. The lid was open and it acted like a rudder, so it turned slowly about its own axis as it drifted along.

Long straps floated out from one side, and from the other, shorter ones with buckles.

The prisoner waited to grab the side of the suitcase. He clutched at the lid. The suitcase didn't hold him and it began to sink.

"That's what he gets for jumping," said the fat man.

At last the prisoner realized he couldn't put his whole weight on the suitcase and maneuvered himself around so it would just keep him above water and he could float downstream with it.

This time, the fat man fixed his sights on the shoulder of the man in the water.

"They still jump," he murmured, taking aim.

"Kill him," said the boy.

"There we go," the fat man said.

The steel cables of the bridge sang in the wind. The columns of prisoners went on their way, going in the opposite direction of the current of the river. After a few seconds, the captives who came onto the wooden bridge had no idea what had just happened.

"At least a hundred of them saw him jump, but it's never more than one that does it. Even at night, there's never more than one."

The fat man slung his machine gun over his head again and

held it against his belly. "You're making a mistake if you think I don't know how to handle things," he said. "What is it that gets into their heads, that they keep on jumping?"

The boy looked over to the other side of the river where there was a pile of sand and stones heaped into a gigantic pyramid, ready to reinforce the riverbank. People were dragging the prisoner out of the water with hooks and poles.

Suddenly, a stake was raised in the middle of a heap of stones. Like a mast or flagpole. After a while, sooty smoke began to curl around it. As if wet wood were burning. Then there was a scream.

"They jump in here and then they pull them out over there on the other side. And burn them like rats. I told you, it reminds me of that story about the fellow who played the pipe."

He kept looking back and forth from the columns of men, to the stake on the other side of the river.

"They can't do anything anymore. Not a thing. They're frozen to the bone. All they do is jump like crazy hoptoads. Like a flyer who jumps even when he knows he doesn't have a parachute. Who'd want to fry like a rat with its tail burned off?"

The boy turned away from the stake which had finally caught fire.

For one split second, he could still see the red brick wall where the showers were and the chambers and the oven. Seven days a week, the smoke rose into the sky and for miles around, the air reeked of burning hair and fingernails and bones, skin and grease. Or as if they were manufacturing glue. Or soap.

That was where he'd been when they picked out his little sister and sent her on the wrong side. By that time, his mother and father and sixty people who had once comprised his family had long since gone up the chimney.

He'd been quiet as a mouse. He was afraid it had gotten inside him, like those worms which work their way inside a person's skin and you can never get rid of them unless you cut them out, skin and all.

It was as if he'd caught some infectious disease which he couldn't give back to those who had infected him.

He'd been in that same camp for twenty-eight days. Every one of those twenty-eight days, he felt as though ashes were falling on him. The chimney was a football field's length away from his barracks.

His sister was in every flake of ash that fell. But she was never alone.

And now, in that split second, which was like a ripple in the river, like a single pulsing of one single ripple, he thought how it would be if now—at this very moment—he could share that half a loaf of bread he had with his sister, the dab of margarine and half a jar of jam. Unless somebody had stolen it from his room in the YWCA in the meantime.

"Isn't this more fun than yesterday?" asked the fat man. "Well, some of them still go on jumping." he added.

The prisoners slouched. These were an older batch. They hardly noticed the burning stake on the other side of the river, but the ones behind them glanced over now and then.

"Look out!" cried the boy.

"Well, what do you know, they're still doing it!" murmured the fat man. This time he began to shoot as soon as he got his gun strap over his head.

The prisoner sank several times and then bobbed up again. From above, he looked like somebody in a diving suit with too much air inside. Or like a frog. His head and arms and legs groped about like feelers.

"He probably felt light as air when he jumped. Now look how heavy he is," said the fat man. "Look how his coat's soaking up the water. Look!"

The water around the coat was turning red. The fat man put in another round of ammunition. The row of prisoners was denser now, coming along one after another. They weren't walking any faster, though.

The stake collapsed with a resounding crash. The wind carried the sound of it across the river. The boy drifted over to a pile of cobblestones at the end of the wooden bridge.

"I'm surprised you've still got the urge," said the fat man. "It's different when they jump."

The boy looked at the cobblestones, at the prisoners, and down into the water. He heard the creak of the cables in the wind. He turned his eyes away as the water turned red around the man, mingling with the current and swirling into the mud and the sediment.

He went back in his mind to the friend he'd had in Poland. They'd belonged to the same fishing commando. His name was Arthur Cohen, and he went out with the German boats to gather gull's eggs on the islands.

The birds on the water were as white as winter stars. They were shy of people. They fed on fish which, in turn, fed on ashes. Then it turned out that there were other things besides ashes they fed on too.

People worked up to their waists in water and sometimes even up to their necks, cutting reeds and catching carp under the eye of Waffen SS guards. Women prisoners carried away the reeds they'd cut, and when the reeds dried, they were used at the front for camouflaging planes and tanks and panzers.

One afternoon, they'd heard someone singing across the water. This was strange, because hardly anybody ever sang in those days.

It was a Greek girl, from a company of Balkan women who'd arrived a few days before.

From that day on, she sang for seven days, and they all looked forward to hearing her. It was beautiful. As if something very far away had suddenly moved closer, bringing with it a sweet and gentle touch.

The song she sang was in a foreign tongue they couldn't understand, but there was none of the coldness in it which they felt around them, none of the dampness which was destroying them as they worked in water from morning till evening. None of the hunger, either, which forced some of them to eat raw fish.

The Greek girl's voice had sunshine in it, like a warm breeze on a summer's night, because there was hope in it and a feel-

214

ing of the future unspoiled by the present.

The song the Greek girl sang may have had a loving sound to it and maybe that was why they looked forward to it for those seven days. As if it were more than just a song.

The eighth day was a Sunday. Just as the girl began to sing, the German guards set their police dogs on her. The dogs tore her apart before her song broke into a scream and before both merged into a single sound.

After that, all they could hear was the water's voice. But now there was always something about the water which contained the song of the dead Greek girl.

One day later, they transferred Arthur Cohen from the fishing squad to another where he was given the job of dragging out and burning the corpses which had been submerged in the mud and suddenly bobbed up above the surface, so there seemed to be more dead bodies than there was mud to cover them.

They were a strange sight, those corpses smeared with mud that water could never wash away.

The guards were annoyed by the stench which the wind blew toward the German barracks.

The ashes of the corpses which had been fished out of the mud and burned were loaded on small boats and taken out into the middle of the pond and dumped in, until finally all the protruding corpses had been converted into ashes.

Cohen was told he'd done a good job and that a similar assignment was waiting for him at another camp. They never saw Cohen after that. Every commando involved in the burying and burning disappeared within three months at most. Usually it was six weeks.

The boy had stayed with the fishing commando, so he was lucky. Sometimes he would stare into the water and listen, as though he were waiting to hear the Greek girl's song, which never came.

He gathered gulls' eggs for a guard's wife whose name was Hilda. He had a nice little rowboat. They'd bring back a basketful in the evening if they'd gone out in the morning, or in the morning if they'd worked at night.

And he knew he'd live—at least as long as there were eggs to be found in the gulls' nests.

"Where'd you get those golf knickers?" asked the fat man.

"Across the street from the Hotel Graf, where the repatriation station is now," the boy replied.

With a practiced eye, the fat man studied the youngster and the pile of cobblestones and the column of older soldiers.

"You're living it up these days if you're staying in a hotel," the fat man said. "Some people really know how to manage." He was waiting to see what the boy would do with the stones.

"What'd you say there was in the hotel now?"

"There's a sterilizer and a delousing station," the boy said. "And a first-aid station and dormitories for people who didn't get into the YWCA or YMCA. That's where they hand out repatriation I.D. cards too."

"So that's where you heard they were still jumping? The word gets around fast, huh?"

The boy didn't answer. He kept looking over to the other side of the river.

On the opposite shore, not far from the heap of sand and stones, a Russian soldier was sponging off his horse. It was a gray horse and it gleamed like a statue in the sunshine.

He could still see those eight captive Russian officers. The Germans told them to undress and bathe, like the other new arrivals. The officers wanted to be turned over to their counterparts—to German officers. Their spokesman was a huge man, big as a mountain. Finally the guard went off to find the commander.

"What is it you want?" the commander demanded.

The giant took one step forward. The others stood in a rigid line, chins high.

"We are officers and we request that we be treated accord-

216

ing to the Geneva Convention. We expect to be handed over to military authorities."

"Ach," chuckled the German. He slapped his riding crop against the palm of his hand. He carried a pistol in a holster at his side, but he didn't touch it.

"So you really suppose you won't obey a German guard because he's not an officer?" Again he laughed. "So you really want to be handed over to an officer?"

"That's exactly what we're asking and we insist on it," the giant said.

"Gentlemen, I'm truly sorry. Truly sorry. We have very few officers in this installation here. So we're forced to use rank-and-file guards."

He laughed a third time. Suddenly he struck the giant across the face with his riding crop. Then he began to shout at them, telling them to realize where they were. And he strode off down the line, striking each of the other seven Russian officers across the face with his riding crop, just as hard as he'd struck the giant.

Blood-swollen bruises rose on the cheeks of the startled Russians. They were unable to defend themselves. The behavior of the German commander had shattered them. Blood trickled over the giant's chin and into his mouth, along his lips and onto his neck and collar.

The commander knew what blood does. He turned away, but even then he didn't draw his pistol or look back. It was as if he were walking away from a dog he'd thrashed. The Russian officers didn't move a muscle.

At one word from the guard, the Russians stripped, folded their uniforms and piled them, with their underwear and shoes, in front of them. Then, at the guard's command, they turned and marched into the showers.

"You didn't think you were better than Jews, did you?" asked the guard. "Everybody here's a Jew—Russian or American, French or English. Whoever's a foreigner in Germany is a Jew, and Jews have to obey orders."

When they'd been gassed, the commander observed, "For

217

us, everybody is inferior, just like the Jews are, and so they end up like Jews. I'm the one who decides who's a Jew."

"What's your name, anyway?" the fat man persisted.

"What's yours?"

"Hey, just for fun, show me that repatriation card of yours, will you?"

The boy took off his cap again. The card was stuck inside the band. It was a two-page identity card listing the places he'd been during the war, his present residence, and how much money he'd been given to start with by the Revolutionary National Committee for Prague II.

He handed the card to the fat man and dug the toe of his white shoe into the pile of cobblestones.

"Theresienstadt, Auschwitz-Birkenau, Neugamme. Neugamme —that's the first time I heard of that one. Buchenwald—I've heard about that. Dachau too," the fat one said. "How can you have lived through something like that, kid?"

The boy stepped back and picked up one of the cobblestones. It was a cube of granite, blue and white.

"Listen, kid, it's different when it's me doing the shooting," the fat man drawled. "I'm not talking about yesterday and last night. That was different. I guess you probably had your share too."

The boy held on to the cobblestone.

"Neugamme, Neugamme," murmured the fat man. He handed back the I.D. card.

"I'd put that stone down if I were you," he went on. "Or just watch if it makes you feel better, but forget the other thing. Unless somebody else decides to jump. If they do, then I'll lend you my gun."

In his thoughts, the boy was back with the children who had come to Theresienstadt from Poland in the middle of the war. They'd raised an awful fuss at the delousing station and nobody could understand why they were so scared of taking a shower.

Terror overcame them in the boiler room and when the

bathhouse personnel asked the nurses and doctors to help un-dress them, the children bit and scratched and fought as if their lives were at stake.

The boilers were heated with coal, the toothbrushes and soap and towels were real and the place was really meant for baths, but these children had other visions.

"Gas! Gas!" they screamed.

In Poland six months later, some of those same Theresien-stadt doctors and nurses and bathhouse personnel under-stood when they were told, "Go and bathe. Don't lose your soap and towel! Remember your clothes hook and where you've put your things. We want you spic and span."

"Did you ever imagine they'd jump this way?" the fat man asked, wondering what the youngster was going to do with the cobblestone. "Did you ever imagine that someday, in just one single city in Europe, you'd see more than one whole division of the German Army going along like a herd of sheep? And that you'd be standing here watching, you and me?"

"As a matter of fact, we used to talk about it," said the boy.

"I'll bet you did."

"We talked about it a lot."

"Did they give you enough time to talk?"

"The older people, the ones who were around thirty or forty, didn't seem to want to talk about anything else finally."

"Whether they were going to jump like this?"

"No. Whether we ought to kill them and burn them or not—and whether we would."

"I can close my eyes for a minute, if you want me to."

The boy was silent.

"You can just pretend I'm not here for a few seconds, if you'd rather," the fat man went on.

The boy turned his back to the lines of men.

"I didn't think they'd jump either, although now it makes sense," the fat one said.

"Some of the people with us couldn't get it out of their heads," the boy recalled.

"You're talking about yourself now?"

"I'm talking about the ones who were obsessed with the idea, but they aren't anymore. They *aren't,* period."

"For a minute—just while I shut my eyes—it's all yours, if you want."

"There's no point talking about it."

"Is that why you came? I hope, in the meantime, they won't drink up all the beer over at the Fatted Calf."

The fat man crossed to the other bridge railing, as if the boy weren't there. The youngster peered intently at the rows of soldiers as they streamed by, tightly bunched and moving faster. The fat man seemed to be indicating that he was turning things over to the youngster now.

"Just for a minute, though," he called.

The boy's little eyes were fixed fast on the fat man's back, then on the column of prisoners. He squinted because he hadn't had much sleep and his eyes were bloodshot.

His gaze stopped on the face of a soldier in a blue uniform. He was trudging listlessly, with no idea that the boy was watching him. He was listless because that made it easier to go—and to face the fact of where he was going.

But in his thoughts, the boy was back at the Demartinka streetcar barns where the Revolutionary Guards had herded all the Germans from the neighborhood.

They were people who had been captured on the other side of the river, which the German commanders had been unable to evacuate. Most of the German civilians had been trying to reach the American lines.

There were three old streetcars in the car barn into which they tossed their belongings—suitcases and clothes and small possessions. Things they wanted to take with them. One flat-bottomed repair car was already heaped with their belongings.

After they'd been registered, the captive Germans had to run the gauntlet through the crowd in front of the car barns. Each got his share.

The people screamed at them and beat them and spat in

their faces. They couldn't seem to get enough of it. Only once were they silent, when a woman with a baby in her arms passed through. They pressed so close, she must have felt their breath on her skin. Then a pistol shot rang out. Someone fell across the streetcar tracks about ten meters in front of the woman with the infant. Five shots were fired.

"Look!" somebody screamed. "She's the one who fired those shots! The woman!"

She had a .635 pistol wrapped in the baby's blanket and she managed to fire six more shots into the crowd. The narrow corridor of people broke up. All there was to see was the baby's blanket exploding into the air.

"So your name's Robert," said the fat man from the other side of the bridge. "That's a nice name. I won't even ask if you were named after your dad."

The boy looked away from the soldier and he knew he wouldn't throw the stone now.

"No, not after Dad," he told the man.

"Well, at least you saw them jump," the fat one said. "You've got a real nice name, kid. Girls'll like to say it. But you're still young for that sort of thing. Not too young for some things, but for others, yes. For messing around in the moonlight and so on. Hey, tell me, what's on your mind all the time?"

"I'm just watching them go," replied the boy.

Back in northern Bohemia, in the Little Fortress, he could still see the superintendent who, before the war, had been a sexton somewhere in the Austrian Alps. He had clear blue eyes, flaxen hair, and a milky skin. He made his rounds through the fortress, impeccably dressed, scrubbed, and neatly combed. Nobody ever saw him hurry or heard him shout. On Sundays, he strolled with a prayer book in his left hand and a pistol in his right. He looked like Jesus Christ. Or the way people sometimes said Christ might have looked.

From every group or transport, the superintendent would

pick out a father and son. First, he had them put in separate cells. For one week, they were given nothing to eat or drink. On the eighth day, they were fed, but at different times. Then the superintendent told them they were going to appear in a bullfight, but without the bulls. Then they'd have a chance to show how smart they were.

On Sunday, the pair were brought out to a dry moat between the ramparts. It looked like an arena in good weather, but it was a soggy sort of stadium when it rained, the turf heavy and slippery with mud.

After a bath, the father and son were led before a podium where the superintendent stood, flanked by trained police dogs on one side and, on the other, the noncommissioned officers. Facing them were the prisoners: men, women and children (if there were any in the fortress at the time). The superintendent lay his Bible on the rail in front of him and, on top of it, his Parabella 9 mm pistol and, alongside these, a pair of kid gloves.

The father and son were told to strip naked. Then they were each given a club heavy enough to kill a man.

At a signal from the sexton and one of the Waffen SS, they were to start fighting and one of them had to win. To win meant that the other had to die.

There were sons who killed their fathers without a word, and fathers who killed their sons. People had been brought together in the fortress from villages and ghettos and prison camps—anybody who was able to work in the nearby quarries or in the underground munitions factories burrowed deep under Kamyk Mountain.

The superintendent watched as if he were seeing something he'd seen before. He'd seen Jewish fathers and sons fighting and Gypsy fathers and sons, people of all persuasions, heroes of resistance movements, people for whom courage had never been a thing that's put to the test, until they discovered that all human qualities have their limits.

Maybe what he saw took him back to ancient times, when sons were a father's property to the last extreme. Perhaps it made him feel like he was returning to some ancient heritage, customs or beliefs, as though he had carved out of reality a new way to compensate for some remote, forgotten lawlessness.

Sometimes the victims just stood there motionless, waiting to be shot. Then he'd set the dogs on them to tear them to pieces and he fired his pistol only when one of his dogs was in danger. The father and son had clubs, after all, and sometimes they would turn on the dogs.

Occasionally, the victims wept and embraced each other. Or prayed. Sometimes they rushed forward to dash themselves against the ramparts, but the moat was too deep.

Sometimes the father and son agreed among themselves to strike a blow at the very same time, to kill each other simultaneously. But there were other stories. Only someone who had been there could understand how such things were possible. For as long as he lived, anyone who wasn't there could only try to imagine how it was.

The superintendent beamed on the victorious son or father, as though he had suddenly brought him back to reality. He studied him with his pale blue eyes while he ran his hand lovingly over the ramparts, as though he were caressing a human being.

The victim was allowed to watch the next performance. To see himself in a living mirror, so to speak.

The superintendent either shot the father for having killed his son or the son for patricide. Nobody ever survived these combats. As patiently as a mother waits for her child, the superintendent would look forward to new arrivals from the ghetto or the transports which came from the occupied countries in Europe.

Afterwards, he would chat with the prisoners who had been ordered to take the corpses off to the crematorium. He would comment on the blueness of the sky, what nice weather it was, about the grass which grew particularly green under the four gallows. He rattled on about how bricks were made in the days when the Spanish Empire reached from setting sun to rising sun (which was how it was going to be with Germany someday) and when the Spanish had built fortresses all over the world, just like this one in north Bohemia. It was called the Small Fortress, but it was small only in comparison with the one in the ghetto at Theresienstadt, a few miles to the southeast.

He used to like to watch the flocks of migrating birds as they flew south each autumn and came back in spring. He used to talk to them, as though he were seeking the real meaning of the words he spoke. "We're on the scent," he said, "but the beast has eluded us again. For stupid animals, a clever trap. They mustn't escape again."

Some of the fathers and sons knew from the start what was going to happen when they were singled out. But no one was ever sure, until he was led into the moat and told to strip naked and was given a club, to kill or be killed.

In the wintertime, the superintendent watched the snow fall for hours and when springtime came, he raised chrysanthemums in the moat.

"For people who've never seen it, you can talk till you're blue in the face about how they jump," the fat one said. "You can explain how we were right here when it happened. You've got some money, don't you? You need some more?"

"I don't need more than what I've got."

"Never refuse money. Only loonies turn down money."

"I don't need any," the boy told him. "Whatever I need, I can get for myself."

He was thinking too about that woman on Rytirska Street. A German policeman was hanging from a lamppost in his burned uniform, just as they'd dragged him out of the police station.

"So we're the same kind of beasts as they were!" the woman yelled.

"Why? You feel sorry for him?" a big-breasted blonde screamed at her, the veins throbbing in her neck and forehead. "You want to keep him company?"

224

"We'll put that bitch on trial too!" somebody shouted from the back of the crowd.

Only yesterday, people had needed somebody to tear apart, to burn or trample. At the YWCA, a rumor spread that the Germans had poisoned the water. Women took jugs of water around to the centers where Germans were being held, to make them drink the water first, although they had no way of knowing whether it had been poisoned or not.

"I told you, I don't want any," the boy repeated. He was still holding on to the stone, the fat man noticed. He was terribly nervous.

"Hey, look at this beautiful mermaid I have on my chest," he said, unbuttoning his shirt. "And the handsome American cowboy beside her." On his belly and chest, he had a naked woman who looked like a worm except for the luxurious bosom where a name was tattooed at heart level: Rosalie.

"That's made the same way as those little numbers and letters on your arm," the fat one said.

The boy glanced briefly at the designs.

"You know what I mean? That's what you can have done with those tattoos of yours. Have them done over."

The fat man kept his eye on the boy's hand with the paving stone.

"Look, Robert, go on home and tie a knot in your handkerchief, if you've got a handkerchief, and if you don't, you'd better get yourself one and tie a knot in it so you don't forget. These guys aren't jumping anymore." He jerked his head toward the prisoners. "So tie a knot in your hankie. Do one for me while you're at it and one for yourself—for what you *didn't* do."

"What time is it?" asked the youngster.

"About ten o'clock. Things have been pretty lively in the little while you've been here, Robert. Come on, let's have a nice, big smile, Robert, O.K.? You won't say no, will you? Throw away that stone and give me a smile. Aw, come on! Look, Robert, you're still awfully young for throwing stones, even if you do have a nice, long list of places in that red I.D. card of yours. I'll grant you that. But you don't have to go around with such a chip on your shoulder, do you? Nobody's going to bite you. You can have those numbers and letters changed into a very pretty little design, you just wait and see.''

The boy stared at the fat man, but he was really seeing those people at the railroad station. They didn't say a word and when he came, they put their fingers to their lips, signaling him to silence. From his shaven head and cap, they recognized him as one of theirs even before he rolled up his sleeves and identified himself by the tattoo.

That same morning, a Revolutionary Guard had shot one of them because he'd said something in German before he could explain himself.

Those people weren't Germans, though. They spoke German and Yiddish among themselves because that was the only way they could understand each other. They hadn't wanted to stay in Germany. They'd wanted to cross the Channel, but the English refused to let them in as if the noun "promise" and the verb "to keep" had nothing to do with each other in some countries. One of their elders explained all this in a whisper.

The old man told him that the brother of the one who had been shot had gone to some station to talk to the head of the Revolutionary Guard.

Actually, he wasn't talking to anybody. He was at an emergency first-aid station after having had a heart attack, but nobody had told the old man because they didn't want to upset him even more.

The people just stood their in silence until late that evening when their train pulled in and the brother of the one who had been shot was well enough to board it with them.

They had nothing to eat and didn't want anything, to the amazement of the railroad workers who kept offering them food. All they would accept was water. The worker said that even then, they sprinkled it first on their hands, as if they were washing them. Only afterwards would they drink it.

"Well, how about it?" the fat one pressed. "Don't things look better now—for us, anyway?"

"Sure," the boy said and he actually smiled at the fat man. It wasn't much more than a flicker, though.

The fat man shoved his machine gun to the side.

"They're not jumping anymore." He took out a cigarette case and offered it to the boy. "You smoke?"

"Sure," the boy replied and helped himself.

"You want me to light it for you too? But you'll smoke it for yourself, I hope."

"I can light yours for you too, if you want me to."

The youngster tossed away the cobblestone. He threw it into the river after a helmet which was floating down the middle of the stream, half-full of water.

"You've got a pretty good arm, Robert," said the fat man. "My name's Tony."

"Sometimes," the boy replied, peering beyond the fat one at the columns of men.

Last evening, at the first-aid station, he'd met a man who had returned from Germany. He was waiting now for the first train back to Krakow. He wanted to go to Auschwitz-Birkenau. So he could be near to his people, he said.

The train he was waiting for came from Vienna and it was going to Warsaw. A lot of prisoners from Mauthausen got off in Prague.

The man told him he could feel at home only where his own people were.

"They aren't jumping, but you can never be one hundred percent sure. Lots of people go quietly out of their minds and they're the only ones who know it, as long as they don't decide out of the blue to make a jump for it. At night, sure, but in the daytime? Does that make sense? I just wonder how many more people are still going to go off their rockers."

When the youngster didn't answer, he went on. "Keep your eyes open, Robert. Look over there—I can see the wall of the slaughterhouse because I've got good eyes and I can almost see the end of the line. And it's still morning. Not even noon yet. Doesn't it look to you as though that's the end of them?"

"It looks like the end," the boy agreed.

Yesterday, at the Powder Tower, when he was walking with Red and the little sister Red had brought back, they'd run into a father and mother who were looking for their son who was supposed to be coming home. His name was Milan. Theirs was a mixed marriage. They'd been questioning so many returnees, they already recognized who had come from where.

Red used to play soccer with Milan at the Hagibor sports club. He could barely remember what Milan had said about his parents, but he told his little sister to go over and stand in the sunshine next to the Tower while they talked.

He obviously didn't want her to hear things she didn't have to hear.

He spoke obliquely, in brief, transparent phrases, but Milan's parents wanted to know more than he wanted to tell.

Red and Milan had been together until early March. When the Germans started to retreat, they loaded the prisoners into freight cars in Gleiwitz and put on an engine only after they themselves were moving out of the camp on another track. They couldn't have had better hostages. The prisoner's train shielded the trainload of soldiers.

The mother wanted to know details. At first, the father did too, but after a while he didn't.

Red tried to sound vague. He went on and on about how long everything took, how their train moved as if it were dragging its feet. And how they got stuck in some little town and how their engine was always the last one to get water, how long it takes for somebody to reach Prague—when he's lucky and doesn't have to walk the whole way, if he finds better connections.

Although he'd been lucky himself, Red said, it had taken him since the fifth of March to get back. Imagine that! And he'd had his little sister with him too.

Since early March, Milan had had no legs. They'd been amputated below the knees because they were frozen. But Red didn't tell them that, of course. He just described what a hard winter it had been in Gleiwitz. More than thirty below. And that time they hadn't had anything to eat for three weeks, so they'd eaten anything—literally.

Red glanced over at his little sister and smiled at her.

Two Jewish and German first-aid helpers carried Milan into one of the camouflaged freight cars. The camp was being evacuated and the Germans wanted to leave things nice and tidy with nobody left behind to tell some scrubbed American or Australian about what had gone on here.

They even took the dead with them.

Again, he looked over at his sister and smiled, as if he were telling her to be patient, that he'd soon be finished and they'd be on their way.

Red had been observing Milan's parents and realized they couldn't take it. He also realized that this wasn't the best way to start his new life—by giving somebody false hopes. His little sister leaned against the Tower, basking in the sunshine.

Suddenly Red had enough when the mother said something to indicate that she didn't think he was telling them the truth.

"If the two of you had been together for such a long time, how come he didn't come back with you, when you even managed to bring your little sister?" she demanded. "You were together for two years, you say. So where is he? Where can he be? What did they do to him? Where did you see him last? You said you were together almost all the time. So how come you got here and he hasn't come back yet? Where is he, for God's sake, where is he?"

"They cut off his legs," Red said abruptly.

The mother closed her eyes and cold sweat beaded the father's forehead.

Red glanced quickly and apologetically at his little sister. He hadn't meant to blurt it out that way. It just slipped out. Like when Milan's mother said it seemed to her that an awful lot of people were coming back. Red knew how many were coming and how.

"Oh, God," the mother whispered. "Is he alive?"

"He was in the same camouflaged freight car I was in, right at the bottom," Red replied.

And he smiled again at his sister and took her back to the YWCA dormitory where they were living. They were a tiny pair with fair fuzz on their heads instead of hair. It had just begun to grow in again. They looked like children. Red had obviously been trying to make a part in his hair, but it wasn't long enough for that and he had scratched his scalp with the comb. He put his arm around his sister's shoulders as they walked along Na Prikope like two young lovers.

The mother bit her lips until the blood ran. The father wanted to take her home, telling her he'd give her some ointment for her lips.

Then it was Robert's turn to be questioned. The parents appealed to him and the mother kept saying his name over and over, as if she were identifying him with Milan, beseeching him, skinning herself alive at the same time. She touched the boy's hands and face and shoulders, as if she wanted to make sure he was real.

"Robert Lustig?" she said. "Before Milan left, he told us he knew somebody named Robert Lustig. You worked together, didn't you?"

"At the beginning of the war, we made pouches for stamps for German soldiers out of white patent leather," he told them.

"And you were together afterwards too?"

"Just until the beginning of 1944."

"What happened then?" the parents asked.

"We got separated. We were both working on a construction site."

The mother's eyes beseeched a lie, and when the father looked at him, it was a silent plea for lies. That would certainly have been better than what little Red had told them.

"We're trying to find somebody who's seen Milan since

that little fellow we were just talking to—Red."

"What do you suppose could have happened to him?" the mother demanded.

The Germans had done other things besides amputating frostbitten arms and legs. It would probably have been impossible to tell them what they'd eaten in those days, when they'd been given no food for three weeks, day after day— twenty-one days. It was better not to talk about that.

He had been in the same camps with Red and Milan. First in Theresienstadt, then in Birkenau. In the Gypsy camp at Birkenau, they went through the reception procedure, passing under a rope stretched some 5 feet 8 inches high. Anybody shorter than that went to the gas. The second qualification was carrying heavy stones. And third was simply who could stick it out the longest, according to the slogan, "Every man for himself."

Anybody who tried to escape was hung by the Germans with the aid of helpers from among the prisoners in the Gypsy camp. They were hung on a thin string, so it took a long time. But it was an entertaining spectacle.

The orchestra played a popular French dance tune. In German, it had a special significance: Komm zurück, ich warte auf dich, den du bist mein Glück...

Milan and Red had wheeled the victims to the execution ground in a wagon with a little roof. Its wheels squeaked.

Three Revolutionary Guards on German horses came along behind the last column of prisoners of war. All three horses were gray and their bodies reeked sweetly, their smell mingling with that of the captives' bodies and the river and the springtime air. The third Guard was leading a white, saddled horse with no rider.

"That horse's for me," the fat man said. "I'm going to leave you now and go on with them. You can take over here if you want to."

He paused, "Well, Robert, I'm glad to see they're not jumping anymore. Hey, look, that horse has an English saddle—the one that's for me. Well, so long, Robert. Look on the bright side of things. This isn't military territory any-more. All it is is one temporary wooden bridge and one broken-down suspension bridge."

The fat man shifted his machine gun onto his hip so it wouldn't get in his way. Gingerly, he kept the muzzle pointed at the ground. He approached the horse.

"How about another nice big smile, Robert, hm?" he said. "And if you still have the idea they're jumping, well, it's not true. You'll spoil this beautiful day for me if you don't give me one more smile."

He'd always waited for this moment—when it would be all over. He'd imagined the date when it would be—the hour, the place, the witnesses, the kind of weather, every circumstance about it. He thought how the Germans would suddenly disappear and nobody would know what became of them. As if they'd never even existed.

Whenever he imagined this moment, he could see a judge in a black robe. He came to him in his dreams three nights in a row, asking what verdict he proposed for the Germans.

"Murder for murder?"

"No," he replied to the judge. "No, I don't think murder will do."

Then the judge shoved back the black cap so the boy could look into his eyes.

"They killed your mother and father, so you have the right to kill them too. You can torture them if you want to."

"But I don't want to kill anybody anymore, and I don't want anybody to torture anybody else either."

On the second night, the judge appeared in a red robe.

"The moment of retribution has come and justice requires you to kill those who wanted to kill you."

"They didn't kill me," the boy said.

"But a thousand kinds of death were prepared for you—by lead, rope, gas, electricity, cold, hunger, whips, thirst, and humiliation."

On the third night, the judge appeared, wearing a white robe.

"It's all over," he said. "From this moment on, there will be no more killing. But you can still do it. You have the right. In your case, killing means defending yourself. That won't stain your conscience."

"No, I don't think I want to."

He didn't. He really didn't want to. After that, the judge never appeared to him in his dreams again. He never told him anymore that if he didn't kill one of those who had taken from him everything a person has only once, he'd reproach himself for as long as he'd live. Everything urged him to kill. He simply wished he could wipe Germany out of his mind, at least until it all wore off, the way a stone wears smooth in a swift river. He had to be responsible for that to himself, including finding an answer to the question of when a person has the right and the duty to defend himself and when the two coincide.

The fat man clambered awkwardly onto the horse's back. He pulled the saddle crooked and the girth slipped back and forth over the white horse's belly. The other Guard, who was riding along after the prisoners, looked back and laughed. Finally, the fat one made it. He perched like a jockey on the horse's back.

"Well, now, you know what I want to say, Robert, but just don't tell me you came down here to watch them jump."

The white horse's hooves danced along the cobblestones. The fat man had a hard time keeping in the saddle. The horse began to move on.

"I hope you'll find whatever it is you're looking for, Robert," he called back to give himself courage. For safety's sake, he kept his eyes ahead. "You want some more smokes?" He managed to toss the boy a pack of cigarettes.

"Thanks," the boy called.

He pulled out a cigarette and stuck it between his rosy lips and the rest he put in his pocket before lighting up.

"Didn't I tell you, Robert?" the fat one called. "They aren't jumping anymore."

Horseshoes rang on the cobblestones. The sound merged with the tread of the last column of infantry. The wind sang through the cables of the bridge. The wood creaked. Below, the water flowed on and on, just as dirty as it had been that morning. It carried with it odds and ends of army uniforms and equipment, human bodies, rags, sewage, pots and pans, logs and planks, blood and oil, and it all rolled on the waves. A cold mist rose from the river. But its surface glittered in the sunshine.

Then the boy went back to the other end of the bridge toward Revolucni Street. He wasn't so nervous anymore. He moseyed along in his blue golf knickers and white shoes with the gold buckles, a cigarette in one hand and the empty machine gun shell in the other. He flicked the cigarette into the river in a long arc. He watched it soar, then land on the surface of the water, and go out.

As he walked on, he whistled into the golden shell casing.